Praise for Nicky Pellegrino

'So much to love about this book. I love the way the food makes you salivate for Italy. I love the matrix of complicated women that interfere in each other's lives . . . Reading this felt like a welcome ticket to southern Italy' *Stuff.co.NZ*

'We love this book . . . absolutely delicious, like a warm hug on a sunny afternoon' *HotBrandsCoolPlaces.com*

'Full-bodied as a rich Italian red, it's a page-turner combining the missed chances of *Captain Corelli's Mandolin* with the foodie pleasures of *Chocolat*' *Eve*

'Three generations of Italian women talk romance and cooking in *Delicious* by Nicky Pellegrino, an evocative food-fest of a novel' *Prima*

'A slice of pure sunshine' *Good Housekeeping*

'A lovely read . . . with a genuine heart and true observation'
Elizabeth Buchan

'A touching story about one woman's search for love'
Sunday Express

'Set against a backdrop of love, friendship and food . . . The descriptions of Italian food will make your mouth water'
Cosmopolitan

'Sink back on the sofa with this delightful read'
Now Magazine

Nicky Pellegrino was born in Liverpool but spent childhood holidays staying with her family in Italy. It is her memories of those summers that flavour her stories: the passions, the feuds but most of all the food. Nicky now lives in Auckland, New Zealand with her husband, two dogs and two horses.

Find out more at www.nickypellegrino.com

Under Italian Skies

Nicky Pellegrino

An Orion paperback

First published in Great Britain in 2016
by Orion Books
This paperback edition published in 2017
by Orion Books,
an imprint of The Orion Publishing Group Ltd,
Carmelite House, 50 Victoria Embankment
London EC4Y 0DZ

An Hachette UK company

1 3 5 7 9 10 8 6 4 2

A CIP catalogue record for this book
is available from the British Library.

ISBN 978 1 4091 5087 9

Printed and bound in Great Britain by CPI Group (UK) Ltd, Croydon CR0 4YY

www.orionbooks.co.uk

'The best thing about ageing is that you have a past. No one can take that away but you'd better like it.'

Diane von Furstenberg

Beginning with an ending

It was the old order books that were Stella's undoing. Shelves of them, neatly stacked, right at the back of the storeroom. She had known they were there of course but it was years since she had bothered to take a look, never mind open one. She did so now and saw her own handwriting, rounder and better formed than it was nowadays, less rushed.

There were orders for pleated fabrics from Maison Lognon in Paris, for fine cashmeres and printed Liberty silks, for jacquard jersey knits in deep blues and heather-toned purples, for soft leathers and supple suedes. Stella flicked through the pages and started to cry.

The tears took her entirely by surprise. Until then she had held firm and stayed dry-eyed. All through Milly's short but brutal illness she'd managed to keep going. Even when she'd had to announce the designer's death to the other staff and break the news that the business was to close. Every day since then, coming into the office to empty it out, closing accounts, packing up boxes, sending the last archive pieces of clothing to fashion museums – it was dispiriting work but it hadn't made Stella cry. Not once.

Now, though, all alone in a half-bare storeroom, she sat down on the floor, leaned back against the shelves, dropped her head into her hands and fell apart. Big, wrenching sobs shook her whole body. The more she cried, the more she felt as if she might never stop.

Those order books held the history of Stella's life. And that life was over.

Soon her cheeks were drenched, her mascara running. Grateful no one else was in the office to witness the state she was in, she struggled to pull herself together. She wasn't going to deal with this today. The order books would have to be thrown away but better to leave it until she felt less emotional. Right now she would make herself a cup of tea instead.

Stella wondered if her hormones were playing up. Perhaps this was the beginning of an early menopause. There seemed no other reason why a bunch of order books, some a quarter of a century old, should have such a calamitous effect on her.

As she boiled the kettle and rinsed her cup, Stella thought about how young she had been when she had written so carefully in their pages. Life was still shiny and new then, and a little scary too. Coming here to work as Milly Munro's assistant, part of the fashion world at long last, she had been desperate to impress, so keen to do well.

What a lovely boss Milly had turned out to be, appreciative and generous, always interested to hear Stella's opinion of a new design for a suit or a little black dress. Milly used to perch on her desk, her grey hair cut into a sharp bob, her mouth a slash of darkest red lipstick, wearing one of her own creations, something plain, slimline and perfectly tailored. Stella would pin up the sketches of each new collection on the large corkboard and together she, Milly and the rest of the small team would examine each one, talk about fabric and fit, discuss what sort of women would wear those skirts and jackets, those gorgeously draped dresses, whether they would be able to run for a London bus in them, sit at a desk, pick up a child.

'These are clothes to live, work and love in,' Milly often said. It was her motto, really. One day Stella had printed it out and pinned it on the wall as a constant reminder to everyone. Now it was the only thing left up there.

Sadly there would be no more collections of beautifully cut clothes. They were finished, the corkboard was bare and the walls too; the desks had been cleared out.

Stella kept wondering if her boss had suspected she was ill. All through that last year, although she worked as hard as ever, she seemed a muted version of herself. It was obvious she was losing weight; those outfits that had fitted so perfectly began to hang off her. Now and then she complained of a stomach ache or back pain. Stella urged her to see her GP but Milly had resisted, claiming she was too busy, saying she was fine and everyone should stop fussing.

In the end Stella had been so worried she had made the doctor's appointment herself and insisted Milly keep it. The diagnosis when it came was devastating. Pancreatic cancer. By then things were pretty far gone and although Milly tried to keep working it wasn't long before she was forced to give up coming into the office. For a while Stella had gone to her home in Kensington every morning to take down lists of instructions and watch Milly become jaundiced and then fade away.

In her will she had been very definite about the future of the business. It wasn't to continue without her, some other person at the helm. She was Milly Munro, her designs were her style and the label would die with her. Stella thought it had been the right thing to do. That was the only thing she was sure of.

She had been working in this office for so long she knew every line of the building, every windowsill, every crack in the ceiling. It was extraordinary to think that someday soon she would lock the door behind her one last time and never come back. Where would she go? What would she do? Stella had no idea.

She knew what she didn't want – to be someone's dogsbody, making coffee and running errands, not trusted with anything important. And even if she were offered a job working for a designer she respected it wouldn't be the same. No, Stella believed she had to reinvent herself. Do something completely different.

Eking out the whole sorry business of closing down the office had kept her occupied for a while. But those order books were almost the last of it. Once they had been cleared out and a few more things tidied up, Stella couldn't justify being here any longer.

She was lucky that money wasn't an issue. A couple of the other girls had been in such a panic about finding new jobs. But Stella had done OK out of her divorce and later, when her parents died, as an only child she inherited all they had. So there was no mortgage to worry about and she had some savings. In fact, if she was frugal she might be able to retire early; but the idea seemed ridiculous.

Forty-nine wasn't old any more, was it? That was what she kept reading in women's magazines. And besides, she didn't feel old. Yes, the chestnut colour of her hair was courtesy of L'Oréal these days and the smearing on of night creams and serums had become quite a process. But Stella still looked in decent shape. One of the few benefits of not having children was that she hadn't gone flabby around the middle, nor been subjected to sleepless nights to leave her puffy-eyed. She had been careful with her pale skin in the sun, had eaten well and exercised. Looking after herself had paid off; she hoped so anyway.

Forty-nine was young enough to start a new career, to see the world, or fall in love again; it meant she had a past but there were still enough good years ahead, or so everyone kept telling her. Lately Stella's future seemed to have been discussed endlessly over cups of tea and glasses of chardonnay. All her friends pitched in with ideas but most of them seemed impractical. Start your own business, suggested one, or launch your own fashion label. Open a boutique said another, become a personal shopper, a stylist. Retrain as a florist or a make-up artist. Teach English as a foreign language. There was no shortage of ideas. Stella was lukewarm about every one. In fact, she almost resented them.

It had been Lisa, the junior assistant at Milly Munro Fashion, who had said the only thing she had been intrigued by.

'Why not have a gap year?'

'A gap year? Isn't it a bit late for that?'

'I don't see why. My gap year was the best time ever. I travelled, got into my photography and tried all sorts of new things. I'd love the chance to take another. Wouldn't you?'

'I never took one in the first place,' Stella had admitted.

'Well then, now is your chance.'

A gap year? What was it young people did on them? Went backpacking, she supposed, worked on a kibbutz or volunteered on a charity project in a developing country. Stella wished she felt bold enough.

This office had been the place she belonged, this room with the heavy sash windows covered in blistering paint, filled with messy piles of fabric swatches and the chatter of other women. Stella knew it was unusual to stay in a job for such a long time but she had never wanted to leave; she still didn't.

Of course, the person she really longed to talk things through with was Milly. In the old days if something was bothering her they would have lunch at the Italian place, the one that was always their favourite. Usually Stella ordered the spaghetti with clams, Milly the chicken salad and if it was a Friday perhaps a couple of glasses of wine. And Milly listened ... she was good at listening.

Stella wanted to tell her how sad she was every morning when she opened the office door and didn't find Milly there, already at her desk, tip-tapping on her laptop. She needed her to know she was angry that she hadn't seen a doctor sooner, when perhaps the cancer might have been caught before it spread so far. To hear about the sympathy notes from long-time clients and the distressed emails, how tough it had been to read them all and draft the right sort of replies. Most of all she wanted to hear Milly's husky voice telling her what she needed her to do, just like she had every single Monday to Friday, and occasionally weekends, for the past busy, happy twenty-five years.

In the kitchenette Stella poured boiling water on the teabag, added milk, then changed her mind and tipped the whole lot down the sink. It was lunchtime after all. She would go to their favourite Italian place and enjoy a bowl of pasta and a glass of wine. She would do it on her own. Surely she was bold enough for that.

The maître d' there was an ancient Italian guy called Frederico who had always made a fuss of them. Stella had never been without Milly and was dreading explaining her absence. Putting on her jacket, she checked her face in her compact. Her eyes still seemed puffy from the storm of tears but once she had fixed her make-up they looked much better.

The restaurant was just round the corner and, walking there, Stella found herself cheered by the thought of sitting at one of the familiar tables and looking through a menu she had read at least a hundred times. However, the instant she walked through the door she saw that the place was different now. The décor had been changed, the starched white tablecloths had gone and the far wall had been covered in blackboard paint that was scrawled over brightly in chalk.

Thankfully it was still the same old guy who greeted her at the door.

'What's happened?' asked Stella. 'Has it changed hands?'

'No, no, it is still in the family,' he reassured her, his accent resoundingly Italian although she was sure he had lived in London for years and years.

'But nothing seems the same,' she said.

He threw up his hands. 'The young people are never

happy to stand still. Always they are wanting to move with the times, even here in Little Italy. And so you see no proper menu any more, just this blackboard.'

Stella squinted at it. 'Do you still have the spaghetti with clams?'

'For you, *signora*, yes. I will tell the kitchen and they will make it for you.'

'But is it not on the menu any more?'

'We are all very casual here now, very relaxed. We serve you small plates filled with meatballs, seafood or crostini, Venetian food, snacks to share.' The old man's mouth turned down. 'I heard about your friend, *signora*. Such a sad loss and I am very sorry. For you there will always be spaghetti with clams. And today a glass of something special to toast her memory.'

He brought a glass of a chilled sparkling red wine that she sipped carefully and thought delicious. Still Stella couldn't get over feeling slightly rattled by the way the place had altered. In her opinion nothing was wrong with how it used to be.

Not that it mattered, really. Once the office was closed she was unlikely to come back here. It was just another part of her old life that was disappearing.

She enjoyed her spaghetti as much as always. The briny juices of the clams, the hit of chilli flakes, the tang of olive oil and white wine – at least the flavours were exactly as she remembered. Comfort food, she supposed it was. And right now Stella needed comfort.

Where would she be a month from now? Stella had never had a plan B. It had seemed enough, her life; it had seemed perfectly good.

A gap year. Stella pondered the idea as she finished her food. Why should they only be for students, anyway? Perhaps taking one was exactly what she needed to recharge. Then she remembered all those order books, relics of the past that for some reason she had chosen to keep. Really they ought to have been thrown out years ago when they had made the switch to computers. Stella put down her fork, dabbed her mouth with the paper serviette that had replaced the usual starched napkin and waved at Frederico to bring the bill. It was time to make a start.

Time running wild

Everything changes, doesn't it? That is what Stella kept reminding herself when she woke in the morning bright and early as always, even though she no longer bothered to set her alarm clock. Nothing stays the same. People die or move on, relationships break up, businesses close or are modernised, jobs are lost and there is nothing you can do so you might as well accept it. Stella told herself this, sitting up in bed with her first coffee of the morning, as she wondered how to occupy the day.

It was three weeks since she had walked out the door of Milly Munro Fashion for the final time clutching a few mementos – an offcut of a fabric she loved, one of the old order books, Milly's own tape measure – so worn it was almost illegible in parts – a few of her sketches and a magazine cover featuring one of her most iconic designs.

Stella carried these things back to her small mews flat and found places for them, then there was nothing else to do, nothing at all.

She tried to fill her time. The first week she painted the living-room walls in a pale duck-egg blue, hated it and re-painted them plain white again. The second week she threw a cocktail party and made ridiculously elaborate drinks that involved much researching of recipes and scouring for in-gredients. The third week she decided she really had to start job-hunting, only she didn't and instead took long rambling walks round London, discovering hidden-away places she hadn't known existed, stopping for sweet treats and cups of tea, and trying not to notice how everyone else seemed to have somewhere to go, someone to meet.

Now it was the Monday of week four and Stella had stopped pretending to herself that she wasn't despondent. She stayed beneath the duvet in the curtained half-light of her bedroom, sipping milky coffee. She didn't even have a cat – that is how empty her life was. Funny, but she had never thought so before.

To Stella time felt like some wild thing she needed to corral and tame. It raced ahead of her, writhing and bucking, and she stayed motionless in bed, half afraid of it.

Simply getting up and taking a shower felt like a triumph. It was late morning by the time she was dressed and had put on a little make-up. That was one of the things she had promised herself she wouldn't do: lie around all day in a bathrobe, with messy hair and a shiny face, giving herself a fright every time she happened to catch her reflection in the mirror. So she slipped on one of Milly's designs, a sample dress she had been given. It was plain black, with off-centre buttons and a shirt collar, and Stella felt a little more businesslike whenever she wore it. This was a dress that demanded some sort of activity. If only there was an errand to run or an appointment she had to keep.

Her friends were all at work and Stella was wary of bothering them. Hadn't she always been impatient at being interrupted by someone just for a chat when she was in the middle of a busy day? There was only one person she thought might welcome the distraction. Her very best friend Nicky Bird, otherwise known as Birdie, was working as a sales rep for a magazine publisher and liked to escape the place and complain how tough it was whenever she had the chance.

Stella texted her, *Free for lunch?*

The reply pinged straight back, *Not really but let's do it anyway!*

They met in a little place on Beak Street. It was part of

a chain but did good sandwiches on crusty sourdough and decent coffee. Birdie was already there when she arrived and had saved her a stool by the window.

'I'm so envious of you being able to flit about catching up with friends instead of imprisoned in an office all day like me,' Birdie said the minute she joined her.

Stella didn't tell her that freedom wasn't all it was cracked up to be, because she knew it wasn't what her friend wanted to hear.

'So tell me, what have you been up to? How's the job-hunting going?' Birdie asked once she had spent the requisite ten minutes complaining about how impossible work was, how difficult her clients and unreasonable her sales targets.

'I haven't even got started yet,' Stella confessed. 'I've just been mooching round.'

'Oh well, you can afford to take a little time off, can't you? May as well enjoy it.'

'Mmm,' Stella agreed.

Birdie looked at her, eyes narrowing. 'What do you mean by "mmm"?'

Stella shrugged. 'The thing is, I'm not enjoying it.'

'Really?' Birdie sounded incredulous.

'It's not like being on holiday and relishing the time you have off because you know it's limited. I have no plans, none at all.'

'Well make some,' Birdie said. 'Book a trip. Go somewhere amazing that you've always wanted to see. Angkor Wat? Petra? Have an adventure.'

'I'd love to but not on my own. It wouldn't be the same.'

'No, I suppose not,' Birdie conceded. 'You know I'd love to come but my credit cards couldn't take the strain right now.'

Stella considered offering to pay for the flights and accommodation but didn't want to seem like she was flashing money around. And actually she had never told Birdie how much she had stowed away in stocks and shares. She was private about that kind of thing, just like her parents had been.

'Someone suggested I should take a gap year,' she said, just as Birdie bit into her sandwich. 'Like a student, you know, but an adult one. Apparently it's a thing now. I googled it.'

'An adult gap year?' Birdie said, swallowing her mouthful. 'Really? What are you supposed to do on it?'

'All sorts of things – voluntary work, learn new skills. There are loads of programmes and expeditions to choose from. I came across one in Ghana helping in an orphanage and another where you work on a building project in some poverty-stricken village without any electricity or running water.'

Birdie looked dubious. 'Would you do that on your own? It sounds a bit awful.'

'You're supported by the organisation that sets it all up so it might be OK.'

'But have you ever built anything in your life? And an orphanage ... you'd fall in love with half the children ... it would break your heart.'

'Probably,' Stella agreed. 'That's not a reason not to try it though. Surely it's better than staying here with no idea what to do with myself.'

Birdie stared out at the lunchtime crowds pushing their way down Beak Street's narrow pavements and she frowned. 'If I had the time and money to escape from all this then what I'd do is go and live in another country for a while and really immerse myself in the culture. I'd choose somewhere beautiful like Paris or Rome, or maybe a smaller town be-cause it might be easier to meet people. And I'd sign up to a language school – yes, I would. That would be me.'

'So would you stay in the same place the whole time?' Stella was intrigued by the idea.

'Yes, I'd rent an apartment, or if I had a nice flat like

yours maybe I'd do a house swap. That way I'd really be living like a local.'

'I don't know if my flat's really all that nice,' said Stella. 'It's tiny.'

'What do you mean? It's in such a cute little mews and it's so central. Visitors would love it.'

From the outside Stella's place didn't look like much, just a plain brick building in a narrow cobbled lane in Camden. But at the back it had French windows that opened onto a tiny courtyard and she had stripped the floors back to palest pine and kept things bright and airy so the pokiness of the rooms wasn't too obvious.

'Perhaps I could try something like that,' she wondered.

'You should look into it at least,' Birdie urged her. 'There are websites, I should think.'

Stella was feeling a little more upbeat as the Northern Line train rattled her towards home. After stopping at the Inverness Street market to pick up some salad for dinner, she hurried back. The afternoon wasn't quite warm enough to open the French doors but she did it anyway and sat on the sofa, laptop on her knee, sunlight dappling the walls, and thought her flat might be nice enough after all.

There were so many websites to explore. Stella picked one to start with then made her way through the rest methodic-ally, taking notes as she went. Soon she realised there was quite a lot to it. The home-exchange companies suggested getting your place professionally photographed, then you had to write about yourself and the neighbourhood, and possibly even make a short video. One site encouraged her to link to her Facebook page so potential swappers could learn even more about her.

Stella didn't have a Facebook page. She had always been slightly scornful about them, maintaining they were for people without enough to do. But now she actually was one of those people, she might as well see what was involved. Facebook sidetracked Stella for ages. It was more fun than she might have imagined making a profile and posting pictures, then finding long-lost friends. The room was darkening and chilly by the time she looked up from her screen.

She stood and stretched, then turned on some lights and went to her small kitchen to put together a quick salad. As she chopped vegetables and whisked together vinaigrette, she thought about a stranger living in her space and what they might think, and what they might do. Would they prefer to shop at the market like she did instead of going to the big Sainsbury's? Would they love the flamenco nights at her old favourite Bar Gansa and drop in to eat Padron peppers and tomato bread? More importantly, would they be tidy or mess up her place? Would they keep the pots in the courtyard watered in a dry spell and double-lock the front door when they went out? It seemed a huge risk to leave some person she had never met in charge of the most valuable thing she owned. Still, Stella thought it worth exploring a little further. There were lots of websites after all, and so many people seemed to be signed up to them; surely it had to be OK?

When she had finished eating she texted Birdie. *I think you may be on to something.*

Two minutes later a reply came back. *Oh my God, are you really going to do it?*

The moment she woke Stella checked Facebook to see who had accepted her friend requests. Then she spent half an hour catching up with what everyone had been doing before forcing herself to set the screen aside and make some coffee. She was beginning to see how this might be addictive.

After breakfast she had another trawl through the home-swap sites. She still wasn't ready to commit but was definitely warming to the prospect. In the meantime there were things to do – drafting a profile and considering how best to describe her neighbourhood, fluffing up the flat so it looked good in pictures and deciding who would shoot them. Stella was busy again; she felt as if she had a purpose.

First she walked through her home trying to look at each room through a critical stranger's eyes. When she bought the place Stella had redone it with lots of white and washed-out pastels. Now she wondered if it looked a little too pared back. New cushions on the sofa would cheer things up, or a bold wall-hanging for the bedroom. Stella had seen some Marimekko ones in a shop at Camden Lock market and might wander down and take a look.

One of the consolations of the divorce had been having her very own space again. Stella had found the mixing and matching of belongings that marriage entailed the least appealing thing about it. The problem was Ray collected things. He was a magpie. Every room in their house in High Barnet had been loaded with his treasures: old train sets and cameras, Tintin figurines, Atomic coffee machines dating back to the 1950s and random stuff made of Bakelite. At any moment his interest might flit away from one thing and alight on another. Stella had drawn a line at the collection of giant pinecones. They attracted dust like nothing else. Besides, by then things hadn't been great between the two of them.

Stella blamed the fertility treatment. It had leached all the life out of her. Even though she feared they had left it too late and the chances of success were so very slim, still Stella had clung on to hope. And when it had been crushed out of her, over and over, she hadn't coped well.

Birdie had told her it was grief she was feeling but to Stella it felt like nothing at all, just a great big blank space inside her where a baby should have been.

For a while life had seemed all disappointments and regret. Stella wasted so much time wishing she had met Ray when she was young and fertile, wishing they had tried to get pregnant straight away like she wanted instead of spending a year or so enjoying each other as he had thought best.

Towards the end they were talking about donor eggs. Even after the split Ray had offered to help her go ahead if she really wanted to. She thought about it, talked to Birdie and a couple of other good friends, and made the toughest decision of her life. She didn't want to be a single mother in her forties, juggling work with raising a child, sending the kid to stay with Ray at weekends. Yes, she could do it, but it wasn't going to be fair on any of them.

Not long after that Stella bought the mews flat in Camden and set about decorating it with no consideration for the sticky fingers and curious hands of small children, with no thought for anyone but herself.

Work was her consolation. Milly had been the only one who had known exactly what she was going through, but perhaps she had thrown out a few hints because all the girls were so kind to her. Still it had been a bleak time. And now Stella could see it in the layers of beige in her bedroom and the barely there blue of the rug on the living-room floor. This place needed more than a whisper of colour, most likely more than just a Marimekko wall-hanging, but that was where she would start.

The thing Stella really loved about Camden was the different lives all rubbing up against each other. There were kids in punk regalia, stallholders with sleeves of tattoos, green-smoothie-sipping girls in yoga pants, homeless people lingering round the Tube station. She liked the mishmash of brightly coloured buildings on the high street, the quirky cafés, the smell of spice and incense, the music blasting from shop doorways as she passed and most of all the fact that eccentric still had a place here. It was more raw and rugged than many other parts of London and, although she hardly added anything to the colour, still she liked looking at it.

Stella felt invisible as she walked towards the market, just another middle-aged woman in clothes that draped her upper arms and covered her knees. She didn't especially miss men's heads turning and definitely not the barrage of wolf-whistles she used to have to brace herself for when walking past building sites. She was way past caring about being noticed. When friends like Birdie nagged her about getting out more or signing up for online dating, she tended to laugh and change the subject. Ray had been a bonus. He came along when she had given up on the idea of finding some-one. Stella thought if it hadn't been for the whole miserable trying-for-a-baby thing they might still be together. But they weren't. And Stella didn't have the stomach for more dis-appointments.

She found the Marimekko store and bought some cushions as well as the wall-hanging. Pleased with her purchases she turned for home, determined that by the end of the afternoon she would at least have decided which of the home-exchange companies to go with.

When Birdie called several hours later she was still staring at the screen. She had been distracted several times, posting a shot of her new wall-hanging on Facebook, reading an interesting newspaper article someone had linked to, looking at a video on YouTube.

'Oh no, you're in a Google coma,' Birdie told her. 'You've got to watch out for that, being home alone every day.'

'I'm not in a Google coma.'

'Yes you are,' she insisted. 'Here's what you have to do. Put down the phone, pick up your credit card and sign up to the company you most like the look of. It's not that expen-sive, right? And it's not like you're committing yourself to anything at this point.'

'I suppose that's true,' Stella agreed.

'Do I need to come round and make you do it?'

'I think I can manage.'

'Good, because I've got a date.'

'Someone new?' Stella asked.

'Yep, I met her on Pink Cupid.'

Birdie too was post-divorce but dealing with it rather differently from Stella. She had declared herself over men, had lost ten kilos, cropped her wheat-blonde hair and started dating her personal trainer – a woman. As far as Stella knew they still hooked up every now and then, but whatever arrangement they had can't have been exclusive because dating website Pink Cupid, and the women she found on it, often featured in Birdie's conversation.

'I'm enjoying my freedom ... you should start enjoying yours too,' Birdie said now.

'So you keep saying, but I'm not as brave as you.'

'You're not as wussy as you think, either.'

Stella laughed. 'I might be.'

She was happy for Birdie. To Stella it seemed as if she had finally turned into the person she was meant to be.

'I'd say you're one of the most courageous people I know,' Birdie told her. 'You just don't see yourself that way.'

It was a lovely thing to hear but she didn't believe it. Stella had never been especially daring. What she wanted from life was all the commonplace stuff – a husband, a family, a nice home, a good job. Well, she had given it her best shot, hadn't she?

'You're going to put the phone down now and find that credit card, aren't you?' said Birdie.

'I am.'

'OK, go for it, and see you soon.'

Stella followed her friend's advice. She chose the company that seemed the most professional and signed up. Immediately a whole world opened up to her. There weren't only ordinary houses and flats available but castles and houseboats, even a couple of yachts. There were French country cottages and villas on paradise islands, a canal house in Amsterdam, an apartment with a view of the Sydney Opera House. Stella found herself amazed. She'd had no idea so many possibilities were out there on the internet, waiting to be discovered.

A lot of doing

If there was one thing Stella was really good at it was making things happen. Once she had set her mind to a task she got it done. So it didn't take her long to set up her profile for the house-exchange website. She was careful to describe her apartment as most suited to a single person and made a lot of how quiet the little mews was but how vibrant the area. She remembered Lisa, the junior assistant from work, telling her she was into photography so had her come and take some interior shots and paid her with a few bottles of wine.

'So you're really going to have a gap year – how cool,' Lisa said, as Stella darted about plumping cushions and arranging lilies in a vase.

'Probably not a whole year; perhaps just a few months to give me time to think about what to do next.'

'Where will you go?'

'I'm not sure. It depends who wants a house swap at the same time and is looking to come to London. And I suppose it doesn't matter where in the world I end up, not really.'

Lisa turned on a few lamps to cast a warmer light, then started snapping pictures of the living room from different angles. She chatted as she worked. 'Is there any place you've always wanted to visit?' she wondered.

Stella thought about it. Compared to most people her age she hadn't done a lot of travelling. She and Ray had honeymooned in Thailand and holidayed in France. Before that there had been beach holidays on islands like Ibiza with girlfriends or work trips with Milly when she had been showing new collections in Paris and New York. But Stella had never spent a decent amount of time in any destination.

'Lots of places,' Stella told her. 'I guess it would be nice to swap with someone not too far away so friends could visit if they wanted. And I'd like a bit of history, and people speaking another language so it really does feel properly foreign, but also a place that's safe, since I'll be there on my own.'

Lisa had finished in the living area so they moved on to the bedroom, Stella smoothing the duvet, arranging more flowers, piling up some colourful cushions she had bought and stacking paperbacks on the nightstand to make it all look welcoming.

'I think it's great that someone your age is so open to new experiences,' Lisa told her. 'I can't imagine my mum doing it. She'd never have the nerve.'

Stella gave her a sidelong look. She always forgot that to girls like this she probably seemed ancient, part of their parents' generation. Perhaps it was not having children but she didn't really feel so different from how she had felt at Lisa's age. More confident in some ways, more cynical certainly, but essentially she was still the same person.

'It's not like I'm backpacking through India or something,' pointed out Stella. 'I'm sure I'll end up some place very civilised having an extended holiday.'

'Well I hope at your time of life I've got your adventurous spirit,' Lisa said artlessly.

It was funny how other people saw you. Birdie had described her as courageous and now this young girl seemed to think she was intrepid. Stella was fairly sure she was neither of those things.

Once she had chosen the shots that showed her home to its best advantage there was nothing to stop her going ahead and posting her profile. After that Stella sat nursing a cup of peppermint tea and searched for possible matches, ideally people who wanted to travel soon, who were interested in London and had homes that seemed appealing but not too flashy. Stella didn't want her place to be a disappointment. She would like whoever stayed there to appreciate it even if it wasn't all that special.

By early evening she had come up with a shortlist – there was a stylish flat in Madrid, a farmhouse in the south of France, a chalet in the Swiss mountains and a small pink villa with terraced gardens stretching down to a rocky coastline in southern Italy. That last place was the one Stella was least sure about. Its owner was a man, and there was a shot of him, silver-haired and quite good-looking, but he didn't have a Facebook profile so she couldn't find out much about him. Plus he said in his blurb that he was looking to swap with a gardener who would be happy to spend time maintaining his grounds. While Stella enjoyed messing about with the pots of herbs and succulents out on her patio she wasn't sure it constituted gardening. What if she killed this man's prized plants or ended up having to spend the entire time digging and weeding? Still, it did look lovely in the photographs. There was a pergola with bougainvillea climbing over it and views to the sea. There were pomegranate trees and a lemon grove, and a courtyard with an outdoor fireplace.

Stella could imagine herself there picking the lemons or reading beneath the shade of the pergola on a hot sunny day. She thought about sending him a message but held back. If she had been the brave, adventurous spirit everyone thought her to be she wouldn't have hesitated, of course. The real Stella was more cautious.

Her phone rang and she checked the number on her screen. It was Birdie so she answered.

'Not Pink Cupiding then?'

'No, I'm having a night off.'

'How did the date go the other evening?'

'It was fine. Not sure if I'll see her again though. There's someone else I've spotted who I may be having coffee with at the weekend.'

'I wish I could find a house swap as easily as you find dates,' Stella told her.

'Did you actually sign up then?' Birdie sounded pleased.

'Yes, you should check out my profile. It looks pretty good.'

'I'll do it right now. Hang on, just let me get my laptop. Here we go ...'

Stella gave the link and heard the keys of Birdie's laptop click as her fingers flew over them.

'Oh yes, there you are,' she said. 'Nice pic of you.'

'It's a few years old,' Stella confessed. 'But I couldn't find anything else decent.'

'Your place looks great too. Yeah, I like it. So what's the problem?'

'Well, actually it is a bit like dating,' Stella explained. 'You trawl through lots of profiles searching for houses and owners you like the look of. You can check their reviews and click through to their Facebook pages. I've found a few possibilities but I'm not sure if I trust my own judgement.'

'OK, let's go through them together then. Tell me where to look.'

Sitting on their sofas, in front of separate laptops, in flats at opposite ends of London, Stella and Birdie spent an evening together. They took breaks to top up wine glasses or smear cheese onto crackers, and giggled over silly things as they ranged through Stella's shortlist and beyond.

Birdie was rude about people's taste in wallpaper and suspicious that several of them might be psychopaths.

'That woman on the olive farm in the south of France looks like a real bitch,' she declared. 'The Spanish couple seem OK but do you really want to go to Madrid? I think the best bet is the guy with the pink house in Italy, the silver fox, I'd go with him.'

'I'm not going to be meeting these people, you know,'

Stella told her. 'They'll be over here while I'm there. They just have to be trustworthy.'

'The silver fox looks trustworthy.'

'I think so too for some reason, although I suppose you shouldn't judge by appearances. Perhaps I'll send him a message.'

'What will you say?' Birdie asked.

'Just that I'm interested in swapping my place for his.'

'You want to make sure you create the right impression. Don't try to be funny because it never works in emails. Just be chatty but not too keen ... you need to intrigue him.'

'This is a house-exchange site, you know, Birdie, not Pink Cupid.'

'Hey, you were the one who compared it to online dating.'

By the time they got off the phone Stella was feeling sleepy and procrastinating was easier. Better to send a quick message in the morning when she felt fresher. She wasn't going to spend hours crafting it though, no matter what Birdie said. If the pink house or its owner turned out not to be right there were other places to choose from.

Writing to a total stranger was trickier than Stella had expected. With a work email she wouldn't have struggled, but brisk and businesslike didn't seem like the right tone for this. She needed to be warm but not over-friendly, to give him a sense of who she was without going on too much.

Hoping for inspiration, Stella looked back at his profile. In the picture he was sitting outdoors, leaning back against a wall of brightly painted terracotta tiles and smiling. He looked a few years older than her. His face was deeply bronzed, his silvery hair a little messy, his build slim with wide shoulders. She reread the words beneath his photograph.

Hello, I'm Leo. I'm a landscape gardener who specialises in creating community spaces and my work takes me to all sorts of interesting locations. I love nature and the outdoors but also enjoy city life. Villa Rosa is my summer house and it lies on a spectacular stretch of coastline near a historic village called Triento. I have beautiful gardens here and would appreciate house-swappers who are willing to do a little to help tend them, but otherwise this is the perfect place to come and relax and reflect, to swim in the sea and take walks, to eat wonderful food and share time with friends. There is a small car that I'm happy for guests to use to visit the surrounding area. I speak fluent English, am single and a non-smoker. Villa Rosa is a simple house but it is kept scrupulously clean and tidy and I would treat any home I stayed in the same way.

He sounded very into his house and Stella wondered if he was gay. Or perhaps like her he was a divorcee. She tried to imagine what his work creating community spaces involved. And just because someone claimed to be scrupulously tidy it didn't mean they actually were. If anything the fact that he had felt the need to mention it made her suspicious. Still, perhaps he would find red flags in the message she was drafting.

Hi Leo, I'm Stella. I'm interested in a possible house swap.

Stella stopped writing and started deleting. She had to come up with something better than that.

Hi, I'm Stella. I think Villa Rosa looks lovely and I may be interested in a house swap with you. I'm planning on taking an adult gap year after many years in the same job, so I'm flexible about dates but am keen to travel as soon as possible. I'm single too but would hope to have a friend or two come to visit over the course of my stay. There isn't a car here for me to offer but really you don't need one because the Underground is a manageable walk away and there are lots of buses ...

This was getting boring and really only repeating things she had covered in her profile. Stella paused, hands hovering above the keyboard.

I'm not an especially knowledgeable gardener but I'm happy to do some basic weeding. I'm very clean and tidy ...

Stella felt she had to mention it since he had.

My place is small and there is no view but it's in a quiet street and close to quirky shops, lively bars and restaurants ...

How to finish? Stella frowned. She needed something brisk and upbeat.

Please let me know if you'd like to hear more ...

She deleted that.

Looking forward to hearing from you and learning more about Villa Rosa. Yours, Stella Forrester

She read it through once and pressed send. Instantly she felt several things at once. Panic because what had she done? Excitement because where would it lead? Relief because now it was up to him whether to take it further.

The website gave no clue how long she should expect to wait for a reply. Stella found herself checking several times as the day went on, and being disappointed. The more she thought about a little pink house by the sea, simple and clean, the greater her longing to be there. London was a constant reminder of how out of kilter everything was and Stella missed the old routines and familiar faces of her job. At Villa Rosa everything would be different. In a way she would be living someone else's life. The idea was quite tempting.

Perhaps Leo wouldn't be interested in her modest little flat at all. Quite likely his inbox was full of requests from people wanting to stay at Villa Rosa, people who had fancier places in smarter parts of London. If so, he would be mad not to go with one of those. Stella wished she had put more effort into selling herself and making a good impression. It was too late now.

By bedtime she still hadn't had any response. She was starting to feel alarmed at how the days were slipping by and how little she seemed to get done. Working for Milly had meant making the most of every moment, packing it full. In comparison to then, Stella felt as if she was living in a daze. The less she did, the less she felt capable of doing.

In the morning she would pull herself together, she vowed. If there was still no word from Leo she would send messages to some of the others – the couple in Madrid, the woman in the south of France – whatever Birdie thought of her. She was going to take her life and make something happen in it.

Hello Stella. Fantastic to hear from you. I'm keen to get over to the UK as soon as I can as I'm working on a community garden project in north London. I think your place may be just what I'm looking for.

My only concern is that Villa Rosa is really designed only for summer living. The kitchen is separate from the rest of the house and this time of year, when we're still having rain, you may find yourself getting wet on your way to cook dinner. The sea will be very cold too.

But there's space for you to have friends to stay, and as I'm keen to be in London for a while to get the garden established, you can have Villa Rosa for as long as you want within reason. It's a special place. I haven't owned it for very long but already I feel a strong link with it. I always feel better for being there. Oh and you will love the gardens. Ciao, Leo Asti.

Dear Leo, so good to hear from you and that's great news that you're interested in swapping.

I guess in the hotter months a separate kitchen is ideal. Don't worry, I'm not concerned about getting a bit wet. I'm not certain how long I want to be in Italy for, though. Could we leave it open-ended? Would that work for you?

I haven't done a house exchange before so I'm not entirely sure how things are meant to work. Do we need to draw up some sort of agreement about bills and things?

I'm attaching a photo of my 'garden'. Yes, it's only a few pots out on my patio! My place is tiny, you know. I think we might have made the rooms look a little bigger in the pictures and I'd hate for you to get here and be disappointed, especially if you have other, grander options. Stella.

Dear Stella, I'm not interested in grand; I prefer simplicity. The inside of Villa Rosa is quite spartan because in the hot summer weather I live my life outside. It's comfortable enough but by no means luxurious.

This is my first house swap also so I'm not sure what the proper procedure is. I think we just agree on a date and mail each other a set of keys – easy! I'm fine with us keeping things open-ended so long as you give me some warning before you want your flat back; what about a *fortnight's notice? My main home is an apartment in Naples so if I need to come back to Italy for work in the meantime I can stay there. At this point I have no plans to use Villa Rosa until late July, when my family will be gathering there for our summer holidays.*

We can each cover the bills for the place we are living in so no need to draw up a formal agreement unless you feel the need to. Villa Rosa has some quirks though – it's an old house after all – and I'll have to give you a list of them.

Now some questions: do you have a pet I need to care for? Will you be happy for me to use all your personal things: bed linen, towels, etc., or should I bring some items over? And you say you don't have a car so are you confident driving? The roads here are narrow and winding, perhaps even a little dramatic in places, but Villa Rosa is some distance from Triento, certainly too far to walk. I don't want you to feel stranded. Ciao, Leo.

PS – Your patio looks charming.

Dear Leo, I used to drive a car regularly when I was living in the suburbs so no need to worry. It's just the last few years, being so central, that I haven't needed one. No pets here, not even a goldfish. I assume since Villa Rosa is a holiday home you don't have any there that I'll need to worry about? Of course you must use my linen, towels, etc. You don't want to be taking up space in your luggage with that kind of thing.

Let me have a think about the start date. I'll come back to you on that.

In the meantime I'm intrigued about your community garden project. What is it exactly? What is involved? Stella.

PS – You're very kind about my patio. It's really not

that charming but it's nice enough to sit outside with your coffee on a sunny morning.

Stella was slightly alarmed about how quickly things were progressing. That was why she had told Leo she would get back to him about a date. Their messages had flown back and forth over the course of a morning. Leo must have been sitting at his computer working and she was on her sofa in what Birdie had so rudely called a Google coma. Then abruptly the communications stopped. He went silent after she had asked him to tell her more about his work. Of course it might have been that he had left his desk to go and do something else but Stella couldn't help being suspicious. He was a complete stranger, after all. Since he had never had a house swap there were no reviews from other people up on his profile. What if he wasn't who he claimed to be? She had no way of knowing.

Google didn't help much. She found a couple of entries for 'Leo Asti, landscape gardener, Naples' but they were all in Italian. There were no more pictures of him; nothing on Facebook, twitter or Instagram – he was practically a non-person on the internet.

Stella had read all sorts of scare stories – identity theft, internet scams, con artists. What if this Leo was dodgy? Some sort of Mafia character? Perhaps there were sinister reasons he needed to get out of the country. Yes, it was unlikely, but not beyond the bounds of possibility.

It was a relief when a reply finally came from him late that evening. He sounded so sane.

Hi Stella. Now you have asked me about my great passion! Sorry to take so long to get back to you but I wanted to wait till I had more time. I could talk about this for ever so feel free to stop reading if you get bored ...
  My real job is as a professional landscape architect.

It is something I have been doing for many years and, while I still enjoy it, I had reached a stage in my life when I wanted to make a bigger difference to people – not just those who can afford to pay me but poorer ones, those who live without beauty and green spaces.

My concern is how isolated we are all becoming. I remember when I was young how people in Italy lived on the streets. We met our neighbours, said *buongiorno*, stopped for a chat, touched lives ... But now even here that is changing. We stay shut inside our homes, on our computers and phones, staring at screens, watching the world instead of being a part of it.

Are you still with me? I haven't lost you?

I began to create gardens to draw people outside and together. To begin with I did it without any permission. I planted things in the night on disused ground. I was a little crazy, yes?

Now my community gardens are organised and official. Often they are in run-down, urban areas. We grow vegetables and fruit trees and flowers in these places. The vision is mine but neighbours come together for the planting and I leave them to maintain what we've created. Often it works, not always. But when I make a gardener out of someone who has never put their hands in the soil ... or I see an old person sharing the knowledge of a lifetime with a young child, then I feel I am doing good work, a thing that counts.

This is enough about me, surely? You said something in an earlier message that I am curious about. You are on an adult gap year? What is that? Tell me more. Leo.

Hi Leo. First of all, that sounds amazing. I really hope I get to see some of your gardens if I come to Italy. Could you send me a couple of pictures?

Adult gap years are a newish thing I think. The idea

is that you take time out from your everyday life for experiences and adventures. Mine was forced on me after my employer died and I found myself out of a job. I'm sure I won't take a whole year but I do like the idea of a gap and this seems a good time for one. I've always lived in or around London and I'd like to be part of somewhere different for a while, get to know new people (hopefully they won't all be inside on their computers!) and their way of life. It all sounds a bit self-indulgent compared to what you're doing. I had thought about volunteering on some project in a developing nation. Perhaps I still ought to. But Villa Rosa seemed so tempting. I looked at all your photos and could imagine myself there. And I've always longed to visit Italy but never managed it ... Stella.

Stella, if you have a feeling that Villa Rosa is where you should be then you must come. It is a house that needs people, I think, and you will be filling it with your voice and your personality, and your friends (and helping keep the weeds down in my garden). You will be doing a good thing.

It must have been a shock to have your employer die and to find yourself without a job so suddenly. You deserve this gap.

I will confide in you now. Since agreeing to work on this project in London I have been feeling a little anxious. I have done only one other in England and I found it difficult. That time I stayed in a motel room and it wasn't a good place to go back to at the end of a tough day. That's why I decided to try this house swap – in the hope I might find a home from home. I would like to be in London soon, however. How long do you think it will take you to decide on a date? I do have a couple of other house-swap options but I'd like to think of you in Villa Rosa ... and I think Villa Rosa would like it too. Leo.

PS – Some pictures of my gardens attached as requested.

He talked about the house as if it was a person and that seemed odd to Stella, who thought him rather intense but supposed that might be the way with Italian men. She clicked on the pictures he had sent and was pleased to find he appeared in one of them. He was with another man, arms slung round each other's shoulders, faces creased into smiles, both holding spades. Behind them was a vegetable bed filled with structures made with willow branches, plants climbing up them. Leo looked more natural, less posed than he had in the first shot. He was older than his companion but striking with his sun-burnished skin and silvery hair.

She wasn't so worried now about him being a conman. Who in the world would create such an elaborate lie? Surely with Leo her little mews apartment would be in safe hands. What was she waiting for?

Hi Leo, I'm free to swap whenever you are. Let's do it soon! Stella.

Curiouser and curiouser

The pictures of Villa Rosa hadn't done it justice, not even nearly. It was early evening by the time Stella arrived and the taxi driver (she had waited half an hour for him – was there actually only one in the whole village?) dropped her off in the wrong place and left her with a pile of baggage to haul up two steep flights of steps alone. There was another house nearby but its shutters were closed so she wouldn't find any help there.

Stella cursed herself for not packing lighter as she heaved the bags upwards. She was irritated and out of breath, so it was several moments before she took in her surroundings properly.

'Oh,' she said aloud, and then again, 'Oh.'

The villa stood with its back to the mountains and glowed pale pink in the setting sun. Its dark green shutters looked freshly painted, its wooden door gleamed with varnish, the terracotta tiles of its roof were weighed down with stones. Everywhere Stella looked there were plants, growing in pots, climbing up walls or sprouting from beds carved into the lawns. In front of the house was a courtyard with a flowering pomegranate tree at its centre. And over by the kitchen there was an outdoor fire and a table she could eat at when the weather was fine.

Stella caught a movement from the corner of her eye and saw it was a small green lizard, disappearing into a crack in the wall. She turned to face the sea and took in the view she was going to see every day for weeks to come.

'Oh my God, this place is perfect. Completely perfect.'

She stood for a while, taking it all in: the rocky outcrops in the distance, the sun glinting off the water, the wide ceiling of blue sky. Then she turned back to the house, eager to see inside.

The bunch of keys Leo had sent her was safely stowed in the zippered compartment of her handbag. There seemed to be a lot of them and she fumbled as she tried to work out which one fitted where. It was a relief to finally get the front door open. The place had a smell she recognised that she thought might be furniture polish. With the shutters closed, it was semi-dark inside and there was more fumbling while she found the light switch.

She found herself in a hallway, small and unfurnished, its far wall completely covered with a fresco that reflected the scene outside, coloured with the vivid blues of sea and sky. As she explored the house she found two more framed paintings in the same style hung in the living room and another upstairs in the larger one of the three bedrooms.

This was where she would sleep, decided Stella, as she opened French doors onto a pretty terrace that gave her a view of the sea through a fringe of wisteria. It was definitely the nicest spot.

She wondered where Leo slept when he was here. He may have arrived at her place by now. Was he doing the exact same thing, opening and closing doors, discovering each small space? If so she hoped he wasn't feeling disappointed, even a little cheated, when he thought about how much Stella had got in exchange for her very ordinary flat.

In the weeks leading up to the exchange the messages between them had become short and practical. Leo seemed anxious she should know about all of Villa Rosa's idiosyncrasies and his emails were filled with instructions about the hot-water supply or the gas delivery. There had been talk of Skyping each other, or at least managing a phone call, but

Leo was caught up with last-minute work and Stella hadn't pushed it.

By that stage she wasn't certain she wanted to speak to him. What if he didn't live up to the way she had imagined him, if there was something about his tone she didn't like or he seemed less genuine? She was anxious enough as her departure date neared, waking in the middle of the night and listing in her head all the things that might go wrong. It wouldn't have taken much to make her back out of the whole thing.

Now she was here, Stella was so glad she hadn't. Digging her phone out of her handbag she tapped out a quick text to Leo. *I'm standing on your terrace looking at the view. I love it here. Thank you.*

A few minutes later he texted back, *I'm on your patio picking herbs for a frittata. I feel at home already. Have you been in the kitchen yet? There's something there for you.*

The kitchen, Stella recalled, was quite separate from the rest of the house. She was pleased to discover steps leading down to it from her bedroom terrace. They would be a morning shortcut and even on rainy days she should be able to dash down quickly to make herself a coffee.

There was more fumbling of keys to find the one that unlocked the kitchen door. This was a narrow room with a rough stone wall and it looked well used, as if many feasts had been prepared in it to be eaten at the table outside on summer evenings.

On the countertop beside the cooker there was an envelope and a gift-wrapped parcel. Opening the envelope first, she found a note, handwritten and very neat, each letter properly formed, each line even, nothing like her own messy scrawl.

Dear Stella, you are standing in my kitchen and I hope you've opened this note first because it contains the instructions for how I would like you to use the gift I've left for you. You don't have to follow them of course but it's taken me some time and effort to put together and so I hope you do. Inside the parcel you will find a scrapbook. Don't skim through or read it from cover to cover. Instead if you have a day when you're feeling perhaps bored or lonely or even homesick, then read a page of the book – any page, pick at random – and do the thing I've described on it. There are walks to take, places to visit, people to meet, recipes to cook, treasures to look for. I've had fun thinking them all up. I hope you enjoy the adventures you'll have just as much. All my regards – Leo.

Stella was almost certain no one had ever done anything quite so lovely for her before. She opened the parcel and found the scrapbook inside; ring-bound, with a plain brown cover and her own name printed on the front. Immediately she wanted to flick through the pages to see what he had written. But Leo was right; she was on her own here and once the novelty had worn off there would be times she felt isolated and perhaps even rather lost. She ought to put this book aside till then and use it just as he had suggested.

It was a curious sort of feeling, being so cherished by a stranger. All she had done for Leo was let her neighbours know he would be staying and jotted down a list of things such as the best places to shop for groceries or buy a decent coffee. She felt faintly embarrassed to find he had gone to so much more effort for her.

Opening the fridge, she discovered he had also arranged to leave her with the makings of a meal: some eggs, salami, cheese, a bottle of white wine.

Right at that moment in her London kitchen Leo was cooking himself a snack. Stella would do the same here in his house and wait until morning to get to grips with the car and brave the coast road he had described as 'dramatic'.

She opened the wine, poured herself a glass and went to stand out on the terrace and watch the last pink strands of the sunset. She was a house-swapper now and what a place she had lucked into. Yet as beautiful as it was, she would have been happy to give it all away to have things as they were: Milly alive, and her days taken up with the work they did together. Whatever the future held, she worried she would always feel that way.

In her dark, shuttered bedroom Stella slept the whole night through without wakefulness or worry. She opened her eyes early to the sound of birdsong and a craving for strong coffee. Today her plan was to make Villa Rosa feel more like it belonged to her. She was going to buy food, and perhaps some flowers, rearrange a few things that could be easily changed back when it was time to leave.

Shrugging on her robe Stella made a quick dash down the terrace steps to the kitchen. It was chilly but at least the day was a dry one. She ground some coffee beans, put the moka pot on the stove then started making a list of all the things she needed.

The scrapbook Leo had given her was still there on the bench-top. Last night Stella had decided not to look inside it for at least a week. Now she suspected it would be impossible to resist opening it before then.

Downing her first coffee, she carried the second cup back to her room so she could follow Leo's instructions for the Wi-Fi and send him a quick message.

Hi Leo. What an amazing and thoughtful thing to do; thank you so much. I haven't opened the scrapbook yet but I'm longing to. I can't wait to see what treats you've got in store for me.

My first night was very peaceful – it's so amazingly

*quiet here! I slept better than I have in ages and now
I'm lazing in bed with my morning coffee. I'm in the
room that leads onto the terrace; hope that's OK.*

*I was wondering about the fresco in the hallway. Is
it by a local artist? Are the other paintings in the house
by the same person?*

*Hope everything is OK over there. I can't help feeling
as though I got the best side of this house-swap bargain.
My flat had better behave itself for you or I'll be very
embarrassed. Thanks again – Stella.*

Triento was a town of narrow lanes and many churches clinging to the slopes of a mountain. It was hardly a large place
but seemed to have everything Stella might need – a market
for fresh produce, a sweet-scented bakery, a butcher's shop
and a *salumeria* selling cheeses and salami. There was a bar
on the corner where she would stop for coffee on another
morning when she hadn't already drunk so much of it.

Her nerves were still jangling from the rigours of her first
drive in Leo's old Fiat. Its gears were clunky and the twisting
coast road held the double threat of a steep drop on one
side and a jagged rock face on the other. Even if she hadn't
been wrestling with the whole left-hand-drive business Stella
wouldn't have dared to more than glance at the view.

Fortunately she had found a parking space just outside
the village, for it seemed cars weren't supposed to stop in its
piazza or cobbled streets. There was an official-looking man
in a white peaked cap blowing a whistle at anyone who did.
It was quite a pantomime actually. Surely the locals knew
there was no parking but many seemed determined to try
nevertheless and there was much waving of arms and shouting to accompany the man's furious blasts on the whistle.
Stella paused to watch.

The whole scene was lively. There were women shopping
with baskets over their arms, just like her. There was a priest

39

in black robes, pausing to chat to an old man; and small clusters of people here and there, neighbours and friends, swapping gossip or exchanging a morning greeting.

Stella heard church bells ringing; she smelt coffee and sweet pastries, and she had that same sense Camden always gave her, of being an onlooker, placed inside the scene but not quite a part of it, almost invisible. It came as a surprise when the woman called out to her.

'*Signora*, you are English, yes? *Signora*, hello.'

Stella glanced over her shoulder and saw a dark-haired young woman standing outside an old-fashioned linen shop where she was pinning up the day's display of tea towels and tablecloths. The woman gave her a friendly smile. 'English?' she asked again.

Stella nodded.

'You are in Triento for a holiday?' The woman was dressed in ice-cream shades, pale blue pants and a pastel-pink jacket with flat silver buttons, clothes that spoke of confidence and suited her slim figure.

'I'm staying here for a while actually,' Stella told her. 'In a place a little way along the coast.'

'In the hotel?' the woman asked in lightly accented English. 'It is nice there I think.'

'No, not the hotel, in a private house by the sea. It's called Villa Rosa.'

'There are many houses along the coast. In the summer holidays when they are full it gets so busy here. But now in spring it is mostly locals, no other English people, no German tourists or religious pilgrims come to visit our famous statue.'

Stella had noticed the statue high on the mountains; a stark white marble figure of Christ with his arms outstretched, you couldn't miss it. Last night from Villa Rosa, it had appeared brightly illuminated against a velvety-black sky.

'I only arrived yesterday,' she told the woman. 'I haven't

had a chance to visit the statue yet but I'm sure I will. I'm Stella, by the way, Stella Forrester.'

'Stella, it's nice to meet you. I'm Francesca Russo and this is my family's shop. You must be sure to visit us also. You won't find linen like ours at home in England. It is artisan-made right here in Basilicata, very good quality.'

Stella was disappointed to find what she had taken as friendliness from an English-speaking local was really just a sales pitch. Still, she supposed it must be a struggle to make a living in a place like this.

'I love fabrics so I'll definitely come in,' she promised.

Francesca beamed at her. 'The Russo family has been handcrafting linens since 1880. I have some special things inside to show you. I think you will adore them.'

'That's great, I'll look forward to it.'

'In the meantime can I help point you in the right direction for your shopping? Have you found the supermarket yet? The post office for sending cards home? The pharmacy? Triento is small but still it can be confusing for visitors at first, with so many places hidden away in the back streets.'

'I'm fine wandering round,' Stella assured her. 'I'm sure I won't get too lost.'

'The nicest places to eat are down by the harbour, especially if you enjoy seafood.' Francesca seemed determined to be helpful. 'You can drive there but there's also a walking path. It's steep in parts, but the views are worth it.'

'Thanks.' Stella began edging away. 'That's good to know.'

'Don't forget to come back and buy some of our linen,' Francesca called after her. 'It's the very best thing about Triento, I promise you.'

She suspected she might get the same hard sell everywhere but Stella managed to buy some bread from the bakery and go from stall to stall in the market with a minimum of fuss. As soon as people heard her speaking her few sentences of phrasebook Italian they immediately switched to English, but aside from that no one seemed too interested by the foreigner in their midst.

Once her basket was full, Stella walked back towards the car. Francesca was still there outside her linen shop, talking to the parking warden now, and she raised a hand in greeting. Stella supposed other faces in the village would become familiar in time. She would get to know the people who served her coffee in the corner bar and the market stallholders where she bought her food. They might begin to exchange a *buongiorno* or make small talk like Francesca had.

Soon the tourists would arrive, and Birdie would visit like she had promised, and some of her other friends might come. Failing all that there was Leo's scrapbook to keep her occupied. Stella was beginning to suspect she might be grateful for it.

Ciao Stella. The artist who made the fresco in the hall is a woman called Aurora Gray. She lived at Villa Rosa for a while, apparently. I look out for her work and buy it when I can. It seems to belong there.

I hope you are finding the house comfortable. You should have seen the place when I first bought it, so neglected and run-down. The paint was peeling from the outside walls, the varnish on the shutters had blistered and the garden was a disaster. Being so close to the sea means it feels the full force of the weather, especially in winter, so I think I may have got to it just in time.

Did you manage OK with the car today? I hope if you drove it up to town everything went well (although a few more dents and scrapes won't matter). Leo.

Hi Leo. More dents and scrapes seem inevitable so I'm relieved you don't mind. That road was never designed for cars, was it? It was meant for people riding horses ...

or donkeys. I'm sure I'll get used to it but I'll be avoiding it at night for a while.

I've never heard of Aurora Gray but I like her paintings. It's obvious she loved this place. Sad to think of it being neglected. Still, you've done a lovely job of renovating.

Does somebody live in the house next door? It's all closed up and I haven't spotted anyone yet so I'm assuming the answer is no – Stella.

Hi Stella. It's a shame about that house. From what I hear the people who have lived there over the years have looked after Villa Rosa and sometimes even taken care of the gardens. But the last one, a very old lady, has died and since then her family has rented it to holidaymakers so I'm not sure when you'll find any company from there.

Do you mind being on your own? You're not nervous at all? For myself I love the solitude of Villa Rosa. But now I'm here and seeing how you live right in the middle of this bustling place I'm concerned you might feel cut off from civilisation. And at night with no street lights and no noise except the sea crashing against the rocks ... well, it's my idea of paradise there but is it yours? Leo.

Hi Leo. It feels so safe here I haven't even thought about being nervous at night. It is pretty safe, isn't it? Do I need to worry? I hope not!

Anyway I'm happy enough in my own company for now. And actually I was befriended by one of the locals today – a woman called Francesca Russo; do you know her? She was actually only trying to sell me some linen from her shop but she was very chatty. I expect I'll have to go in at some point and buy a couple of tea towels.

It's a beautiful day here, sunny with a blue, blue sky and a chilly breeze that's making white caps in the sea. It looks like one of Aurora Gray's paintings come to life and I think it's anyone's idea of paradise. I'm sure I'll be fine – Stella.

Stella, sorry if I worried you. It's very safe, I promise. In the summer holidays, we never even lock the doors. Be reassured you can relax in paradise – Leo.

It was difficult to find any clues about him from looking round at the house, even if he had renovated it. On the shelves in the living room were a few novels in English and Italian but they were the sort of thing friends or family might have left behind, thrillers and romances. The small storeroom off the kitchen held what you would expect to find in any holiday home: sun loungers and table-tennis sets, spare sets of wine glasses. There were no photographs in frames, none of his clothes, no personal belongings at all, really. In one of the bedrooms was a locked cupboard but none of the keys she had been given opened it so Stella assumed that was where everything was stored.

Perhaps Leo was doing the same thing right now, looking at her place for clues about her. If so he would find a locked cupboard that he couldn't open. Inside were photographs and bank statements, old birthday cards from her parents, the wedding album she had never been able to bring herself to throw away. Now that Stella considered it there were plenty of things about herself that she hadn't shared with him.

Still, she was curious. As she tweaked the place to suit her tastes, shifted furniture, tidied a few glass ornaments away in cupboards, arranged fruit in a bowl and filled a vase with spring flowers taken from the garden, she found her eyes searching for little things that might say more about him. And when she found none, she felt disappointed.

Sky blue

On the second morning the sun was shining and the sky seemed the exact shade as in the fresco on the hallway wall. Stella threw on a long cream cashmere cardigan over her pyjamas and drank her coffee sitting beneath the pomegranate tree in the courtyard. She'd had another incredible night's sleep and when she had woken in her dim, shuttered room there had been a disorienting few seconds when she wasn't sure where she was. Villa Rosa; it came back to her and she felt her spirits lift.

Today she was going to see about taking some classes. Hopefully there was a language school she could sign up to, or maybe cooking lessons or some sort of walking group. Stella didn't care so much about learning to speak Italian or being taught how to make the local dishes but it seemed a route into the place, a way to begin to experience it properly.

Yesterday, busy shopping and rearranging the house, the whole day had been filled up. Stella hadn't even walked down to the sea yet. According to Leo there was a path that led down to the rocks so, without bothering to get dressed, she slipped on some shoes and went to find it.

The pathway dropped down through the terraces of the garden, past vegetable beds and more fruit trees, and beneath a shady strand of pines. At its finish Stella found a low wooden gate and a short flight of stone steps that took her onto the rocks. The sea was unsettled and she could hear it crashing into the land and see frothy fingers of spume shooting up.

She walked across the flat parts of the rocks, well back

from the edge, and found the beginnings of another path carved into the cliff. As she followed it, she saw more houses, all shuttered and closed up. She walked on, continuing to a small stony beach tucked into a cleft in the rocks.

This might be a place to swim on warmer days, as the sea seemed more settled. Stella kicked off her shoes and, leaving them on an upturned rowing boat, walked to the shallows and let the waves wash over her bare feet. There was someone fishing from a small boat out way beyond the breakers. She started to raise a hand in greeting but then, remembering how eccentric she must look, paddling in her pyjamas, changed her mind about attracting attention.

Leo had said he loved the solitude. Stella could see its appeal but she was used to having people around – Milly and the girls, to starting each day with inconsequential chat about what they had cooked for dinner or watched on television, to the hum of them talking as she was trying to work. There were times back then that she had wished for peace and quiet but now she had so much of it, Stella missed their noise.

When she was younger Stella never imagined reaching this age and being alone. Back then the future seemed clear, almost predestined. You had fun for a while then met the right man and settled down. You worked hard, bought a place together and had a couple of children. That was how it went, right?

The having fun part had worked out pretty well. At university there were lots of friends, and wild weekends and a couple of boyfriends, although neither lasted long. In her twenties she had quietened down, especially once she started her job with Milly. It was such a female office; and work took up so much of her time. Stella had dated now and then, hoping to meet the right person eventually.

Other friends got married. Lots had babies and afterwards their lives seemed to fall away from hers. They were busy, tired, distracted; even if they did find time to see her, things never felt the same. Stella always swore she wouldn't be like that when her turn came.

Ray didn't appear until she was in her late thirties. He was a fabric supplier Milly had started dealing with and was charming from the outset, often popping into the office with a takeout coffee for Stella and sometimes even a little sugary treat. She had assumed his charm was all part of doing business.

'He likes you,' the girls in the office kept saying but she shrugged off the idea.

'I like him too,' was her response. 'But only for his beautiful merino.'

It was Milly who intervened in the end. She seemed half-amused, half-exasperated by Stella's mishandling of her own love life.

'For goodness' sake, give the man a break. He's dying to ask you out, isn't that obvious? All he needs is the tiniest amount of encouragement. You like him, don't you?'

Did she like him? Stella wasn't sure. Ray was tall yet soft-looking and his pale shaven head didn't seem quite large enough for his body. But Stella always noticed clothes and his were good, tailored by someone who knew what they were doing. And besides he was engaging, lively and funny, interested in her. She thought he would be good company.

So the next time Ray came in she mentioned a film she wanted to see, a documentary about a fashion designer. And he seized the chance, saying he was keen to see it too and why didn't they go together.

There were more films and dinners; there were Sunday walks and drinks with her friends then his. They started to merge their lives, not always comfortably, but bumping along. When Ray proposed and Stella said yes, everyone was happy.

Thinking about it now as she sat on a rock and stared at

the sea merging with the horizon, Stella wasn't sure if she had been in love with the man or the life they had together. She adored waking up with him on weekend mornings, grabbing the newspapers and going somewhere for coffee or brunch. She liked being part of a couple at parties, always knowing he was there to moor to in a roomful of strangers. And she enjoyed the quiet evenings, drinking a bottle of red wine while cooking dinner together, then sitting side by side on the sofa watching something rubbishy on TV.

Ray was a nice guy and mostly she had been happy sharing lives. Still, it hadn't been so hard to be without him.

Good morning Stella. I hope you slept well last night. I've realised that I didn't answer your question about Francesca Russo. Oh yes, I am very well supplied with her tea towels and tablecloths, napkins, pillowcases, bed covers, even some of those linen doilies people used to have out on their sideboards. But I'm sure she will have me buy more next time I'm in Triento. She is difficult to say no to – Leo.

Hi Leo. How funny. Still I suppose you can never have too much linen.

I slept beautifully, thank you. I'm just about to drive up to the village where I'm going to treat myself to a pastry and a cappuccino for breakfast, so if I spot Francesca Russo I'll say hello from you … possibly I'll even buy you a few more tea towels! Stella.

The drive to Triento might have been marginally less hair-raising than the day before although Stella did squeak once or twice when an oncoming car looked about to hit hers. Arriving unscathed, she parked near the same spot as last time and walked to the bar on the corner of the piazza where she ordered herself a coffee and a vanilla-scented pastry.

Sitting at a table near the open doorway, she watched people come and go. It was their clothes that told her who they were. The dirt-stained trousers of an old farmer, the tight skirt of an Italian mamma who spent half her day in the kitchen, the narrow-legged trousers of a young woman who may have lived miles from the city but still read fashion magazines.

Different as they were, each of them belonged here. They had families and jobs, places to be. For a moment Stella wondered if it had been madness to come to Italy when all she had really done was swap one sort of loneliness for another. At least at home there were people who cared enough to ask how she was doing; here no one knew her at all.

Still, as Stella had recently learnt, friends came with complications. Far too often lately some of hers had looked at her with an expression that she recognised as pity and Stella hadn't liked it. The idea they were discussing her situation and feeling sorry for her ... while she must have done the same to them many times, now it was her turn and it felt horrible.

Perhaps it was better to be in Italy after all. Here she wasn't the poor thing who was failing and floundering; she was just another visitor and her life was her own business.

Stella sipped her coffee, watched the passers-by and made plans for her day. She would stop in at the linen shop and ask about language schools or cooking classes. Francesca Russo seemed the busybody type so surely she would know.

Except when Stella glanced across the piazza she saw it wasn't Francesca this morning, pinning up the day's display of napkins and tea towels beside the doorway, but instead a man who might be her husband. He was taking his time over the task. Every few minutes he stopped to chat, first to the parking warden, then a couple of older men, a pretty girl cycling past with wheels juddering over the cobbles, a mother with a toddler at her feet; he seemed to know everyone and have a few words to offer.

Stella decided to wander over anyway in case Francesca was inside. Leaving some cash on the table, she shrugged on her jacket.

The man smiled as she approached his shop. He gave her a look that seemed to sweep from her face right down to her toes, and then he called out, '*Buongiorno*.'

Stella supposed he was handsome. He had a spare, athletic frame and dark hair that was cut so it flopped onto his face, a style he was really too old for although it did kind of suit him.

'*Buongiorno*,' she replied. 'Is Francesca around?'

'Around somewhere but not here,' he said, in perfect English. 'Can I help? You are looking for something special; a gift or a souvenir?'

'Oh no, I'm not here to buy linen; at least not today. I wanted to ask Francesca about something else but I can leave it till another time.'

'She is a friend of yours?'

'No ... and really it isn't important. I'll talk to her next time I'm passing.'

'Shall I say who was asking for her?'

'Just tell her the Englishwoman, Stella, but she might not remember me.'

'Stella.' He held out a hand to shake hers. 'I am Roberto Russo and I'm not going to let you walk away from my shop without looking at some of my linen. I know you want to. I see it in your face. Come on in; I absolutely insist.'

She found herself following him inside. For a moment she was stilled by the scent of the place. Fabric was piled up on shelves and tables, and there was more stacked in the room beyond, all smelling so wonderful that she could only close her eyes and breathe it in. Cinnamon, she thought, vanilla, warm butter, toasted sugar, perhaps even honey.

She opened her eyes to see Roberto watching her, his expression curious. 'You like it in here?'

'Yes,' Stella agreed, and she let her hand drift across the nearest pile of cloth, crisp beneath her fingers, its weave so fine.

'You have a passion for fabrics?' he guessed.

Hemmed in by sheets and coverlets, Stella nodded.

'Francesca says it's like a love affair for some people. They see a beautiful piece of cloth and they can't resist picking it up, stroking or crumpling it in their hands. They need to be close to it.'

'That's me,' Stella admitted. 'Most of all I love the way it smells.'

He smiled at her. Pulling a wooden ladder over to the shelves, he climbed to the highest and took down a quilt. It was patterned with flowers in shell pink and pale yellow and when he laid it out on the wide polished-wood counter Stella could see the design was old-fashioned and intricate.

'Help yourself, *signora*,' he told her.

Stella couldn't resist. She leaned down until her face was almost pressed against the fabric. It smelt like the lavender biscuits Milly used to love to buy from Fortnum's. The fragrance took Stella right back to her little ritual of making afternoon tea if they had been working especially hard. Lavender biscuits piled on a plate in the middle of the work-room and Earl Grey drunk from old-fashioned china cups.

'Try this one now.' Roberto Russo was unfolding a table-cloth, starched and white. To Stella it smelt of fresh air and sunshine.

Finally he offered her a table runner, rough-woven and the colour of butter. This one was musky, like an older woman's fragrance, heavy and a little oppressive.

'My mother has one like this,' he told her. 'She has place mats and napkins to match. But I don't think it's your taste. You love the quilt, yes?'

'It's beautiful but it looks expensive.'

'I would sell it to you at a good price.' He said it casually as if he wasn't interested in pushing her.

Stella looked at the quilt. She could imagine it lying over her bed at home but knew she shouldn't be spending money on things she didn't really need. 'Maybe ... I'll think about it.'

'Come back and visit it. I'll keep it aside for you. And I'll tell Francesca you were here.' With quick, efficient hands, he began to fold away the linens that he had pulled out to show her. 'It's her day off but she'll be back tomorrow.'

It was difficult to leave the linen shop. Stella might have spent half the day in there and hardly noticed the time pass. Out in the piazza, she stared back towards the tea towels fluttering round its doorway and thought again of lavender biscuits. She had never really liked the way they tasted, only how they smelt, and the ritual of drinking tea with her colleagues had been such a comfortable one.

Strolling through the village, she glanced in windows as she went. There was a *pasticceria* with a display of garish marzipan sweets. A souvenir place selling mini replicas of the statue on the mountain and painted wooden Pinocchios. Stores filled with coral jewellery and silk scarves. A wine merchant and a flower stall. Nothing else quite like the linen shop, however.

The walk seemed to be clearing her head so Stella decided to keep going and see if she could find the pathway Francesca Russo had said would lead her down to the harbour. Luckily it was signposted, otherwise she might have missed the steep flight of steps cut into the rocks. It was so narrow she had to move aside and press against the wall to let a man pass by, an aged-looking priest who nodded his thanks and kept climbing upwards, barely out of breath.

Three flights down, Stella reached a terrace and found the view. From here the sea looked like a piece of cloth, an aqua satin or a shimmery silk, with boats studded on it like crystals. She could see the terracotta roofs of houses and the line of the harbour wall, all of it far away and in miniature. Only then did it occur to Stella that if she walked all the way down then at some point she would have to climb back up, unless she managed to find Triento's elusive taxi.

The next fight of steps was uneven and crumbling so Stella had to be careful where she put her feet. Every now and then she stopped to drink in a little more of the scene beneath her. As she drew closer she could see striped sun umbrellas outside what she assumed was a restaurant and a few people moving about.

Eventually the steps finished and Stella found herself on a path that zigzagged downwards beneath a stand of pine trees. It seemed to go on for ever and she didn't see a single person after the priest. She kept thinking of the lunch she would deserve after so much exercise – definitely a bowl of pasta and maybe a second course, even a dessert.

Finally she reached the outskirts of the little settlement, a ruined house with half its roof missing and then a couple of others that seemed equally old but in better shape. A final flight of steps and she was there, standing on a promenade besides the water's edge.

It was all very picture-postcard. Layers of pastel-coloured houses perched on the rocks that half-circled the harbour. There was washing fluttering at windows and people were out on balconies, an older woman knitting, a younger one snatching time for a quick cigarette.

Stella needed to sit down. She could feel the muscles in her legs aching. A little further on was the place with the fluttering sun umbrellas and several people sitting beneath them. She headed to it, finding a table that was sheltered from the breeze by a clear plastic canopy.

It was a relief to be off her feet and Stella tried not to think about the climb she faced returning to Triento. She would have a glass of wine with lunch and perhaps that would help power her back up.

Usually when eating alone, she brought a book or magazine but since Stella had neither, once she had finished with the menu, all there was to do was look about.

It was early in the season and things were fairly quiet. A few people were idling in the sunshine, a couple of men in suits seemed to be having a business meeting over coffee, and a trio of teenagers who probably ought to have been in school were hanging about on the narrow strip of beach, sharing a cigarette.

At the table beside hers there was a couple who seemed mismatched. He was heavyset, poorly dressed and flushed from the wine he was drinking. She was very elegant, not young, but finely groomed. Stella stole another look and realised she recognised the suit the woman was wearing – a light wool in navy blue with a peplum jacket and a narrow skirt. It was one of Milly's designs, a few seasons old, but a classic you could wear for ever. The woman, with her slender figure, tanned skin, and mane of mahogany hair, looked great in it. There was a peep of a camisole above the jacket and a touch of gold at her throat, but she had added nothing to spoil its careful simplicity. Stella wondered what she was doing with this man whose belly swelled above the waistline of jeans that looked distinctly grubby.

As the waitress left with her order, Stella watched the man stand up, knock back the dregs of his wine, and walk away. The woman stayed where she was, tapping on her phone. She looked up, caught Stella's eye and raised her eyebrows.

'*Buongiorno*,' said Stella.

The woman nodded at her then returned her attention to her phone.

About ten minutes later, as Stella's pasta arrived, a man approached her table. He seemed uncertain, looking from her to the woman in the navy suit, and then he said, 'Tosca?'

Stella shook her head. 'Not me, sorry.'

'*Signore, sono Tosca.*' The woman in navy waved at him from the next table.

For a moment Stella thought she saw him hesitate but then he greeted her and, sitting down, launched into conversation.

The pasta was good, thick ribbons of pappardelle in a buttery sauce with gems of tender baby broad beans and crisp rocket leaves. Between mouthfuls Stella found her attention tugged back to the glamorous woman at the neighbouring table. This man she was chatting to was much younger than the last and better dressed. He was wearing rather a nice red scarf and dark-framed spectacles. She might easily be his mother but Stella had a feeling that she wasn't, and wished she understood some Italian so she could eavesdrop.

The man ordered an espresso and after he had drunk it, fidgeted with his cup and teaspoon. His conversation seemed to be flagging and when he stood up to go the woman shrugged and, picking up her phone, barely bothered to say goodbye to him.

A third man arrived as Stella was eating her dessert, a sweet tart of ricotta and candied lemons. This one appeared to recognise the woman. She stood, and they kissed on both cheeks before settling at the table together. He was pleasant-looking with a downy layer of thin grey hair covering his head and a round face that was softening with age. He stayed chatting to the woman while Stella finished eating and wondered if she could manage another coffee.

Then the pair stood, touching cheeks to say goodbye, and when the man left, the woman took her seat again. Stella was curious about what was going on. Were these men her business contacts, friends or something else? She stared at the woman rather too obviously and her reward was an amused look.

Stella smiled apologetically.

The woman inclined her head and half-smiled back. 'Speed-dating,' she said.

'I'm sorry?'

'That is what I'm doing. Speed-dating. I could see you were wondering.' She spoke in English with an accent that held a slight American inflection.

'Oh I see.' Stella was taken aback.

'None of them today have been worth the effort. That last one, much too old, and nothing like his photograph.'

'Did you find them on the internet?' Stella asked.

'Yes of course, where else? There is one more to come. I hope he isn't another disappointment.'

But the final man didn't appear. The woman sent a text, then made a call and left a message. She seemed irritated, tossing her phone back on the table.

'It appears I have been stood up,' she said to Stella coolly.

'Would you like to join me? I was about to order coffee if the waiter ever comes back.'

'Why not?' The woman gathered up her things. A small quilted handbag with a gold chain Stella thought might be real Chanel, her phone, her glass of water, a pair of sunglasses, a copy of Italian *Vogue*. Taking the seat opposite, she introduced herself.

'I am Tosca.'

'I'm Stella, nice to meet you. I love your suit. It's a Milly Munro, isn't it?'

'You have a good eye.'

'Actually I used to work for her. I remember that suit. It was one of my favourites that season.'

'I have other designs of hers,' Tosca told her, counting them off on her fingers. 'A wrap dress, some pencil-slim pants, oh and a trench coat. I read somewhere that she died recently. Is that true? What happened?'

Stella managed to flag down the waiter and order coffee for them both. As it was sipped, she found herself sharing the whole sad story. She told it in clothes. The pale grey blouse with the Peter Pan collar that Milly had been wearing on the day she was diagnosed with cancer, the apple-green cashmere cardigan she had been wrapped in the last time Stella had seen her alive. Tosca nodded as if she could imagine each scene quite clearly.

'At the funeral, every woman wore one of her designs,' Stella told her. 'Row after row of them in the church, from the youngest to the most elderly: black coat dresses, suits like yours in darkest blue, simple shifts warmed with woollen shrugs. It was like the most astonishing fashion show you could imagine, a tribute to her really, an amazing ending.'

'How old was she?' Tosca asked.

'I'm not sure; she never would say. In her early sixties, I think.'

Tosca frowned. 'Too young for an ending then.'

'Yes,' Stella agreed. 'She had so much passion for what she did. She was sketching out ideas for designs right to the very last. All that brilliance just snuffed out, gone from the world, such a waste ... it's difficult to make sense of. At least we still have the clothes, I suppose. She's left something of herself behind.'

Tosca shrugged. 'Is that so important? Do you care what you leave behind? Once you are gone what does it matter?'

Stella thought about it. 'I'm not sure I agree. Milly would be pleased if she knew I was here, talking to a woman I've just met who is wearing one of her designs. She liked her clothes to be out in the world, used and touched, taken places. And I'm sure she'd have hated to think of herself as forgotten.'

'So then ...' Tosca leaned her elbows on the table, resting her chin on her hands. 'What will you be remembered for? Good things or bad?'

Stella was taken aback. It wasn't something she had ever considered. 'I'm not sure; good, I hope. What about you?'

Tosca shrugged. 'I expect that will depend on who is doing the remembering.'

Stella was intrigued by this woman; she was very attractive and everything about her had been carefully curated – the hair coloured in caramels, the brow almost certainly Botoxed, skin plumped by something, make-up flawlessly applied, fingernails squared and buffed to a shine. If Stella had been asked to guess her age she would have said late fifties, perhaps a little more but she didn't think so. And, while she was definitely Italian, there was that mysterious American lilt to her voice.

'I can't quite place your accent. Have you spent time in the US?'

'Yes, but this is where I was born. Years ago my father used to be a fisherman. I've come home.'

'It's a lovely place,' Stella said warmly.

Tosca shrugged. 'Tell me, how long have you been here?'

'Just a couple of days so far, but I'm staying for a while.'

'Well I hope you continue to find it lovely. I have been back for long enough that I'm about to die of boredom.'

'Hence the speed-dating?' Stella guessed.

'There are no men in Triento as far as I can tell,' Tosca told her. 'They are either married or almost dead or they're still children. Now I'm looking further afield. So far no luck, as you have seen.'

'You want to be in a relationship?'

'Of course, of course.' She sounded surprised by the question. 'I want a companion, a person beside me. What is life without that?'

'I'm single,' Stella admitted, 'and I'm fine with it. Life has plenty of other things to offer.'

'Perhaps it does in other places, but not here.'

'Surely there is still adventure, possibilities, freedom?' said Stella. And then she told her about her gap year, about the pink house nestled against the mountain with its sweeping view of the sea and her plans to spend time there, get to know the area and experience life as a local.

'It's called Villa Rosa and it's beautiful. I'm loving it so far,' she said.

'Villa Rosa?' Tosca repeated. 'Is it an old house that's been restored, just along the coast a little way?'

Stella nodded.

'But that is Leo Asti's place, yes?'

'Do you know him?'

'Not well, but I went to a party last summer, a lunch in the garden to show off how beautiful it was looking. A friend took me and Leo Asti was very charming. He walked us round his property and explained what he is doing and what he plans to do. Tell me, is he with that woman, the blonde one who trails after him like she's frightened he'll escape?'

'I've no idea,' Stella said. 'I don't know him at all. I'm just staying in his house for a while.'

'You've never met?'

'No, with house swaps usually you don't. He's in my place and I'm in his until we swap back again.'

'But you've spoken to him.'

'Only via email,' Stella admitted. 'I've built up an idea of what he's like from that. Of course, I may have got him entirely wrong.'

Tosca gave a wry laugh. 'On email those three men you saw me with today all seemed ideal. They sent photographs that flattered them; what they wrote made them seem funnier and smarter; they showed me their best selves. You can't rely on email.'

'Oh no, don't say that. He's in sole charge of my home. I need him to be the kind, considerate person he seems.'

'I'm not saying he isn't ... only that you can't be sure.'

Stella felt a stab of anxiety. 'What did you think of him when you met at his lunch party?'

'What was my impression?' Tosca stared out to sea,

considering the question. 'I wondered if he was a little dull. All the talk of gardening and restoring old houses; I couldn't be less interested.'

Stella was cheered. 'But you liked him?'

'He was very pleasant, so yes,' said Tosca.

'Better than any of the men you speed-dated today?'

Tosca threw up her hands. 'My God, there is no comparison. That first one, what a slob, and I couldn't get rid of him. Two glasses of wine he drank and I had to keep a conversation going for all that time. The second said he was looking for a younger woman than me. And the last one, the *nonno*, very sweet but I'm not planning to be someone's nurse in his old age. I'd far rather be alone than that.'

'So what next?' Stella asked.

'I will try again. Why not join me? With two it will be more fun. There was a man from Salerno who couldn't make it today and a couple of others, maybe even the one that stood me up if he has a reasonable excuse.'

Stella laughed. 'Thanks, but I don't think so.'

'Give it a go,' Tosca urged. 'What else are you going to do with your time here? Maybe the man of your dreams is somewhere in this part of Italy.'

'I'm not dreaming of a man right now. What I really need is a job that I love as much as I did my last. Can you find me one of those?'

Tosca looked at Stella and smiled. 'No job and no man; it seems we have some things in common, you and I.'

Learning that Stella had walked all the way down to the port, Tosca insisted on driving her back up the hill to her car. She had an old Fiat 500 with scraped bumpers that she drove quickly with little consideration for the hairpin bends or other traffic, all the while talking, trying to change Stella's mind.

'Give me your email address and I'll send you links to

some profiles. You might like the look of them, perhaps even a few of those I've rejected. We like the same clothes but our tastes in men may be quite different.'

'Really, I'm not interested,' Stella insisted. 'I'm not sure I can think of anything worse than speed-dating, to be honest. But I'll give you my email address and my mobile number. It'd be great to catch up for a drink or a meal.'

'OK, but not at that place you ate at today. There is a better one further on, right at the end of the point. We'll go there for lunch.' Tosca beeped at an oncoming car, even though it was she who had crossed the centre line. 'You like seafood I hope; and a glass of chilled white wine while sitting in the sunshine beside the sea? It may be boring here but at least the view is usually good.'

Tosca dropped her at the far side of Triento and Stella walked back through the village to her car. The shops were closed, the place almost deserted and she assumed everyone must be having a siesta. The pace of life was so slow here, she could see how a woman like Tosca might quickly grow tired of it.

Still, speed-dating; Stella smiled to herself. She wasn't going to be caught up in anything like that. The thought of sitting with some man she had met online and trying to eke out a conversation, while sizing each other up ... no thank you.

Dear Leo – I had lunch at the harbour today and met someone else you know, a woman called Tosca, very glamorous. She came to a lunch party of yours; do you remember? I liked her, although she's slightly frightening; at least her driving is. We bonded over clothes and we're going to catch up another time, I hope. It would be good to get to know some locals. Do you spend much time here or do you only come in the summer?

Oh, and how are things in London? Is the garden project coming together? Stella.

Hi Stella. In London it is raining and the garden – or at least the space where it will be – is nothing but mud. I have to keep in mind an image of how it will be once it's transformed. I also have to buy more wet-weather gear in case this rain never stops.

I am missing Villa Rosa. I keep thinking of you sitting on the terrace in the sunshine. While the renovations were in progress I visited all the time, of course. Since then I've returned as much as I can. I've made some friends in the village. I think it's where I will retire one day and dig my own gardens instead of planting them for other people.

Now let me tell you about Tosca. She is our local celebrity, an actress who's appeared in a few movies. By all accounts she's had an interesting life. She turned up in the village when her father was sick and after he died moved into his house. It caused quite a stir when word got out, but that died down pretty quickly as she seems to keep herself to herself. So that is Tosca's story, or as much of it as I know.

Did you buy any linen yet? Leo.

Hi Leo. I came pretty close to buying a quilt but I managed to extricate myself. The problem is the linen shop is right beside the place that has the most delicious pastries and I don't see how I'm going to be able to avoid either.

That's fascinating about Tosca. I've just googled her and found a couple of pictures from when she was younger. There's a bit of the Sophia Loren about her, isn't there? I wonder what made her move back to Triento. She complains it's boring here. When I met her she was speed-dating!

Hope the rain stops soon … although I can't promise it will – Stella.

Dear Stella, speed-dating? Oh please don't tell me that is happening even in Triento now – Leo.

Hi Leo. Don't worry, I think she is a lone speed-dater so far. I just found a clip of one of her films. She looks amazing. I'm a bit obsessed now. Is Tosca her real name, do you think? I'll have to do more googling – Stella.

There wasn't a lot more to be found online. A fragment of an interview, all in Italian, and a couple more clips from American movies she had appeared in but nothing recent and no real details. Bored with looking, Stella resisted logging on to Facebook and put her laptop aside. It was a waste to stare at a screen when there was all this beauty to behold. She sat out on the terrace, the way Leo imagined her doing, until the sun faded and the breeze picked up. She thought of him here on other occasions, doing the same, solitary and happy. It was a nice thought. It warmed her.

Where the heart belongs

The light spring breeze had turned into a cold wind and the sky was slate grey. Stella drank her morning coffee in the kitchen, huddled for warmth inside her cashmere cardigan. An empty day stretched ahead of her. How was she going to fill it?

The scrapbook Leo had made was still lying on the counter. Its cover was so very plain; Stella longed to know what lay inside. Her curiosity was overwhelming. Where would it send her? Who had he thought up for her to meet? What treats were in store? She truly had intended to hold off a while longer before taking a look but suddenly there seemed no point. She was bored and lonely now. Surely Leo had made it for days like this one.

Stella reminded herself he didn't know her. It was entirely possible that the things he thought she might enjoy wouldn't be to her taste at all. If that was the case it was going to be tricky and she wasn't sure what she would say to him; he had gone to so much trouble after all.

Almost nervously Stella opened the book at its centre pages and saw his neat handwriting.

Dear Stella, if this is a Monday then choose another page quickly. Otherwise read on. Today why not take the coast road and drive north. I'm sending you on a treasure hunt. You will pass some stunning scenery and a few small villages beside the sea. Keep driving until you reach a slightly larger town. San Nicola is famous

for its flea market, open every day except Mondays, and
there are always bargains to be found. If you're not a
person who enjoys browsing round such places then
go directly to the music stall right in the middle. There
Sandro sells records, CDs, even a few cassettes – he's an
old-fashioned guy! Tell him who you are. He is expect-
ing you.

Stella glanced out of the window and saw it was raining now. She could imagine the coast road twisting and turning north and didn't fancy the idea of tackling it in the wet. Still, she was tempted by the idea of a treasure hunt; and picking her way through flea markets seeking out special pieces was one of her favourite things. If only the weather would clear up she would go like a shot, but the sky was leaden and the terrace puddled and slick.

It was difficult to resist flicking through the rest of the scrapbook but Stella managed not to; it seemed too much like cheating. Better to enjoy it day by day than gorge on the whole thing at once. She gazed out at the rain, practically coming down in sheets now, and willed it to stop. Being stuck indoors all day would give her cabin fever.

Even running the short distance across the terrace to the main house left her dripping. Stella took a hot shower to warm up, hoping that by the time she stepped out of it, the rain might be falling less heavily and she would see a hint of brightness streaking the sky.

Nothing had changed. The wisest thing would be to curl up in the living room and let this weather pass. Stella ran her fingers along the spines of the novels that lined Leo's shelves, paged through a magazine and looked back at the rain-spattered window.

She wanted to know why this music-seller Sandro was expecting her, what he was going to say, or perhaps even give her. It was exactly like being a child and impatient for Christmas ... a frustrated anticipation. Stella couldn't remember feeling that way in years.

She tried to distract herself with clothes, by choosing what to wear, an outfit to meet the day in. But this was weather that narrowed the options and in the end Stella put on the same black trousers with the forgiving stretch she had worn the day before, a long-sleeved striped T-shirt and the trusty cashmere layered over it. When she couldn't stand it any longer, she shrugged on her most waterproof jacket, grabbed her keys and bolted out to the car, keeping her head down so the hail of raindrops wouldn't blind her.

Thankfully there was hardly any traffic. Stella took it slowly, negotiating the hairpin bends and corners where the jagged rock face seemed to lean into the road. The route followed the curve of a mountain and took her through a tunnel. As she came out into daylight there was a definite blueness to the sky and by the time Stella reached the first village, the rain was no more than a damp veil on her windscreen.

She took the next section of road more quickly but still the drive was longer than she had expected and by the time she reached San Nicola it was mid-morning. Hopefully this wasn't one of those flea markets that packed up early; what a pain if Sandro had left for the day.

There were a few shabby-looking stalls on a bridge just beyond the edge of the small town and Stella saw the rest of the market sprawling beyond. It was huge and heaving with people so finding the right stall was likely to take a while.

She pushed her way past displays of homemade jewellery, cheap socks, second-hand clothes and kitchenware, and on through the press of people, intent on finding the centre of the market as Leo had directed. At last, hearing the throb of bass and the wail of an electric guitar, she knew she was getting closer to the music stall.

She found it piled messily high with records and CDs and

music blasting loudly. Behind the counter was a young man with a bushy beard and an Asian boy with his hair cut in a Mohican. Stella stood, jammed in with the other customers, flipping through the jumble of records on the racks, finding treasures, old Dusty Springfield albums, Lulu and the Beatles, as well as Italian singers whose names she didn't recognise.

Catching the eye of the bearded man, she called above the music, '*Buongiorno*, I'm looking for Sandro.'

'Yep,' he said dismissively.

'Is he here?'

'Yep.' He pointed to himself.

'Oh right, well in that case you might be expecting me. My name is Stella Forrester.'

He glanced at her again. 'Expecting you? No, I don't think so.'

'Leo Asti sent me.'

He looked at her properly, then smiled and nodded his head. 'OK, OK that guy. So you're the one. He said you would come. Now wait, let me see what I did with it. Stay there.'

Ducking down beneath the counter, he disappeared for several minutes. When he resurfaced he was holding a record-sleeve-shaped package, wrapped loosely in brown paper.

'He had me hunt this down for you.' Sandro handed it to her. 'He is the romantic type, yes?'

'Can I open it now?' Stella asked.

'It's yours; you can do what you like.'

Ripping off the paper, she found a record as expected, but not one she recognised. The photo on the sleeve showed a middle-aged man singing, his eyes half shut, and the title was in Italian.

'What does it mean in English?' she asked, holding it up to him.

'*Where the Heart Belongs*. It is an album of love songs from Napoli. Very nice; I think you will like it.'

Love songs. Stella wasn't sure what she thought about that. Was it a strange thing to be presenting her with, given that she and Leo didn't really know one another?

'Did he say why he wanted me to have this one in particular?'

Sandro shrugged. 'I guess it must be one of his favourites. It is in excellent condition, no scratches. Enjoy the music, *signora*.'

He left her puzzling over the album. She wasn't sure how she was supposed to listen to it, even. Did Leo intend for her to buy a record player from somewhere? Stella hadn't noticed one in Villa Rosa and she'd had a pretty good look around.

She made her way more slowly back to the car, taking detours to rummage at stalls that caught her eye, the record bundled back into its wrapping and tucked beneath her arm. Love songs from a stranger. Of course Leo couldn't have predicted that particular page would be the first she would choose and perhaps the other suggestions in his scrapbook were more impersonal.

Driving home, she tried to remember if she had ever heard any Neapolitan love songs. *O Sole Mio*, was that one? If so, wasn't it a bit corny? Stella liked upbeat music, not a bunch of old men caterwauling.

The first thing she did when she got back to Villa Rosa was fire off an email.

Hi Leo, I opened the scrapbook. Curiosity got the better of me. I've spent an enjoyable morning at the flea market in San Nicola and Sandro passed me your gift. Thank you; it's very generous and thoughtful. I'd like to listen to it but I'm not quite sure where to find a record player. Is there one in the house somewhere? I've looked but can't see anything. Hope things are good over there – Stella.

She checked for a reply several times as the day wore on but nothing came. He was busy with his garden project, she reasoned, and nowhere near a computer. She ate boiled eggs for a late lunch, then tried to settle down with a novel but gave up a couple of chapters in and opened her laptop. Nothing from Leo; he was still working, of course. That was the problem with email: everyone expected an instant response.

Yet she couldn't help wondering if he had read her message. Did he feel awkward about the gift? Was he disappointed with her for starting on the scrapbook so soon or irritated she couldn't find a record player without his help?

She emailed Birdie instead, hoping her friend was stuck at her desk and online.

Hi Birdie – Big news from Italy today! Leo arranged a gift for me, a record of love songs – yes, actual vinyl. But I don't have anything to play it on. So frustrating. Bit bored right now, to be honest. When are you coming? Stella

Hey Stella – A record, how retro. Are you sure there isn't anything to play it on? I think sometimes in those European houses they're disguised to seem like furniture. Have another look.
Love songs from the silver fox ... ooer – love Birdie.

Yes, Neapolitan love songs apparently. I know, weird. I still want to have a listen though – Stella.

One woman's weird is another woman's sexy. No one ever sends me love songs. Jealous – Birdie.

Stella had another poke around the house and discovered Birdie had been right. An intricate carved wooden sideboard turned out, on closer inspection, when Stella removed the vase on top, to have a lid that could be lifted to reveal a turntable hidden inside.

Pulling the record from its sleeve, she put it in place and lowered the needle carefully, an action that reminded her so much of being a teenager, of noisy parties at university and dancing to the Rolling Stones. The nostalgia rushed at her and swept through, leaving Stella feeling as if something had been lost without her noticing.

The music didn't do much to cheer her up. It was designed to tug at the heartstrings and while she didn't understand the words, the melodies spoke to her of lost loves and time passing. Listening, she wondered if Leo had known how she would be affected.

Hi Leo, ignore my last request. I found the record player. Such sad songs! I've been sitting here listening to them, almost with tears in my eyes. Have Neapolitan men traditionally been very unlucky in love?

Anyway it's been nostalgic playing a record again after so many years. I may have to go back and buy some more music from Sandro. Thanks again – Stella.

At 5 p.m. Triento came alive. The shops opened and the piazza filled. Stella had only driven in to buy something for dinner but she found herself wanting to linger. It felt too late to drink coffee, and too early for wine, so she walked, looping through back streets so narrow she almost had to turn sideways, peering into windows and wondering who lived there and what their lives were like, climbing steps and finding new places: a hidden-away church, a hardware store, a shop selling wine by the demi-john.

A little lost and with the light fading, she turned back and tried to find her way towards the main street. Perhaps this evening Francesca Russo would be behind the counter of the linen shop and Stella could ask for her advice about signing up for some sort of class.

There was music coming from the bar in the piazza and people gathered at tables behind its lighted windows. The linen shop was closed, a sign on the door asking customers to please return tomorrow. Stella felt cold and very alone. She thought about home, the vibrancy of Camden and how there was always something to look at and somewhere to go. For the first time she wished she were back there.

Birdie, stupid love songs have made me all melancholy. It seemed such a great idea, this house swap. I was so carried away when you talked about settling in a foreign place and becoming part of the life there. But now I'm not sure if it's possible. These people all know each other – and I'm a stranger to them. Oh, they're very pleasant and helpful but still I'm an outsider and on my own. I can't help wondering if I'd have been better off in a city where there are language courses and tours to take. Instead I'm sitting alone in this house in the middle of nowhere and it's started raining again and I can't watch television because I don't understand any of the channels Leo's got. I think I've made a mistake coming here. Bugger. Stella.

So Stella, you're in Italy, one of the most beautiful countries in the world, with amazing culture, food and wine; and you're thinking you've made a mistake? I feel like slapping you. Get out and meet some people. Surely it's not that hard – Birdie.

Argh, Stella, no. I shouldn't have pressed 'Send'. I didn't mean it! I've just had a crappy day and I was feeling sorry for myself ... and struggling to feel sorry for you. So look, I do really want to come over, but right now they're restructuring and I feel as if I have to be here, getting results and proving my worth. I can't afford to lose this job. But as soon as things are settled I'll put in for some leave. And in the meantime try not to get too down. Just talk to people, be warm and funny, your usual lovely self. They might not all want to be friends but some of them are bound to stick. This is such an opportunity; you absolutely cannot come back so soon with your tail between your legs. I won't allow it.

I do love you and I'm sorry for being a grumpy cow – Birdie.

Bright Italian star

Hi Leo, is everything OK? Just a little concerned as I haven't heard from you in a while. I'm sure you're very busy ... in fact I know you are ... but it'd be great if you'd flick me a quick email and let me know all is fine with you and the flat. Regards, Stella.

Perhaps she had made a mistake being so quick to dismiss the idea of speed-dating. At least it would get her out and meeting people – Birdie was right, that was what she needed to do; it was half the point of being here. Stella was mortified when she remembered her whiny email, considering how lucky she was to be enjoying her freedom rather than living month by month, dependent on a regular salary, like so many of her friends.

In Triento, bright and early, she treated herself to the most fat-laden, sugary pastry from the tempting display in the corner bar and sat out at a table in the morning sunshine waiting for the linen shop to open.

She saw Francesca Russo, head down and hurrying across the piazza, unlocking the shop and shutting herself inside. A short while later she re-emerged with a selection of linen to pin up for the day's display. Stella gave her a few moments to get organised before wandering over.

'*Buongiorno,*' she called.

'*Si, si, buongiorno.*' Francesca looked up from her task. 'Ah the *signora* from England. You came in the other day, yes? Roberto mentioned it to me.'

'Your husband showed me some beautiful things.'

'My husband?' Francesca said uncertainly. Then she laughed. 'Oh no, Roberto and I are not married. He is the brother of my husband. Sometimes he comes and works here when I need a day off. What exactly did he show you? Something you are keen to buy? If so, I can finish this later.'

'Actually, I thought you might be able to help me with a little local knowledge. I'm hoping there is somewhere I can go to take a few classes, perhaps a language school that teaches Italian to foreigners, or even a cooking course?'

'I don't think so; and I'm sure if there were I'd have heard of it.'

'Oh that's a shame, never mind.' Stella made to leave.

'Wait.' Francesca stopped her. 'I might be able to help. After all, I'm Italian and I cook. Why shouldn't I teach you?'

'Would you have time?' asked Stella, although it wasn't quite what she'd had in mind.

'That depends how often you want to do it. We could try one session. We cook and we speak Italian so you learn both things at once. If you enjoy it we can do more, if not then no problem.'

'How much would you charge?'

After a moment's thought Francesca named a figure that seemed a little steep. When Stella frowned she added, 'Remember it will include the food we buy and cook. We will eat together. You can meet my family and practise your Italian on them for as long as you want. It is a bargain really, I promise.'

'OK then.' It was the idea of spending time with an Italian family that swung it for Stella.

Francesca offered her a dazzling smile. 'Fantastic. Come on Sunday morning. We will prepare a traditional lunch together, a little pasta, some meat and vegetables. Then we will sit down to enjoy it, drink a glass of wine, get to know each other a little. Fun, yes?'

'That sounds great,' Stella agreed.

Francesca wrote down her address along with detailed instructions on how to find it. 'If you get lost then stop and ask for directions. Everyone knows the Russo family. You will be shown the way.'

'Thanks. Sunday then.'

'Yes, come early and bring cash.'

Feeling as if she had taken a positive step, Stella returned to the bar and ordered a second coffee. It was worrying that she hadn't heard back from Leo. She couldn't send another email; he would think she was stalking him. Still, her mind kept filling with images of her bathroom flooding or the place being burgled, and him being too wary of her reaction to break the news.

She checked her phone to see if anything had come through in the past few minutes and found a text from a number she didn't recognise. *Dying of boredom here. Dying! Didn't we say we'd have lunch? Come today. I insist. Tosca.*

The movie star! Stella hadn't held out much hope she would get in touch when she had given Tosca her contact details and, pleased to hear from her, she texted back straight away.

Yes, I would love to. Where? When? Stella.

Very good! Midday at Raffaella's trattoria. *At the far end of the harbour wall. Everyone knows it.*

Lunch with Tosca required a change of clothes. A piece by Milly Munro, casually stylish rather than an outfit that screamed 'look at me'. She mentally flicked through the pared-down contents of her wardrobe and considered her options as she drove back to the house. It was what she most loved about going out, transforming herself with frocks, hats and scarves. Stella didn't understand people who dressed as if they were wearing a uniform, all in black every day. Where was the fun in that?

By the time she drove back through the gates of Villa Rosa, she had made a decision. But before getting changed into the pale blue shift dress and a fine merino cardigan she checked her emails again. Still silence from Leo; she was starting to feel irritated as well as worried. How hard was it to take a minute to send a quick message? The longer she waited, the more convinced she was that something had gone wrong.

Stella couldn't see any *trattoria* at the end of the harbour wall. From where she was standing it seemed like there was only a row of houses. She stopped a passer-by, an older woman with violently hennaed hair.

'I'm looking for Raffaella's *trattoria*.'

The woman stared at Stella, head tilted. 'Raffaella?'

Stella nodded. '*Si*.'

Pointing in the direction Stella had been looking in, the woman said something in Italian, finishing with '*Va bene?*'

'*Si, grazie*,' Stella replied, although she hadn't understood a word.

There were no sun umbrellas, no signage to show anything was there, and only as Stella drew nearer did she spot a blackboard with a few Italian words scrawled on it in chalk. The day's specials, she supposed, so this must be it after all.

She had another moment's doubt, opening the door and stepping inside. It looked very much like someone's living room. Against one wall was an antique sideboard stocked with plates and glasses, and there were a few tables and chairs, but not many. Stella could smell some sort of food cooking but the place was empty.

'Hello ... *buongiorno*,' she called, hovering by the half-open door.

'Hello,' a woman's voice called back. 'One moment please.'

From her voice Stella hadn't expected her to be so old ... or so beautiful. She had thick grey hair that fell in waves to her shoulders, full lips and the sort of bone structure it was impossible not to stare at, olive skin dewy from the heat of the kitchen and scored with lines from a long life. Her clothes were black and so was her apron.

'Are you Raffaella?' asked Stella, hoping the woman spoke decent English.

'That's me.' Thankfully she seemed fluent, although her words were heavily accented. 'You are here for lunch? You are meeting Tosca, yes?'

Stella was slightly taken aback but reminded herself this was a small place and everyone knew each other's business.

'At midday; but perhaps I'm early.' She glanced at her phone. 'Oh no, I'm exactly on time.'

'Yes you are,' Raffaella agreed. 'And this proves you don't know Tosca so well. She will be late as always.'

'That's fine. If you have a table available I can sit down and wait.'

'You are welcome to sit at any of my tables. But what I would prefer is if you come and talk to me while I prepare your lunch.'

'In the kitchen?' Stella was surprised.

Raffaella smiled and nodded. 'I'm on my own in there.'

The kitchen was so tiny Stella wasn't sure where to put herself. Wherever she stood, she felt in the way, but Raffaella didn't seem to mind.

'So tell me,' she said, pouring out two glasses of a fruity chilled white wine. 'Tell me who you are, why you're in Italy, how you know Tosca.'

As Stella gave her a shortish version of the story, Raffaella busied herself, chopping and stirring, tasting a little of this and that, adding a pinch of whatever was missing.

'Ah yes, Villa Rosa,' she said when Stella mentioned it. 'I know that house. I worked there once, many years ago before I had a family. It's a strange place; lots of people pass through but no one stays there long. And yet it is so beautiful.'

77

'Were you the cook there?'

'Cook, cleaner, I did whatever needed to be done.' She glanced around at her kitchen, adding ruefully, 'That at least hasn't changed.'

'You run this place on your own?'

'For the past few years since my husband Ciro died. My sons would like me to close it. They think I'm too old. But what would I do? They are busy with their lives; why shouldn't I be busy with mine? So I keep things going and open up when I feel like it, today only because Tosca called. Then I had to hurry to buy fish from the boats, carry vegetables from home, make a quick sauce. It will be a simple lunch, but good.'

'I'm not much of a cook myself,' Stella told her. 'Although I'm going to have some lessons with a woman in town.'

'Oh yes, which woman?'

'Her name is Francesca Russo; she runs the linen shop.'

The laughter seemed to burst out of Raffaella. 'Francesca Russo is going to teach you to cook?'

'Yes.' Stella wished she hadn't mentioned it.

Raffaella was laughing still. 'This is the best joke I've heard in some time. Please tell me you're not paying her.'

'Um, actually I am.'

'Well then, you must cancel.' Raffaella sounded serious now. 'It's not too late?'

'We made a pretty definite arrangement. I don't want to mess her around. And it's only one lesson.'

'*Va bene.* You have that one lesson with Francesca and then you come to me and I show you how to do it properly. I charge you half what she does; not even that, only the cost of the food. You will go back to England a real Italian cook.'

'But aren't you busy with the restaurant?'

'No, not until later when everyone comes south for the summer holidays. If you're still here then, you can help me.

You wouldn't be the first English girl I've trained up in this kitchen.'

'I wasn't looking to be trained up,' Stella hurried to explain. 'I only wanted to learn to make a couple of the local dishes and meet a few people.'

'Exactly. Perfect then.' Raffaella's tone was brisk. 'You will come to me and that is what we'll do.'

Stella watched the old cook as she prepared the food. She carried herself well; that was part of her beauty. Her face was free of make-up, her hair untouched by dyes or serums, but there was a pride in the way she moved, a gracefulness. She must have been quite something when she was young.

'How many sons do you have?' Stella asked her.

'Two, they both have restaurants in London.' Raffaella named a couple of places that sounded vaguely familiar although Stella didn't think she had eaten at either.

'I'm more into fashion than food,' she said apologetically.

'*Si*, *si*, like Tosca, this is what you have in common.' Raffaella glanced at the clock on the wall. 'Speaking of our friend, she is now half an hour late so we are in the zone of time when she might possibly appear.'

Stella smiled. 'Is she really that bad?'

'Terrible ... Tosca thinks the rules other people live by don't apply to her. Once you accept that then she is less infuriating.'

'Have you known her for a long time?'

Raffaella nodded. 'Our fathers were fishermen and our families were neighbours. When she was a girl I knew her well. I didn't see her so often, of course, when she was living away from Italy. But she hasn't changed as much as she likes to think.'

It was another fifteen minutes before Stella heard a door banging open and then the sound of Tosca calling out their names.

'Ah there you are,' she exclaimed, finding them in the

kitchen together. Today she was all glamour in a fur stole, almost certainly real, over a butterscotch silk dress that showed off her extreme slenderness.

'It's not even 1 p.m. – what are you doing here?' Raffaella said drily.

Tosca rolled her eyes, and shrugging off her fur, she tossed it on a stool. 'I locked the door behind me,' she told Raffaella. 'You're cooking only for us so you must eat with us. What are you making? Remember I said, no pasta.'

'We are having pasta but you don't have to,' Raffaella replied.

'I never touch it.'

'Yes, you do, I've watched you eat it many times.'

'No.'

'If Ciro were here, he'd back me up,' Raffaella insisted.

'That means nothing; I'm sure that Ciro always backed you up.'

'Tosca, a little plate of pasta is not going to make you instantly fat. It's food, it tastes good, so enjoy it.'

'I will bloat.'

'We will not care if you bloat, *cara*.'

'Yes, but I will care.'

Stella listened to the two Italian women bickering in English, hands waving, faces alive, clearly enjoying the fight. They were very alike she realised, not so much in looks, although both were lovely, but in the way they spoke and the confidence they seemed to have that whatever they said was right.

'Go and sit down and I will bring out the food,' said Raffaella. 'And stop arguing with me. You are driving me crazy.'

Tosca had the last word. Exiting from the kitchen she said to Stella in a loud whisper, 'She has always been crazy. She can't blame me for that.'

It was a beautiful lunch. The pasta that Tosca stubbornly

refused to touch was a ravioli filled with a garlicky cream of prawns, resting in a light sauce that tasted of the sea. Next Raffaella brought out plates of herb-crusted fish soused in wine and fat green olives. She couldn't sit still for long. One minute she was up fetching salt, although the food hardly needed any extra seasoning, the next she was filling wine glasses or clearing plates or seeing to the next course. Only at the end of the meal, when they were eating sweet biscuits and drinking dessert wine, did she seem to relax.

'Will you open up this summer for lunch and dinner?' Tosca asked her.

'I'm not planning so far ahead right now. I'll take each day as it comes,' Raffaella replied. 'And what about you ... what are your plans?'

Tosca sighed heavily. 'I am planning to be bored. Today, tomorrow, next week, next month, only boredom.'

'Why don't you go back to America?' asked Raffaella.

'And do what? If I'm going to be bored anywhere, better it is here.'

Raffaella looked at Stella, explaining, 'She is an actress.'

'Used to be,' Tosca corrected.

'A very good actress,' Raffaella continued, 'who is letting her talent go to waste for some reason that she won't explain even to me, her oldest friend.'

'Oh stop, please ...'

'Who has had such an interesting life and now seems content with a dull future.'

Tosca slammed her hands down on the table so hard everything rattled. 'I said stop.'

'Yes, OK, I heard you.' Raffaella was calm.

'I don't want to talk about it, I have never wanted to talk about it.'

'Yes, yes,' Raffaella agreed.

'What I would prefer to discuss is what we three single women are going to do to make our lives more interesting.'

'*Madonna mia*, please not the speed-dating again,' begged Raffaella.

'Do you have a better idea?' Tosca asked. 'Just think, if there were a few of us we could organise a proper event. Make an evening of it; get more men to come from further away. It would be fun and don't we all need a little of that?'

'I've buried my husband and I'm an old lady; what do I want with another man?' Now it was Raffaella who was sounding heated.

'I don't understand why you won't try it once.'

'For the same reason you won't eat the pasta. I don't want to. And anyway, why do you think a man is going to fix all your problems? Has that ever happened before? No, I don't think so.'

'This is not about my problems.'

'What then?'

Tosca lifted her glass to her lips and took a small sip of the sweet wine. Then she placed it back onto the table and sighed. 'Quite honestly I'm lonely,' she said. 'So are you, Raffaella, that's why you can't let go of this place. Stella, I don't know you so well but it seems to me that you feel the same way. Three lonely women.'

'Three woman who are enjoying each other's company, not lonely at all. Isn't that right, Stella?' Raffaella looked at her.

Stella shifted uncomfortably. 'Well ...'

'Oh, so you too are looking for a man?'

'No, although I'm looking for something,' Stella admitted. 'I'm just not sure what it is.'

'Whereas I am absolutely certain,' Tosca put in. 'For just once in my life I want to be loved, the way your Ciro loved you, Raffaella. I want to be able to rely on someone other than myself. So far I've never really had that.'

'I suppose you chose another sort of life which led you away from it,' Raffaella said.

'It isn't too late though. I am going to make it happen.'

Raffaella groaned and dropped her head into her hands. 'Oh please no ...'

'Excellent,' said Tosca brightly. 'I will organise it; you two only have to show up. We could hold it here. Why not? Drinks, nibbles, an elegant evening, almost a salon. Yes, that's it.'

'If we do it then it's for one time only,' Raffaella warned her.

'Yes, *cara*, yes, of course.'

Stella had forgotten to check her emails. She remembered later that night while she was making some toast for a quick supper. But there was no word from anyone, not even Birdie. Had they all forgotten her?

She stood, leaning back against the kitchen bench, crunching the toast down quickly. Tosca had called her a lonely woman and Stella hadn't denied it. Now in the silence of Villa Rosa, licking butter and honey from her lips, she wondered if she really was so happy being single as she was always claiming. Someone to love and to rely on – perhaps Tosca was right; it didn't sound so bad.

She took a cup of tea back to the house, stopping for a moment to appreciate the view. Hovering in the inky blackness, the statue of Christ was illuminated and starkly white. Moonlight touched the tips of the trees and palely lit the garden; the sky was ceilinged with stars. There was one right above her, twinkling far more than all the others. Perhaps it was a satellite but Stella preferred to think not. It was her star, she decided, her bright Italian star.

Sanctuary

*Dear Stella – I am so sorry not to reply to you sooner.
I have been sick, a very bad flu. No, not the man flu – I
know you must be thinking that – a real one with fever
and aching. All I've done for days is sleep and now I'm
out of bed but still feeling terrible. I blame the rain –
what happened to spring? Did I leave it behind in Italy?*

*Anyway, I'm glad to hear you started on the scrap-
book and I hope it's going to amuse you. Perhaps
some of my ideas won't be to your liking since I don't
know much about you of course – although living in
your apartment I feel as if I'm getting to know you in
a way. I think my favourite spot is going to be your
little courtyard. As soon as the weather improves that's
where I will spend all my time. I hope that is soon! Leo.*

*Hi Leo – I don't know if I have a favourite spot in
Villa Rosa, it's all so lovely. This morning I lay in bed
with the doors wide open because it's a perfect morning. I listened to the bird song and smelt woodsmoke
coming from somewhere. Things are flowering in the
garden and spring is definitely here. I feel quite guilty
to be enjoying it all when you're stuck in London and
everything seems so gloomy.*

*Sorry to hear about your not-man-flu but hopefully
you're on the mend. I'm going to choose something else
from the scrapbook today so think of me off on some
adventure. Take care – Stella.*

Leo was sending her to a church. Stella had opened the scrapbook at the very first page and found instructions to take the road south and drive for half an hour until she reached a large Calabrian town beside a stretch of sandy beach. This town's secret was its church, he explained. From the road she would see it pressed against the mountains but she had to go inside to understand what made it special.

Perhaps he was the religious type. Stella hadn't sensed that about him but you could never really tell. It was years since she had last been inside a church, her wedding day perhaps. A country church in winter, decked out with creamy white flowers and red ribbons, and the pews crammed with friends and family. Ray was the one who had wanted a traditional ceremony and Stella had been happy to go along with it. She had worn a Milly Munro dress designed especially for her, cream shantung silk and simple lines. She shimmered down the aisle in it, smiling faces turned towards her and Ray waiting at the altar. It had been such a joyful day. Stella felt vestiges of that joy thinking about it even now – everyone she loved gathered together, dressed in their finery, primed for a celebration. Afterwards at the reception they had danced till 2 a.m. and the shantung had been stained with red wine but Stella hadn't cared.

No, of course there had been one more church since then: Milly's funeral. Some of the same people had been there, all clothed darkly and desperately sad.

As she drove through tunnels and down roads that seemed to double back on themselves before plunging over high bridges, Stella thought about all the people who had gone from her life with such finality – her parents, then Milly, and Ray too she supposed, although for a while after the split they had stayed in touch with one another. That petered out when he met someone else and Stella didn't mind too much. He deserved to have companionship, it was what he wanted, and by all accounts he and this new woman were good together.

Stella insisted she wasn't lonely, but perhaps she was and hadn't recognised it. She remembered Friday evenings and hanging on at after-work drinks until the wine and crisps were finished, then home to an empty flat with the whole weekend ahead. Yes she had lots of friends but they couldn't always include her and she hadn't expected them to. Loneliness? She had never said the word out loud to anyone. It seemed a thing not to admit to, a failure. And after Birdie followed her into divorce, they had kept each other busy with movies and museums, long lunches and even longer late-night phone calls.

The final stretch of road was wider and straighter. It led to a town with boulevards shaded by tall trees. It was busier here than in Triento and Stella noticed a row of shops it might be worth taking a look in: fashion boutiques and homeware stores. She kept driving, however, following Leo's instructions and taking the road that climbed into the mountains. From there she had her first glimpse of a pale terracotta building with a tall bell tower, backed by a steep wall of rust-coloured rock. The Sanctuary of the Madonna, Leo had called it. Stella wondered why he thought she would find it interesting.

To begin with it seemed like any other church. Stella climbed a long flight of steps, passed through an archway and then stopped in surprise. She was in a cave and there were more steps ahead of her, carved through a great boulder.

Breathless by the time she reached the very top, she found herself in a dimly lit chamber filled with dripping stalactites and worn limestone statues. The air was chill, the floor damp and at one end there was an altar illuminated only by thin rays of sunshine finding their way through an opening in the roof of the grotto. It was a cold, strange place and eeriest of all was the silence. Stella could hear only the dull thud of her own footsteps. Here she truly did feel lonely.

There were a few rows of white plastic chairs arranged in front of the altar. Stella sat down on one and tried to imagine how it might be to worship in a place like this. Despite its gloom it must be used for all the usual things, weddings and christenings, Sunday Mass. Families would come here each week, as part of the ritual of their lives, and possibly Leo was a regular among them, kneeling in prayer or whispering to a priest in the confessional box. Stella closed her eyes and tried to imagine it.

She had never been attracted to religion, although as a child her parents insisted she go to the local church's Sunday school every week. She remembered Bible readings and nativity plays; giggling with her friends instead of paying attention; and then arriving home to find her parents locked inside their bedroom. Only much later did she realise they hadn't cared about religion either; her attendance at Sunday school was their way of getting time alone together.

Even when they were older they were one of those couples that held hands all the time. It can't have been perfect, their relationship, but if they fought it was in private. Her mother once told her the whole point of being married was to make everything better for each other. In their suburban house, with their quiet lives and small dreams, she thought they had managed that; until they died barely a year apart, leaving Stella devastated and all on her own.

By then she'd had her other family, the girls at Milly Munro's. And when the house was packed up, everything sorted in piles for charity shops or keepsakes, and a For Sale sign planted on the front lawn, it had been such a relief to get back to work and slip into the usual routines. That was what Stella had drawn comfort from, not a church or religion.

Opening her eyes, she looked around the grotto, noticing

that near the altar there were candles, not those awful modern electric things but real ones to be lit with matches. On a whim Stella felt for some coins, enough to pay for three of them. She supposed you didn't have to be Catholic to light them in remembrance.

She stayed there for a while, watching the candles flicker and burn down, thinking about losses and endings as around her the stalactites dripped and water trickled down the walls. Finally leaving, walking down the steps back to the car, Stella hoped the next activity she picked out of Leo's scrapbook would be a little more cheering.

Hi Leo, a church in a cave! That was a novelty. It's spooky though, isn't it? As I was heading out I met one of the priests and he told me about its history. He said it was a safe place, where people could worship without fear of being attacked by the bandits that used to roam the mountains. I suppose that's why it feels so cut off from the world, so tomb-like – it was designed to be that way. I must admit I was quite glad to get back into the world, back to seeing shops and people. The priest gave me a list of when Mass is held, but I can't imagine I'll be using it.

How are things with you? Are you feeling OK? Are you making any progress with the garden? Stella.

Hi Stella, I too have been into the world! The sun is shining and this morning I felt much better so I got up early and went for a walk. I'm back at your apartment for a few moments to get changed and then I'm going to see what all this rain has done to my garden site.

I take it you didn't much like the Sanctuary of the Madonna? For me it is an extraordinary place – bleak, yes, but also filled with a power. If there is a God that's where you'll find him I think, not in some great cathedral

*amid the carvings, paintings and gold. I've never been
to a Mass there; I'd like to though – Leo.*

Stella was beginning to feel as if Leo was someone she had
actually met. There was a real sense of him coming from
his emails, especially that last one, which she suspected had
been dashed off and not as carefully considered as others
he had written. She reread how he described the Sanctuary
of the Madonna; he felt power where she had found only
darkness. Stella wasn't sure what that said about them both,
but she found it interesting.

She had been planning to have lunch at one of the cafés
along the main boulevard. But when she got in the car she
changed her mind, and drove back towards Triento instead.
Raffaella had told her to come and find her any time she
wanted company. She had pointed out a house, painted
the colour of peaches, clinging to a rock right beside the
harbour, and said that was where she would be if she wasn't
at the *trattoria*. 'I don't go far from either these days,' she
had admitted.

Stella found the *trattoria* closed up, not even the blackboard left outside, and so retraced her steps and found a
narrow lane that seemed as if it might lead to the house
Raffaella had shown her. She went through a tunnel and
it brought her into a small courtyard with a few pots of
herbs in the sunny spots, and stone steps leading up to a blue
wooden door.

There was no knocker so she rapped with her knuckles,
and when there was no reply tried the doorknob. It twisted
easily in her hand and she pushed open the door. 'Hello, is
anyone there?'

She heard Raffaella calling back in Italian. 'Hello, who is
it?'

'It's Stella. I just came to see if you'd like to come out for
a coffee.'

'Stella, come in, I'm in the kitchen.'

It seemed this house had been built to fit round the curve of the rock. The whole place was narrow and cramped, but the narrowest part was the kitchen where the wall was carved into the rock itself. Brightly coloured plates danced across the rough grey slab and on a high shelf was a clutter of things: old bottles arranged alongside jewels of glass worn smooth by the sea; photographs in gold-painted frames.

Raffaella, dressed in black pants and a baggy top, was filling a pot with coffee, heaping the grounds into a pyramid so tall it was in danger of collapsing all over the table.

She smiled at Stella. 'This is perfect timing.'

'Are you sure you wouldn't like to go out? I really wanted to treat you to a coffee and something sweet as a small thank you for all the trouble you went to yesterday.'

'It was no trouble. Besides, here I have biscotti, baked fresh this morning; and the best view in Triento.' Raffaella gestured towards a window that looked out over the harbour and to the sea beyond. 'Sit down; this will only take a moment.'

Stella slid onto a wooden bench and leaned back against the rock wall, watching as Raffaella clattered biscotti onto a plate and poured a stream of black coffee into two small white cups so old their glaze was starting to crack.

'So, Stella, what have you been up to?' she asked.

When she mentioned her visit to the Sanctuary of the Madonna, Raffaella nodded and smiled.

'Yes, yes, I know the place. It's extraordinary, isn't it? Like a children's storybook come to life.'

'I thought it was gloomy,' Stella admitted.

'Really? Perhaps that's just the way you're feeling and nothing to do with the Sanctuary at all.'

Stella sipped her coffee. 'You may be right – I haven't been feeling like myself lately,' she conceded. 'I had the same job for so long; I guess I'm finding it difficult to adjust.'

'So that's why you decided to make this life swap?'

'Well it's a house swap, really.'

'Surely it's the same thing; a house is a life, isn't it? This one is mine.'

'Were you born here?' Stella asked.

'Yes, in the bedroom above us. My family used to gather round this table; me, my sister and brother did our homework here; my mother made coffee in the same moka pot I used today and she stood at that window watching as my father's boat returned from sea. Now I'm the only one left; the others are all dead or moved away.'

'You said you have sons in London. Have you ever thought of moving there?'

'I have considered it. Tonino and Lucio are always saying they would welcome me and I have grandchildren there but ... the past is here. And I'm an old woman now; the past is what I have; I don't want to lose it.'

'You don't sound old; and really you don't look it,' Stella told her.

Raffaella touched her fingers to her face, pushing at the soft skin beneath her eyes. 'You're kind, but yes I do. These last few years have left their mark; since I lost Ciro.'

'Your husband,' Stella remembered.

Raffaella stretched up to the high shelf and reached down one of the framed pictures. 'This was my love,' she said, showing it to Stella. 'He was and he always will be.'

The man in the photograph was dark and had a sharp-featured face that might have seemed stern were it not for the smile flashing over it. But it was the woman beside him that drew Stella's eye. Her dark hair fell in glossy ringlets to her waist; her lips were full and her olive skin flawless.

'This is you? You were totally gorgeous.'

Raffaella laughed. 'The most beautiful girl in all of Triento is what they used to say. Still, back then it was a very small village so there weren't too many other girls ... and lots of people hated me for it. Ciro was always my friend though; he was my best friend before he was ever my husband.'

'And you ran your *trattoria* together?'

She nodded. 'We also had a pizza place up in the main town but we closed that when Lucio left us to move to London. Soon I suppose I will have to close the *trattoria* too.'

'Couldn't you hire in a chef to help you?'

'That is what Tosca tells me to do. She thinks I should dress up in fancy clothes and drift around talking to my customers while someone else cooks in my kitchen.'

'Why not?'

Raffaella looked at the picture of her younger self, sitting beside her husband, smiling down the lens. 'I expect Ciro would say the same thing. Why not? And I think the answer is that, just like you, I am struggling to adjust.'

Stella wanted to be comforting, to say something warm and inspiring, but all she managed was: 'Maybe try it just for a summer; see how it goes.'

'Perhaps I will or perhaps I won't; it's not so interesting to anyone except me.' Raffaella poured another coffee and offered her the plate of biscotti. 'But more importantly, tell me how do you think we can escape this ridiculous business with Tosca?'

'The speed-dating?'

'Yes, yes. Really I don't see how a woman as glamorous as Tosca can be struggling to find a man, but if she is so desperate, surely there are other ways?'

'I would have thought so too,' Stella agreed. 'I'd have thought she could have any man she wanted.'

Raffaella picked up one of the biscotti but didn't take a bite. 'Maybe once she could … maybe for a long time and she took it for granted … until suddenly she couldn't.'

'Is that what she says?'

'No, Tosca says nothing: this is what I assume because it's

what happens. One moment they are giving us those looks, you know the ones. The next they don't see us at all. Surely you have noticed?'

'Yes, I have, but I can't say it bothers me too much,' said Stella.

'Well it bothers Tosca. It bothers her a great deal, I think. And that is what this speed-dating is all about. She thinks it's the answer.'

'I'm not even sure how it works,' Stella admitted. 'Would we all sit at tables and have the men move between us and spend ten minutes with each?'

'Ten minutes ... oh dear God ... and all to stop Tosca being bored and lonely. I am a good friend, aren't I?' Raffaella snapped off the end of her biscotto and put it in her mouth.

'Yes, you are,' Stella agreed.

Hi Leo, apparently I'm going speed-dating! I know, I know, but it's a favour for a new friend I've made. Two friends actually – Tosca, the movie star, and a woman called Raffaella who runs a little trattoria down by the port.

I like these two women. I'd call them commanding (that's a nice way of saying bossy!). They're older than me, Raffaella by quite a lot. Her husband has died and she says she's not interested in meeting anyone else but has agreed to the speed-dating to keep Tosca happy. Whatever happens I'm certain it's going to be interesting.

Oh and it's not that I didn't appreciate the Sanctuary of the Madonna. You're right; it's an amazing place. If I do end up going to a Mass there I'll let you know what it's like – Stella.

Dear Stella: mud, nothing but mud ... it's what I ex-pected of course but still it is discouraging. I'm worried that I didn't take into account how different this garden will be from what I've done before. I don't want to let anyone down. I'm emailing you now in the middle of the night because I can't sleep for thinking about it. Perhaps I need to reconsider my whole approach. Or maybe in the morning the sun will be shining again and the mud will start to dry out and we'll have something better to work with.

I'm intrigued that you've become friends with the movie star. You must tell me all about her. As for the speed-dating, you are braver than I am!

I'm going back to bed now to see if I can get at least a little rest. I hope you're sleeping peacefully at Villa Rosa – Leo.

A lesson in something

Stella had been looking forward to her lesson with Francesca Russo. She was interested to see her home, imagining it as rather bohemian and over-filled with beautiful fabrics: antique linens and hand-stitched quilts collected by her family over the years. She put on a dress the colour of lemons and drove there in bright morning sunshine against the sound of church bells ringing, car windows wound down and a breeze on her face.

The house lay at the far reaches of Triento, an imposing three storeys with a driveway sweeping up to it through a neat garden of clipped shrubs and hedges. Stella remembered her assumption that the linen business must be struggling and instantly revised it.

There was no sign of Francesca. When she knocked on the door, she found it was ajar. As it swung further open what she could see of the hallway looked rather formal: highly polished furniture, gold-framed mirrors, a glass chandelier. There was a smell that reminded Stella of almond essence but it might have been some sort of cleaning product. She didn't want to walk straight in, but when no one responded after she'd called out several times, there didn't seem another option.

'Hello,' she repeated, taking a few steps inside. 'Is there anyone home?'

'Who are you?' The woman was half-hidden just inside a doorway, all dressed in black, grey hair severely plaited. Her skin was pale, her expression unfriendly.

'Oh, hello.' Stella was startled. 'I'm here to see Francesca. She's expecting me.'

The woman stared at her blankly.

'Is this not the right place? I'm looking for the Russo house.'

'This is the Russo residence.' Her English was slow. 'But Francesca, she is busy. She does not have time to see you.'

'We had an arrangement but she might have forgotten. Perhaps if I could just see her for a moment.'

'What arrangement?'

Stella was about to launch into an explanation when she heard Francesca's voice. 'Ah, my English friend, you're here. I've been looking out for you but you must have arrived when I was distracted.'

The couple of times they had met at the linen shop Francesca always seemed very composed but now she sounded flustered. Her cheeks were pink, her feet bare and she was wearing jeans rolled at the ankle and a mint-green top that was crumpled as if she had only just thrown it on.

'Are we still OK for today?' Stella asked her.

'Yes, of course.' Francesca turned to the older woman and said something in Italian. There wasn't so much as the faintest smile in response but she didn't seem concerned.

'Come, come,' she said to Stella brightly. 'We are going to make a *timballo*. It is a traditional dish for celebrations. You will like it.'

Francesca led her through a reception room, equally as formal as the hall, with ornaments laid out in neat formation, and chairs that didn't look as if they were intended for sitting on.

The kitchen was three times the size of the one in Raffaella's *trattoria* and considerably less tidy. Pots and pans cluttered the surfaces along with a jumble of pasta packets and bags of flour.

'Do you have the money for me?' Francesca asked.

Stella produced the sum they'd agreed on. 'In cash like you wanted.'

'Excellent.' Francesca tucked it away quickly into a pocket in her apron. 'Now the *timballo* is a little tricky and takes some time to make so we should begin straight away.'

'I don't know that I'm ready for tricky,' Stella told her dubiously. 'I'd imagined us making a simple dish and learning a few Italian phrases as we went along.'

'*Timballo* has lots of elements but when you bring them all together the result is simple,' Francesca reassured her. 'We will begin with the *melanzane*.'

Rounds of aubergine were dipped in egg and breadcrumbs then fried until they were golden, the pan smoking and Stella quickly becoming as red-cheeked as Francesca. Next they used rolling pins to pummel pieces of pork into slender slices, sprinkled them with Parmesan, rolling them up into parcels with thin leaves of cured ham.

There was no time to rest: meatballs needed to be shaped in Stella's hands, a sauce simmered with tomatoes and chicken stock, pastry dough kneaded and all the time Francesca hovering, referring to a handwritten recipe in a book, issuing instructions, throwing in the occasional Italian phrase, and panicking when things seemed to be going wrong.

'No, no, the dough has too much water in it. Add some flour, not that much. Careful now.'

The process of rolling out the dough into two neat circles didn't go well. Stella had two tries and then, clearly frustrated, Francesca took over, leaving her to boil some penne and mix the cooked pasta with the meaty sauce.

'How often do you go to this much trouble for lunch?' she wondered.

'Only once a year,' admitted Francesca. 'This is my mother-in-law Angelica's favourite dish – you met her earlier in the hallway. On her birthday she requests that I make it.'

'And it's her birthday today?'

'That's right. And so we prepare the *timballo* to celebrate. Don't worry, it is nearly done.'

Francesca produced a deep, round mould that she carefully greased and then lined with the larger circle of pastry. With Stella's help she filled this up with layers of penne, aubergine, mozzarella, meatballs and Parmesan, then sealed the top with the second circle of pastry, brushed it with egg and cut a neat hole in the middle.

'A pasta pie,' said Stella. 'I've never seen anything quite like that.'

'It is not so unusual here although different families make it their own way. This is the Russo recipe, passed down for who knows how many generations.' Francesca gave a little sigh. 'While it bakes in the oven we must prepare the vegetables. Then I will call the family together and we will eat what we have made.'

Stella's pretty lemon-coloured dress was dusted with flour, most probably so were her hair and face. But there wasn't time to fluff with her appearance. Francesca was directing her to make a puree from some dried beans that had been soaked and simmered.

'It is to be served together with steamed wild chicory and lots of olive oil,' she instructed. 'And then there will be broccoli rabe which we will fry with slivers of garlic. And for dessert a tart of almonds sprinkled with grated chocolate – I prepared that last night, thinking you wouldn't want to do so much in your very first lesson.'

'No, indeed,' Stella said drily.

The *timballo*, when it emerged from the oven, all burnished brown and steaming, was an impressive sight. While it rested they set the dining table with cloth napkins, weighty crystal and shining silver cutlery. Then Stella seized a moment to tidy herself while Francesca gathered the family.

Her mother-in-law Angelica didn't seem any less frosty when she reappeared; even the sight of the *timballo*, miraculously freed intact from its mould and posing at the centre of the dining table, failed to cheer her.

From Roberto, who recalled Stella from her visit to the linen shop, there was considerably more warmth. He insisted she sat beside him and admired the feast she had helped prepare.

'Now we are just waiting for my husband Gennaro, then we can make a toast to Mamma and open the *timballo*,' said Francesca.

The old woman said something in Italian, her tone impatient. Francesca turned away and left the room, not bothering to reply.

'My mother is complaining that Gennaro moves so slowly the *timballo* will be ancient by the time he appears,' Roberto explained, sounding amused. 'It is true that he is always the last to arrive anywhere.'

'Is he involved in the linen shop as well?' Stella asked.

Roberto nodded. 'All of us are. We live under the same roof; we work for the family business. Mamma too – it is her dynasty.'

He emphasised the last word in a way that to Stella's ears sounded rather bitter. 'It's an impressive house,' she murmured politely. 'And I really love your shop.'

'The shop is only a small part of it,' Roberto explained. 'There is the manufacturing and wholesaling side of things that my brother and Mamma are involved in.'

'And what do you do?' Stella asked.

'A little of everything; I help out where I'm needed.'

The old matriarch frowned. 'My son has been living abroad,' she announced. 'Now he is home he will be taking a greater interest in the business. And I will be able to step back at last.'

'Where have you been living?' Stella asked Roberto.

'I've travelled all over – Australia, New Zealand, Bali, Hawaii. I love to surf. But now I'm home to settle down.' He sounded resigned.

Stella had imagined having lunch with a large, noisy Italian family. She envisaged it like a scene from a movie, everyone talking and eating, a room filled with sounds of laughter and smells of delicious food, lots of children running about, maybe even chickens roaming under the table. Instead she found herself trapped in a grand but grim dining room, a not especially welcome part of this family's celebration.

It was a relief when Francesca returned, her husband in tow. He was an attractive-looking man, not unlike his brother, but with shorter hair and gold-framed spectacles.

'My Gennaro was working on his computer. Always working, even on a Sunday,' Francesca said.

'There is lots to be done,' Angelica remarked.

Wordlessly they settled round the table. Roberto opened a bottle of champagne that had been chilling in an ice bucket, and poured each of them a glass. There was a toast, a few 'happy birthdays', then Francesca stood and carefully sliced into the *timballo*, passing the first portion to her frosty mother-in-law.

Stella only realised how hungry she was when her plate was set in front of her. Had she been with her own friends she'd have taken a fork and carved off a slice to try. But here it seemed the proper thing was to hold back, while the vegetables were passed round and the red wine poured and while Gennaro disappeared for a few minutes because he really had to check something and it couldn't wait.

The *timballo* had cooled by the time she tasted it but if anything that made the flavours bigger.

'Worth the effort?' Francesca had been watching her.

'Delicious,' Stella replied truthfully.

The conversation as they ate was mostly in Italian, although now and then someone remembered to translate. Roberto was the most solicitous. He made an effort to talk, asking questions about her life in England and what she was planning to do in Triento.

'Tourists don't normally stay here so long. I think you may be bored,' he said.

'Hopefully not. I seem to be making friends already,' Stella told him.

Then she mentioned Tosca's name and everyone's attention turned to her.

'She is the movie star; the one that went to Hollywood? You know her?' Francesca was wide-eyed. 'People tell me she is living in town but I've never recognised her.'

'Movie star.' Angelica was scathing. 'How many films was she in? I have never seen any.'

'She was in some, years ago, I'm sure,' Francesca insisted.

'Yes, yes, I think I watched one on television once,' Roberto agreed. 'She will be older now so perhaps that's why we haven't recognised her. Stella, you must introduce us; I would like to meet this Tosca.'

Angelica hissed in impatience. 'She was never anyone special. Just a fisherman's daughter.'

'You knew her then, Mamma?' asked Gennaro.

'No, I never noticed her. And what if she did go to Hollywood? She was no Sophia Loren.'

Normally Stella didn't take a dislike to people unless they gave her a really good reason to. This woman, though, had put her back up. She turned to Roberto. 'Actually Tosca is a lot of fun. I think you'd like her. Why don't I arrange for us to catch up for a drink one evening.'

'Oh and me too, I would like to come,' put in Francesca. 'She may not be Sophia Loren but she is the most famous person Triento has ever produced.'

'Yes, of course,' Stella promised. 'I'm sure she'd be happy to meet you.'

Roberto laughed. 'Here we are, the Russo family who have been here for generations, and we are asking this stranger to introduce us to someone from our town. Mamma, you must have met her.'

Angelica shook her head. 'Not that I remember.'

'Well then, I wonder if you know the man whose place I'm staying in?' asked Stella. 'His name is Leo Asti and he's a landscape gardener with a house a little way along the coast called Villa Rosa.'

Angelica considered the question. 'I may have heard his name perhaps, but no, I've never met him. The house I know: Villa Rosa.'

'You've been there?'

'Not me; but many years ago the Russo family brought a man from America to build Triento's great blessing, the statue of Christ the Redeemer you have seen up on the mountain. Villa Rosa is where he stayed. Now that man was worth meeting; he was a person who achieved something important, not like this Tosca who is famous for doing nothing.'

'Yes, but he is dead, Mamma, so we can't meet him,' Roberto said. 'Tosca is still with us and if she's lived in Hollywood she must have some good stories.'

'I don't want to hear them. Everyone is obsessed with celebrities these days. I don't understand it.'

'Stella says she's fun,' Roberto countered.

'Fun, well then.' Angelica was stone-faced. 'That's what is important, isn't it?'

Stella drove back to Villa Rosa faster than normal. She couldn't wait to get to her laptop and write to Leo, to introduce him to this family: the toxic mother, the unhappy sons and the cunning daughter-in-law.

Dear Leo, let me tell you about my Sunday. I'd arranged to go to the Russo house for Francesca to give me a cooking lesson. I thought it would be entertaining and it was; but not for the reasons you'd imagine. First the house – it's the complete opposite to Villa Rosa, very grand, one of those places that seems as if it's been staged and no one really lives there. I hadn't been there for very long when I realised Francesca had tricked me. She wasn't teaching a lesson; she was getting me to help cook her mother-in-law's birthday lunch. And I paid for the privilege!

I should have walked out. I'm not sure why I didn't, except that I was sort of fascinated to see how things would develop. We made this giant pasta pie, a timballo, which took for ever to put together. There was a bad moment when I thought the whole thing was going to collapse as Francesca turned it out of the mould but somehow it stayed in one piece. It tasted great but never, ever will I make another one. I may not even be able to bring myself to cook again.

Anyway aside from the food, lunch was deadly. The matriarch of the Russo family is this snooty old woman who didn't have a good thing to say about anyone, not a single thing. And then there's her son Roberto who is clearly the black sheep. And Francesca's husband, Gennaro, who seems to only care about work. I'm sounding like a bitch, but you really should have been there. It was one of the most awkward lunches I've ever sat through. Never again!

How are things with you? Is the mud drying up? Stella.

The trouble with food

It was a perfect morning for the scrapbook, a warm day that beckoned Stella outside. She sipped her coffee sitting at the outdoor table, the book set in front of her, trying to decide where to open it, finally settling on a page close to the beginning.

On it Leo had drawn a quick sketch, a line drawing of the tall white statue up on the mountain behind her.

Dear Stella, possibly by now you have already driven up to the statue of Christ the Redeemer. The view is wonderful so it is the obvious thing for visitors to do. But today I would like you to go there for an experience few others have had. Between the church and the statue there is a small bar that serves food. If you spot it you may assume it's a place only for tourists – it even has a sign outside with photographs of some of the things they offer, simple pizza and pasta dishes, breads stuffed with salami and cheese. Go in and introduce yourself to Benedetto Pippo or his wife Maria. Tell them I sent you. Go hungry! – Leo.

Stella hadn't visited the statue, mainly because she had seen the road snaking up to it and thought it looked perilous. But she felt more confident in Leo's car now, and besides, with the day so clear, there couldn't be a more perfect time to go and appreciate a view. Recalling how bored Tosca had claimed to be, she sent her a text suggesting she come too.

Ten minutes later a reply came back. Tosca was certain there was nowhere worth eating at up on the mountain; still, the view was good so she would meet her there.

Stella put on white jeans, a crisp broderie anglaise top and a denim jacket in case it was chilly on the mountain. The route up was a series of hairpin bends with dizzying drops. The car's engine screamed as it climbed the steep rise and she tried not to think about how many vehicles might have crashed through the flimsy barrier and hurtled over the edge.

Reaching the summit, the road finished at a potholed car park. From there some steps led round the side of the church and out into a wide piazza where Stella found a souvenir shop and spotted the bar Leo must have meant. Ahead was the towering statue, its back turned to the sea, head bowed and arms stretched wide. Perched on the highest rocky point it was an impressive sight, even for a non-believer like her.

Another flight of steps took Stella to the base of the statue and she walked around it slowly, looking down on the line of the harbour wall, the curve of the coastline, the blue of the sea and the distant mountains melting into the sky.

She had been there for a while when she heard her name on the breeze and turned to see Tosca, in high-heeled boots, a hat and sunglasses, climbing the steps, Raffaella beside her, wrapped in a long black cardigan.

'My God, it's years since I was up here last,' she exclaimed, when they had greeted each other with a kissing of cheeks.

'I have never been,' Raffaella admitted. 'Not since it was completed.'

'Never?' Stella was surprised.

Raffaella stared up at the statue. 'It is striking; I will admit that now I'm here. Maybe it was worth all the trouble.'

Turning her attention to the view, Raffaella began pointing out landmarks: the terracotta roof of her own house far beneath them, the ruins of a settlement that once clung to the rocks, the old convent now a smart hotel. 'Everything seems so small from here, and so unimportant,' she remarked.

Neither Raffaella nor Tosca were convinced they would find a decent lunch in the little bar. They suggested driving back down to the harbour instead but Stella was adamant she wanted to stay.

'There is a surprise arranged for me there. I have to see what it is.'

Both were intrigued when she explained about Leo's scrapbook, Tosca especially. 'But you told me you haven't even met this man. Why would he do something so romantic?'

'I don't think it's meant to be romantic; just kind.'

'And you have looked only at three pages of this book? No more?' Tosca sounded disbelieving.

'Yes, because I want to enjoy it the way he intended.'

'When I met him that one time I didn't pick Leo Asti as the romantic type,' mused Tosca. 'To me he seemed practical, driven, passionate about his house and garden but not much else. Clearly I missed something.'

Even Stella had to admit the place Leo was sending them to looked unprepossessing. Plain tiled floors, old wooden furniture and a bar selling a selection of lurid-looking liqueurs, it was empty aside from a couple of old men; still it was clean, she noticed. The man behind the counter, bald-headed and middle-aged, greeted them with a polite nod and a *buongiorno*.

'*Buongiorno*, I'm Stella and I've been sent here by Leo Asti. He said I should introduce myself to you.'

The change was instant. Smiling widely, he came out from behind his counter to embrace Stella and her friends, shouting to his wife as he did so. 'Maria, *vieni qua*. It is the English woman. She has come like Leo said she might.'

His wife appeared, drying her hands on a tea towel – a large woman, with lots of black hair and large gold-hooped earrings. 'You have chosen the perfect day,' she told Stella.

'And you have brought friends. Good, good. Take a seat and Benedetto will serve you an *aperitivo* while I cook for you.'

Tosca glanced at Stella as they chose a table and sat down. 'Yes, very romantic,' she said. 'Impossible to believe this man Leo does not know you at all.'

'He's seen a few photographs of me.'

'Then I think he must have liked them.'

Stella felt herself flushing. 'It's not that way at all. He was concerned I'd be lonely at Villa Rosa on my own, and the scrapbook is how he's tried to help. It's a lovely thing; but thoughtful rather than romantic.'

Tosca raised her eyebrows. 'You are wrong, in my opinion.'

When Benedetto delivered their drinks, Tosca stopped him. 'Can you tell us about Leo Asti? Do you know him very well?'

'Certainly, he's my friend. We were at school together in Napoli. In fact, he is the reason I am here in Triento. He helped me.'

'Sit down and talk to us,' Tosca demanded. 'What did he do?'

'I shouldn't, *signora*, I am working ... my wife will expect ...'

'Only five minutes.' Tosca help up the fingers of one hand. 'Sit and tell us about Leo Asti.'

Obediently Benedetto perched on a chair. 'Well, Leo is a successful man as I imagine you're aware,' he began. 'He has worked hard and built a business. But he's never lost touch with his old friends. A few months ago he came to visit me in Scampia and, seeing how bad things were, said he would help us to get out. And Leo kept his word. He learnt this place was available, put our names forward, let us borrow one of his vans to move our belongings and now here we are, me and Maria. It is quiet now but once the tourists come things will be busier I'm sure.'

'Where is Scampia?' asked Stella.

'It is in the north of Naples, a hellhole with a lot of crime. The people there are very poor. There is no work, no future; only the gangs.'

Raffaella interrupted. 'Better here than Scampia, I'm sure. But in winter up on this mountain you will see no customers. You will struggle. Did your friend Leo Asti tell you that?'

'The rent is very cheap and the place has possibilities, *signora*,' he said. 'We haven't been open for long. When they hear what Maria can do, people will come.'

'I hope so.'

Benedetto seemed unconcerned. 'My friend Leo believes in us,' he told her. 'When you taste my wife's food perhaps you will too.'

The first thing he brought out was bread, coarse sourdough with creamy curls of browned butter. Then there were loaded *antipasti* plates, almost too many to fit on the table, and Raffaella began tasting, murmuring between each bite.

'The red melanzane they have found in Rotonda, the olive oil is the very best from the Santi Estate, the croquettes of salt cod couldn't be any lighter, the grilled squid is stuffed with both Parmesan and anchovy and tastes exactly right. He is right: his wife knows about food.'

Tosca ate with more restraint. She didn't touch the bread or the fried croquettes, grazing only on the seafood and vegetable dishes. When the pasta arrived – tagliatelle coated in a gluey slow-cooked ragu, she tasted only a little of the shredded beef in thick tomatoes.

'My God, I watch her eat and I want to cry,' Raffaella told Stella.

'Don't be ridiculous.' Tosca was haughty.

'It is true, though.' Raffaella was still addressing Stella. 'Would it be such a disaster to gain a couple of kilos? Would she be any less beautiful? I don't think so.'

Stella licked sauce from her lips and looked from one

woman to the other. 'I suppose when Tosca was making films she had to keep herself slim,' she said reasonably.

'True. But now she says she is finished with that so she doesn't have to stay hungry. She can enjoy food, indulge in it, fill herself up.'

'I expect it's hard to break the habit of being so careful.' Stella tried to be tactful.

Sighing, Tosca forked up a piece of the tagliatelle, put it in her mouth, chewed and swallowed. 'There, I have enjoyed some pasta, my life is complete,' she said. 'Is everyone happy now?'

'It is you we want to be happy, *cara*,' said Raffaella.

'But to me food isn't happiness.' Tosca looked down at her plate. 'It is only food.'

'You are wrong; food is everything,' argued Raffaella. 'It is pleasure, happiness and love; most of all it is memory.'

'I don't care to remember. I'd rather look forward than back.'

'You don't like your past then?'

'I'm finished with it.' Tosca put down her fork. 'Just as I am this pasta.'

The next dishes were the most interesting: hyacinth bulbs fried in a light batter and dusted with pecorino cheese, briny mussels snug in coats of breadcrumbs, a stew of pork and pickled sweet peppers, braised wild fennel flavoured with garlic and anchovies. Even Raffaella's appetite seemed to be flagging by the time she'd tried a portion of each.

'Will they be successful do you think, Benedetto and his wife?' asked Stella. 'Their food is good, isn't it?'

'The food, yes, but success is about more than that.' Raffaella sounded grave. 'Atmosphere, location and, here in Triento, who you know matters a lot. Perhaps they'll get through the summer but by winter I fear they'll be back in Scampia.'

'That seems a shame.'

Tosca took a forkful of the pork and chewed it carefully. Next she tried a wedge of one of the hyacinth bulbs. 'The solution is obvious, isn't it?' she said, once she had swallowed.

'It is?'

'Yes, Raffaella, *cara*, completely obvious. They need a better place than this and meanwhile you are needing help in your *trattoria*. So you come together and there it is, perfect.'

'Oh really?' Raffaella said tightly.

'Yes, yes.'

'I will decide the future of my *trattoria*, Tosca. I will say what is perfect.'

'This woman can cook; even I can tell that. You should at least talk to her, see if she and her husband might be interested.'

Raffaella shook her head. 'Why do you feel you must interfere in my life?'

'Because I am right.'

'So she gives me one good meal and I give her my *trattoria*?'

'You come to a business arrangement. Lease the place or hire them to work in it. Why are you so stubborn, Raffaella? You know you can't keep it going for ever. You will need to slow down.'

'There is a young woman inside me.' Raffaella said it sadly. 'She feels no different from how she did twenty or thirty years ago. It is only her body that aches when she tries to do what she used to.'

'Then get this Maria to do it for you,' Tosca urged. 'That is the solution. You can still be involved with the menu and the planning if you really want that. Work out a deal that suits you.'

Raffaella said nothing. She picked over the remains of wild fennel with her fork, eating a few more fragrant, oily strands.

'I suppose there is no rush to make a decision. They will

be here all summer as you said,' Tosca conceded. 'We can come back.'

'We could meet Roberto here one evening,' suggested Stella.

'Who is Roberto?' asked Tosca. 'And why are we meeting him?'

'Ah, that's right, I haven't told you about my experiences on Sunday yet.' Stella smiled. 'It's quite a story.'

She regaled them with the making of the *timballo* and the awkward lunch at the Russo house, doing her very best impression of the vicious old matriarch presiding over the table and Francesca in a tizz in the kitchen. The change of subject lightened the mood and by the story's finish both women were laughing so hard they were dabbing the tears from their eyes with serviettes.

'Roberto is very keen to meet you,' she told Tosca. 'He wanted me to set up a time.'

'Really?' Tosca sounded intrigued. 'What does he look like? Do I know him?'

'You must have seen him around town,' Raffaella said. 'He is the eldest Russo son. But too young for you; Stella's age, possibly less.'

'Never mind his age, what is he like?'

'Very charming,' Stella told her. 'Quite good-looking, too.'

'But young, much too young,' Raffaella insisted.

'Will you stop saying that?'

'I'm sorry but it's true. I know how old you are, I was there when you were born.'

'I don't look my age,' Tosca insisted.

'Yes, because every time a wrinkle appears you attack it with Botox. Meet this boy Roberto for a drink by all means but remember you could be his mother.'

Tosca put her hands over her ears. 'No, no, I refuse to hear this. In fact I'm going to leave now.' She got to her feet. 'I'll pay the bill. Today is my treat, I insist.'

Watching her stalk towards the counter, Raffaella smiled at Stella. 'I think perhaps we may be able to escape the speed-dating.'

'But you said he's too young for her.'

'Of course I did, and now she is determined to prove me wrong.'

Benedetto refused to give Tosca the bill. He said their money was no good there, that Leo had everything covered, and he wouldn't hear any argument. All he wanted was to know if they'd enjoyed the meal and he flushed with pride when they praised his wife's cooking.

'We'll be back very soon,' Stella promised.

'Bring your friends,' he pleaded. 'Tell people we are here and what we can do.'

Stella felt sorry for him and also a little guilty. They had eaten a feast and she would have to find a way to pay him or Leo back for it; after all, neither had expected her to arrive with friends in tow.

She drove back down the hill, thinking about Raffaella and Tosca, how they never stopped clashing yet seemed to care for one another, how being with them was always such a good time. They were starting to feel like friends.

Birdie, I've realised I never thanked you for being so straight-talking. You were completely right of course and all I had to do was make an effort. I'm getting to know people now; you'll meet them when you come to visit I hope; and I'm seeing a glimpse of lives very different from my own. It's fascinating.

Being here doesn't feel like a mistake any more; it may even be the best thing I've done. So thanks. And love you – Stella.

Hi Leo – Today I went up to the statue and met your friends Benedetto and Maria who gave me the most

*amazing lunch. Thank you but please let me pay the bill.
I had people with me and we ate a lot. I can't let you
cover it all and I'd hate to think of your friends being
out of pocket when they're trying so hard to establish
themselves.*

*What I'm really writing for is to say the scrapbook is
proving to be such a brilliant idea. When I first arrived
in Triento it was like I was only partly here. I couldn't
stop thinking about home and how sad everything has
been lately. Now at last I'm feeling as if I'm properly in
the world and that's largely down to you.*

*I don't think I'll be opening up the scrapbook tomor-
row. Raffaella has come up with some plan for us to
meet in town and go to the market together. I have a
bad feeling she wants to give me a cooking lesson. I'm
not over the day of the* timballo *yet but if she's made
up her mind there'll be no point in trying to argue. She's
formidable!*

*Anyway, I'll be choosing another page from your
book very soon. And I'm looking forward to it. Stella.*

*Hi Stella – I hate to admit it but I can't remember half of
what I put in that book. Everything except this garden
has gone out of my head. But I'm glad you went to see
Benedetto and Maria. They are good people and I hope
they can make a go of it in Triento. The place they're
in isn't perfect but it's better than before and Maria is
clever, she understands food.*

*So speed-dating, cooking lessons – you are so busy.
I had always thought of Triento as such a sleepy place,
but apparently not. Perhaps Raffaella wants to show
you her way of making the* timballo. *How funny would
that be? Leo.*

Hey Stella, of course I was right; I always am. Pleased to hear things are better. In fact, it sounds like they're great. So my news is I still have a job … oh and I think I may have found a girlfriend! We met at a party, the old-fashioned way, not online. I really like her; so much it's scaring me a bit. I'd got used to things fizzling out after a few dates and I'm really desperate for this not to. I'm seeing her tonight – we have plans for a glass of wine after work and we'll see where that takes us. Wish me luck! Birdie.

Stella, I am not as old as that crazy woman thinks. Ignore what she says because her memory is shot. Friday would be good for drinks with Roberto. Will you organise? Tosca.

A pale green heart

Stella's day began with coffee as always, this time drunk early in the café in Triento with Raffaella sitting beside her and complaining about the pastry on her plate.

'Too much cinnamon,' she said. 'Someone has a heavy hand. It is a shame because otherwise it would have been perfect.'

'Have you always cared so much about food?' To Stella the pastry seemed perfectly fine.

'I don't remember a time when it wasn't important. My mother loved to cook and she taught me to look for the joy in it rather than the work. Even today I still make many of the dishes she showed me.'

'My mother was a fan of instant mashed potato and foods that could be heated in the microwave,' admitted Stella. 'She always said life was too short to be stuck in a kitchen and I think I agree with her.'

'But a kitchen is the best place in any home,' Raffaella protested. 'There is warmth, the smell of good things cooking; people come to taste a spoonful and they stop to talk. For many families a kitchen is where lives touch.'

'Ours touched around the television set and our favourite night of the week was when Mum sent me out for fish and chips. Food isn't a big part of my memories.'

'Then you need to make new memories. We can start today.'

Aware of what was coming, Stella tried to head her off.

'You know I'm not especially keen on another cooking lesson. The *timballo* was enough.'

'*Timballo*.' Raffaella rolled her eyes. 'Still, I'm impressed that Francesca Russo managed to make one. I never would have thought it.'

There was no arguing with her. Presenting Stella with an empty basket, she declared that first they would shop for ingredients and then go to her *trattoria* and prepare a delicious lunch with what they had bought. 'You will enjoy it, I promise.'

'OK then,' agreed Stella, knowing that even if she hated every minute she wouldn't dare admit it.

They spent half the morning in the market. Everyone seemed to know Raffaella and she stopped to ask after mothers or children, to enquire about family members who had moved away from Triento, or simply exchange a few words about the ripeness of some fruit or the freshness of a vegetable. It was as much a social occasion as grocery shopping, lives touching, thought Stella, food bringing them together.

Some stallholders offered them tastes of what they were selling: a sweet wild strawberry, a spoonful of fruity olive oil, wedges of earthy caciocavallo cheese, slices of garlic-laced sausage. As they moved from one to another, Stella's basket grew heavier.

'This market hasn't changed much since I was a girl,' Raffaella said, as they sat down on the low wall beside the town hall to take a moment's rest. 'It's a little bigger now but many of the stalls are still run by the same families.'

'Has the rest of Triento changed much?' asked Stella.

Raffaella considered the question. 'In many ways, no,' she decided. 'The buildings, the cobbled streets, the churches; they've been here forever. We've always shopped for bread in the same bakery, and drunk our coffee in the bar in the piazza. Even the Russos linen shop has stood there for as long as I can remember. But when I walk through Triento I can't help but see what is missing now. The pizzeria my husband owned that used to be hidden up that narrow lane, the woman who ran the bakery and was the town's biggest gossip, the priests who were kind to me and those who weren't. The whole place is a patchwork of my memories these days. Perhaps that's what happens when you reach this age.'

Stella wondered if some day she would feel the same way about London.

'How old was Tosca when she left?' she asked.

'Young, too young probably, only sixteen. Her mother took her to Rome to find work and a few months later came back without her. I heard nothing for a while then suddenly the talk was that she had been discovered and they were going to make her into a star like Claudia Cardinale or Gina Lollobrigida. Whenever anyone asked after her we were told how much she was loved, how well she was doing. The times she came back, the fuss that was made, as if she really was as famous as those others.'

'But she never was?'

'Tosca was in some films. I remember going to watch one with my husband. She was very beautiful of course and in my opinion she is a fine actress, but whether she was ever famous is another thing. I'm not the one to judge that.'

'She's still very glamorous,' said Stella.

'Yes, she is holding on to that as tightly as she can. It won't be easy for her when it's completely gone.'

Stella looked at Raffaella, her skin bruised and lined from decades of laughter and tears, the soft fold of her jaw, the slight droop of her mouth, her clothes as black and shapeless as usual.

'Old can still be attractive, can't it?'

'It's not the same. They used to say I was beautiful and I didn't understand what that meant till they stopped. People treat you differently; somehow you stop mattering so much. And so Tosca has her Botox and her special diets and whatever else she does, to postpone the moment for as long as possible.'

Stella knew she was often admired for being stylish. People said they liked her hair colour or envied her slim figure or loved what she was wearing. But never in her life had she been called beautiful; listening to Raffaella made her think she should be grateful.

'Whatever Tosca is doing is working,' she remarked.

'Why then is she back here, wasting what's left of her precious beauty?' wondered Raffaella. 'She cares so much about her brow being smooth and the grey not showing in her hair, and her body being slender, but who is all of that for now she's given up on her career?'

'For herself perhaps, just to feel good. Or to attract a man?'

'A man who wants you only for your beauty isn't worth having; I know that much,' said Raffaella. 'And I worry about Tosca. I think there is something more going on but I can't pin down what it might be.'

'Do you ever wish you'd left this town like she did?' Stella asked.

'No, I've been happy here. My life may have been smaller than hers but it's just as worth remembering.'

Stella couldn't imagine how the contents of their baskets could be brought together to make a meal. From the fish stall they had bought octopus with pinkish-purple legs and from the vegetable sellers glossy tomatoes, leafy greens, tender buds of artichokes and tiny red chilli peppers. There were two types of cheese, a bottle of local olive oil and a jar of anchovies. When she asked Raffaella what the menu was to be she only smiled and said, 'You will see soon enough.'

At the *trattoria* they drank more cups of strong black

coffee before unpacking their purchases, Raffaella exclaiming over the briny freshness of the octopus and the beauty of the broccoli rabe.

'Italian food is all about good ingredients and doing as little as possible to them,' she told Stella, giving her an apron to cover her clothes. 'In my kitchen simplicity is the greatest virtue.'

Not that making orecchiette was especially simple. Flour and water was mixed and massaged until it was transformed into smooth, dense dough. Raffaella showed her how to roll it into curled ears of pasta, with a quick flick of a thumb. The few that Stella attempted were misshapen but they were put on the wire rack anyway to dry along with the others. 'They will taste just as good,' said Raffaella.

They prepared the octopus, simmering it in a garlicky sauce with lashings of red wine. Then they stripped the thorny outer leaves from the artichokes until all that was left were the pale green hearts.

'And now we rest, enjoy a glass of wine and a few *taralli* to nibble on,' declared Raffaella, 'and when we're ready to eat we cook the pasta and make the artichoke salad. Simple, you see?'

'A lot easier than the *timballo*,' Stella conceded.

They phoned Tosca, inviting her to join them, then sat out in the sunshine crunching into the *taralli*, little savoury biscuits flavoured with fennel seeds, while Raffaella talked about her *trattoria* and how it used to be.

'In the summer this whole area would be filled with tables and chairs and we'd feed crowds of people with the dishes we created from whatever the boats had brought in. Ciro and I worked long hours, our sons too when they were here to help, but we were successful, we were doing what we loved and we were together.' She rubbed at her eyes tiredly. 'The last summers without him I've halved the number of tables out here and hired people in to wait on them, but all the joy seems to have gone. Just the thought of doing it again this year makes me want to lie down for a very long time.'

'Perhaps Tosca is right about ...' Stella began.

'Oh yes, Tosca is always right,' Raffaella said tartly.

Stella risked pressing her point. 'They seemed so nice, those friends of Leo's, and their food was delicious. They might be the right people to lease this place.'

Raffaella looked around at the empty terrace, as if imagining it filled with diners, with waiters taking orders and people finding pleasure in the food on their plates.

'Once I give this up there is no going back. It will really be the end of it all.'

'Endings are difficult.' Stella could sympathise.

'They always come eventually, though, don't they?' Raffaella sighed. 'And Tosca may be right this time, I know that.'

The orecchiette tossed with swiftly wilted broccoli rabe and vibrant with garlic and chilli; the octopus so meltingly tender in its rich red sauce; the raw artichoke hearts sliced thinly and married with shaved pecorino cheese and shredded mint leaves; Stella ate another lunch completely delicious from start to finish. Tosca joined them, but only at the end to nibble round the edges of what was left. Long into the afternoon they stayed at their table. Eventually Raffaella brought out walnut biscuits with a sweet/sour lemon icing. Stella made coffee; Tosca poured more wine and the sun slowly sank lower in the sky.

'So tell me, Stella: tomorrow what is your scrapbook sending you to do?' Tosca asked. 'Something exciting, I hope.'

'I don't know. I never look until the morning.'

'What happens if you open it to a page with something on it that you don't like the idea of?'

'Obviously I don't have to do it.'

'Remind me what there has been so far?' Tosca seemed entranced by the whole business.

Stella counted them off. 'The market where he left me the record of Neapolitan songs, the church in the cave, and the lunch up by the statue.'

'What next I wonder?'

'I'll open the book in the morning and call you straight away,' Stella promised. 'Do you think you might come with me to wherever it is?'

'That depends ... but I do want to know.'

Stella wondered how they usually spent their days. Did Raffaella cook intricate meals and eat them alone? Did Tosca make herself glamorous purely for her own eyes? What would be filling their afternoon if she weren't there?

'I'll call you first thing then.'

Dear Leo, the scrapbook is proving to be a hit with my new friends. They may even come and join me on whatever adventure you're sending me on tomorrow; I hope it's something good!

Tosca can't believe I haven't read the book from cover to cover. It's not that I haven't been tempted but it's more exciting this way. It's funny, I've never thought of myself as a person who likes surprises but apparently I do. I guess before life just didn't offer many to me. I was always so organised, my week planned, my diary in order with no double bookings or even last-minute cancellations, not if I could help it. But now I love not knowing what's coming next. My days feel full of possibilities.

Today my cooking lesson with Raffaella was a lot less stressful than the last one – no timballo by the way – and sharing the meal was much more pleasurable. It has to be one of the nicest things in the world, sitting in the sun for an entire afternoon with nothing to do but eat good food and chat to friends. When I think of London and everyone rushing to get from one place to the other, so much to be done and all those crowds, I wonder how you're finding it all? It's not exactly ideal for a person who loves peace and solitude! Stella.

Ah Stella, there is no peace here, you are right about that. I can always hear the rumble of traffic, wherever I am. In your apartment I play music to blot it out – yes, sometimes even Neapolitan love songs, although they make me miss home. Of course, Napoli is as frantic and noisy as London, probably more so, which means I'm used to living like this even though I'd prefer not to. Given a choice I would stay at Villa Rosa all the time. I love that feeling when I close the gates and it's as if no one can intrude on my small piece of the world. Of course I enjoy company too. Being there surrounded by friends and family, swimming in the sea, cooking meals together – it's the way to spend a summer. Still, Villa Rosa is at its best when you're alone I think. The peace there is somehow different to any other place I know.

Having said that I am going to shatter your peace for a day. I'm sending a crew to tidy up the grounds. This time of year a garden won't stay tame for long: the temperatures are warmer, spring growth is in full flush and before you know it the weeds will be waist high. I hope you won't mind the intrusion; they're nice guys and I've told them not to bother you. Perhaps they'll take care of everything while you and your friends are out somewhere.

I look forward to hearing what you choose from the scrapbook. Don't forget to let me know – Leo.

Dear Leo, I know that exact feeling you describe when the gates are closed. It's how I feel every evening when I shut them. And I play music too to screen out the noise of the buses roaring up Camden High Street.

*Usually jazz or opera, maybe some 70s disco if I feel
like dancing round the living room! Funny, isn't it, this
house-swapping? It really is like exchanging lives. Love
Stella.*

Sweet and sour

Stella had left the scrapbook beside her bed the night before so the first thing she did when she opened her eyes was lean down and pick it up. Opening it at random as usual, by the light of the bedside lamp, she read Leo's words.

> *Today I think you should call the number at the bottom of the page and ask to speak to Elena. Tell her I have suggested you visit her vineyard for a tour. Hopefully it will be convenient but if not then arrange another time. At this vineyard they are doing something different. It's a bit of a secret, not something they've advertised yet anyway, and I doubt you'll find many people in Triento that know about it. I helped them with their garden and learnt what they are up to. It's intriguing ... and delicious! I'm not going to say any more. I'll let you discover it for yourself.*

It was still too early to be bothering people with phone calls so Stella put on her robe and went down to make breakfast. Most mornings, if she wasn't going to eat pastries in Triento, she boiled an egg or sliced up a tomato to have on toast. Her cooking lesson with Raffaella had made her feel as if she should be more creative.

Instead of going straight to the kitchen, Stella detoured into the garden and checked the vegetable beds to see if anything seemed ready to eat. There were lots of herbs: small bushes of flat-leaved parsley shading leafy sage and mint, a straggle of rosemary, some tidy upright thyme.

Beyond the herbs were pea plants basking beside the sun-warmed wall and a crop of leggy fava beans that someone had neatly staked – Leo's gardening crew, she supposed, on their last visit. There were towering artichokes, tender spring onions, a few plants she failed to identify and one she thought was wild fennel. Stella couldn't believe she hadn't bothered to take a proper look before. She picked a handful of herbs, and stuffed the pockets of her robe with pea pods. Some of the rest she might harvest later and give to Raffaella or surely they would spoil.

Breakfast was a scramble of eggs mixed with fresh herbs and sweet, green peas. Stella never would have bothered to make something like it at home. During her time at Milly Munro's breakfast was a sandwich picked up from Pret a Manger on the way to work, or nothing at all. Lunch meant sushi most days, and for dinner – if not eating out – at best she would assemble a salad. When she was married, Ray had been the one who made all the effort in the kitchen and she might chop an onion or stir a sauce to help. It wasn't that she didn't enjoy eating the results; but the fuss of preparation, gathering ingredients, having the right equipment, following a recipe ... it just seemed easier to buy a ready-meal from somewhere. Ray called it factory food and was always quoting the latest scare story – horsemeat in burgers, evil E numbers, that kind of thing. Stella preferred not to think about it; the food looked and tasted fine, she argued. Ray said that wasn't the point.

In their final year together it became one of the things they argued about. In Stella's opinion Ray was obsessed with what he put in his mouth. He kept giving things up – first wheat, then dairy, next bacon. In the cupboard were solid loaves of gluten-free bread bought from some wholefood store, an endless proliferation of things labelled organic and natural, a giant jar of homemade sauerkraut – he took that with him when he left.

For Stella, reverting to foods packed in plastic almost felt like rebellion. She bought white sliced bread, those baked beans with little pink sausages in them, jars of pasta sauce, a pie in a tin. They were the foods of her childhood; she was asserting herself again. Perhaps some of it wasn't especially healthy but she told herself there was no point filling the fridge with fresh stuff that would only go off.

It was Raffaella's artichoke salad that made Stella fear she had been wrong about food all along. Those tender green hearts protected by layers of thorny leaves and a spiky beard. Once they were freed they had to be cosseted, their surfaces rubbed with lemon then plunged into water so they wouldn't brown. But the taste of them, the clean crispness against the salty cheese, it had made her feel nourished. She began to see why people cared so much about what they fed themselves.

Pleased with her attempt at scrambling eggs, she finished them off, made coffee in the moka pot and went to find her phone so she could call this person Elena at the mysterious vineyard.

A woman's voice answered almost straight away. '*Pronto.*'

'Oh hello, is this Elena? Do you speak English?'

'Yes, who is this?'

'My name is Stella. Leo Asti suggested I call you.'

'Ah Leo, how is he? I haven't heard from him in a while. He is in London still?'

Stella gave her the quick-version explanation of their house swap. 'Leo said you might give me a tour of your vineyard and I was wondering if today is convenient,' she finished.

'He mentioned there was someone he might send over. I'm here all day doing dull paperwork. Come mid-morning if you like. I'd welcome the break.'

'A couple of friends might want to join me. They're locals,

so is that OK? Only Leo mentioned what you are doing is sort of a secret.'

'A secret?' Elena laughed. 'Oh, Leo is funny. He loves his secrets and surprises. It was only that we weren't ready to tell people, but now we are. And it will be good to have outsiders come, to see what you think of what we're making.'

Elena gave her the address of the vineyard along with some complicated directions.

'Great, mid-morning then, see you soon,' said Stella, hoping Tosca or Raffaella would join her and be some help in finding the place. She sent a text to both of them.

Mystery tour of a vineyard where they are doing something special. Come soon.

Tosca sent a thumbs-up in reply.

An hour later they arrived, Raffaella at the wheel of a dented old car, hooting the horn as she drove through the gates.

'I'm so sorry,' she called out of the open window. 'I know you said come soon but to Tosca that means something different than it does to the rest of us.'

'Oh stop complaining,' Tosca said from the passenger seat. 'We're here now, aren't we? Get in Stella quickly, or you'll be the next one in trouble.'

'Actually there's no hurry,' Stella said. 'I only said to come soon because I know you tend to run late.'

'What are you talking about? I'm never late.'

Raffaella laughed at her. 'Oh no?'

'Well, what is the point of rushing in a place like this where everyone is moving at a snail's pace and nothing ever happens anyway?' Tosca was defensive.

'You always say that.'

'Because it is true.'

'That is no comfort for the people who have to wait for you.'

'It gives you something to complain about, doesn't it? You love complaining.'

As they bickered Stella tried to make space for herself on the back seat. It was cluttered with a rubble of things – tomato seedlings in plastic trays, soil that had spilt from them, old magazines, a pair of cork-soled sandals, a straw hat, a box filled with bags of flour, a wool rug.

'OK, I'm in,' she said, giving the door a good slam to make sure it stayed shut.

Raffaella drove with terrifying confidence, foot down on the accelerator, one hand on the horn and talking over her shoulder. 'Sorry about the mess, I really must have a clear-out some time. Do you need more space? Tosca, move your seat forward.'

'I'm fine,' Stella lied, trying not to think of the soil sticking to the back of her white Milly Munro sundress.

'It's half an hour's drive at least so you'd better be comfortable,' Raffaella warned. 'Although if I put my foot down we may get there faster.'

'Your foot is down as far as it needs to be,' Tosca said. 'Can you even see properly in those sunglasses? Shouldn't you be wearing spectacles?'

'Now who is complaining?'

'I'm only trying to make sure you don't kill us all. How old is this car anyway? The engine might explode if you try to make it go any faster.'

'There is nothing wrong with my car. Ciro looked after it. And usually I don't drive it so far. Just up and down the hill.'

'That's what concerns me.'

'I am no worse a driver than you are, Tosca. Much better in fact.'

'Now you're talking like a crazy woman as well as driving like one.'

Sitting quietly on the back seat Stella stared at scenery blurring past dirt-fogged windows and listened to the two old friends. There weren't many things she missed about home; in fact a lot of it she was glad to have escaped – the noise, the traffic, the crush of bodies in overheated Tube train carriages, the unrelenting greyness of rainy days. But the familiarity of good friends, the ones like Birdie who you didn't always have to be the best version of yourself with, that she missed. Stella hadn't realised how important such closeness was to her until she'd come to Italy and been without it. Oddly, she had even been nostalgic for Ray. Several times she had caught herself wondering what he would think about a meal she was eating or some little thing she spotted. Of course, he wouldn't have agreed to spending weeks of his time in one place. Her few trips with him had been carefully plotted, a night here, a couple of days there, no photo opportunity missed. Ray was a high-energy person and easily bored – Type A was how he liked to describe himself. He wouldn't have driven for half an hour in this old banger of a car, with no real idea of what was waiting at the destination.

The vineyard wasn't as picturesque as Stella had imagined it might be. It lay on the suburban fringes of a dull-looking town and the exterior of the building seemed very ordinary.

Walking inside, it was the smell Stella noticed, clean and sharp, not wine but something like it.

'*Salve*. Lovely to meet you.' Elena was a young woman with skin that seemed to glow with good health and a petite figure sheathed in denim. She welcomed them in and showed them through to a small shop, its shelves half-filled with dark cork-stoppered bottles.

Raffaella was the first to pick one up and take a closer look. 'What is this you are selling? Vinegar?'

'These are drinking vinegars,' Elena announced, pride in her voice. 'They are our big secret.'

'Why would anyone want to drink a vinegar?' Tosca screwed up her face. 'It's for dressing salads, surely. Wine is for drinking.'

'This vinegar was once a fine wine. When you taste it you'll find it's very different to any you've had before. But first we'll take a small tour and I'll show you how we make it.'

She led them through a doorway and down some stone steps to a dark cellar lined with wooden barrels. The smell was much stronger here and Stella breathed it in as she listened to Elena.

'My family has always made vinegars, but only for ourselves. A few years ago I suggested we produce some for sale. You will find the ones designed for drinking are less acidic than those you put on your salads. They are good to sip after a rich meal or to take as a palate cleanser between courses.'

'How exactly do you make them?' asked Raffaella.

'They are a labour of love. First we must grow the grapes on our estate, make them into wine and age it. Only then is it fermented into vinegar and matured in these barrels.'

Raffaella seemed especially fascinated as Elena explained how bacteria turned the alcohol in the wine into an acid and how it could take years for the results to be perfect.

'Some people might say you are ruining perfectly good wine,' she observed.

'Not once they have tasted the result,' Elena promised. 'Centuries ago it wasn't so unusual to drink vinegar. People believed it was medicinal and perhaps they were right. No one in my family ever catches a cold or flu.'

From the barrel room they were shown through to another chamber where the air was heavily laced with the scent of herbs and spices. Here Elena talked about the way they flavoured the vinegars and how she liked to use them. 'The fig one is good drizzled over fresh strawberries, the wild cherry I pour onto ice cream, some of the herb vinegars I splash into a pasta sauce, others are perfect with cheese. Today we will sip them as if they were good Marsala. I have selected a few I think you will like. They are waiting for us outside.'

She took them to a pretty courtyard where plants climbed the walls and rioted from barrels and baskets. In the centre was a table, set out with several of the dark glass bottles along with three sherry glasses, a plate of bread and a small dish of chocolates.

Elena uncorked a bottle and poured them each a taste. 'First smell it, then sip and hold it in your mouth for a while before swallowing.'

Raffaella closed her eyes as she lifted the glass to her nose. 'Vanilla,' she said. 'Figs, cherries ... and something else ... I'm not sure.'

'Very good.' Elena sounded impressed. 'The last ingredient is apricot.'

'Yes, yes, of course,' murmured Raffaella before taking a careful sip.

Stella followed suit. To her surprise her mouth was flooded with sweetness. Only after a moment was there a pleasant tickle of sourness at the sides of her tongue.

'How unusual,' she said. 'It's like an explosion of flavour. My tastebuds are tingling.'

'Leo called it magic for the mouth when he tried it,' Elena told her. 'The next one you will try was his favourite.'

This time it was Stella who recognised the flavour. 'Gingerbread,' she said after her first sip. 'Leo is right, it's amazing.'

'This is our Christmas vinegar. We flavour it with spices like cinnamon and star anise.'

Raffaella nodded thoughtfully. 'I would use it to baste a piece of roasting meat or make stewed fruits more exotic. It would be wonderful with chestnuts.'

To Stella the final bottle they tried smelt like a summer meadow. Elena told them it was a special tonic produced by steeping herbal remedies in vinegar and spiking it with orange peel. It tasted medicinal, rather like a cough mixture.

'So what do you think?' she asked.

'I need to try more of them and then I want to buy lots,' declared Raffaella.

'I'm afraid the shop isn't open yet.' Elena must have seen the impatient look flashing across Raffaella's face because she added quickly, 'Perhaps we can still sell you some. I'll check with my father.'

She led them back to the shop where a man was busy arranging bottles on one of the empty shelves. He had fine features, looking almost like an older version of Christopher Plummer in *The Sound of Music*, and he beamed a smile as they came through the door.

'You are Leo's friends, yes?'

'Well not exactly ...' Stella began but he interrupted, keen to know if they had enjoyed the vinegars they sampled, waving his hands around excitedly in a way that made her fear for the safety of the bottles he had been arranging so carefully.

'This shop is my daughter's dream but so far only our very good friends have tasted what we've produced and now we are about to open and we are nervous,' he told them. 'What if people don't like our drinking vinegars or believe they are only good for salads?'

'That's what we thought,' admitted Stella. 'I think we've all changed our minds though.'

Raffaella was moving from shelf to shelf, brow knitted in concentration. She pulled a crumpled piece of paper from her handbag and began scribbling on it.

Tosca sighed. 'She is very excited.'

Stella glanced over. 'Really? She doesn't look it.'

'Oh, but she is, I know the signs.'

The older man introduced himself as Antonio Colloca. They chatted to him about the estate and his grapes as Raffaella made the rounds of the store, checking each shelf carefully.

Antonio watched her. 'There are more flavours that I haven't put out yet,' he said worriedly. 'We have twenty different ones altogether. Shall I tell your friend?'

'Certainly not,' said Tosca. 'She'll never leave.'

Raffaella had come up with a list of the vinegars she had to try right then – flavoured with lavender and rosemary, gilded with saffron, infused with raspberries, scented with orange blossom. She huddled at the counter with Antonio, talking rapidly in Italian as she sniffed, sipped and scrawled more notes.

Low on patience Tosca disappeared, back to the car most likely, but Stella stayed and watched, marvelling at how intent they were. Raffaella's cheeks were flushed and her eyes seemed brighter than usual. She was nodding vigorously at whatever Antonio was saying to her and he was waving his hands in the air to make his point, even more excitedly than before.

When at last they left, they were carrying two boxes clinking with bottles she had selected. Antonio helped to cram them into the cluttered car and stood on the pavement, waving and smiling, as Raffaella pulled away.

'He can't believe his luck,' said Tosca. 'How much did you spend in there anyway?'

Raffaella seemed distracted. 'I'm sure it was worth it,' she said shortly.

'A shop that only sells vinegar – what sort of terrible idea is that?'

'You like shops that only sell clothes,' Raffaella pointed out.

'That is entirely different.'

'I don't see why.'

Tosca sighed. 'No, I suppose you don't.'

'These vinegars will bring me more pleasure than any new outfit. Can you imagine the sweetness of the chestnut in a rich sauce to dress a roasted duck? Or a salad of raw asparagus with one of the sharper herb vinegars? Or the pomegranate elixir in a summer cocktail?'

'Will you make all those things?' asked Stella.

'I will play in my kitchen and when I've refined a few dishes I will think about holding a dinner; I'll invite you and Tosca, perhaps even Antonio so he can see what I've done with his products.'

'You know he's too young for you,' said Tosca.

'What are you talking about?'

'I didn't think we'd ever prise you away.'

'I was interested in his vinegars, not him.'

'Good, because he's much too young.'

Raffaella gave an exasperated hiss and stared over the steering wheel. She didn't say much for the rest of the drive and Stella assumed she was busy mentally pairing vinegars with local game and aromatic cheeses, dreaming of turning them into glazes and marinades.

Tosca was less settled, drumming her fingers on the car door, shifting in her seat. It was more difficult to imagine what might be going through her mind. Not vinegar, that was for sure, decided Stella.

Dear Leo, it's entirely thanks to you that the latest event on Triento's social calendar may be a vinegar dinner. Raffaella has disappeared home with boxes full of bottles from the Colloca estate and Tosca says we shouldn't expect to hear from her for a while. Experimenting with them will keep her occupied for days apparently and then she's going to let us taste the results.

Your gardening crew was at Villa Rosa when I got back and I'm very grateful since I haven't so much as pulled a weed the whole time I've been here. I don't have any excuse for there has been plenty of time. I just seem to be drifting through it and not getting very much done at all.

For once I don't mind my lack of productivity. Also, as I was pottering around listening to the men working outside I realised that I've entirely stopped worrying about what will happen when I return to London. I've heard people talking about living in the now and never thought it was possible but here I am doing it. I go from day to day, not knowing what will happen or where I'll end up. Your scrapbook is a part of that, of course. When I woke up this morning I had no idea there were people in the world creating vinegars to be sipped like fine wine. (I bought a bottle by the way, the gingerbread one that Elena told me is your favourite.)

I can't remember ever feeling like this. Even when I was a child there always seemed to be things I had to do – homework and chores, usually. And much as I loved my job, looking back now it feels as if I was always working. It makes up so much of my memories and they all meld together somehow, days at a desk staring at a computer, and then those days becoming weeks, months and years until they were a huge block of my life. If Milly hadn't died I'd still be there ... and as much as I miss her I'm so glad I'm not.

So thank you again for Villa Rosa and the scrapbook. I think you might have changed my life – Stella.

Sand and sea

Too much wine on an empty stomach – that was the only excuse for pressing *send* on an email like that, thought Stella. She hoped Leo didn't think she was an over-sharer. In the clear light of morning it was with some trepidation that she checked her laptop for his reply, clicking on it a little nervously.

Dear Stella, you are learning to be impulsive just as I seem to be forgetting how. Perhaps London is to blame or maybe this is just the way my life has to be right now.

I lay awake after I read your email and remembered how I used to go out in Napoli after dark, with fruit trees filling the bed of my truck, and plant them wherever I thought they were needed. There was never a plan. I'd find a patch of earth beside a school or in some desolate hell of apartment blocks and I'd dig a hole and put one in. Many wouldn't have survived because I was relying on there being rain or other people caring enough to give them water. But I know some are still there and I imagine children picking the fruit to eat on their way to school.

It's not like that any more. I can't go out and plant a tree wherever I choose. You would be amazed how much paperwork is involved in creating a community garden, how many meetings and special permissions and safety reports. Sometimes by the end of the day I feel like screaming (I don't, of course, at least I haven't so far). It can feel like the plants are an afterthought rather than the reason we are all here.

At Villa Rosa where things are simpler it is easier to be impulsive. Make the most of it – Leo.

PS The gingerbread vinegar is amazing over baked peaches in the summer.

Dear Leo, I love the idea of you planting trees under the cover of darkness like some sort of guerrilla gardener. Is that what they call it? You'd probably be arrested if you tried to do that in London.

Today in Triento it feels like summer. I'm sitting outside and thinking about being on a beach, with a picnic. I'm thinking about the sun on my skin, swimming in the sea and getting all salty and letting it dry on me. Shall I do it? Yes, I think I will! – Stella.

Dear Stella, you may have that beach to yourself. No matter how hot it is summer hasn't officially begun yet and in Italy we are quite rigid about these things. But you should go and break the rules and have a wonderful time doing it. I will be thinking of you – Leo.

Picnic essentials were easy to gather in Triento. The market stalls were groaning with local cheeses and cherry tomatoes, the bakery provided a warm loaf of dense crusty bread, the man in the *salumeria* sliced up salami and prosciutto thinly and sold her jars of olives and bottles of chilled beer. As Stella was stowing it all in the boot of her car she heard her phone ringing and saw that it was Tosca.

'What's happening? You haven't texted me this morning,' she complained.

'I'm giving the scrapbook a break for today and going to the beach for a picnic instead. Do you want to join me?'

'The beach at this time of year?'

'It's a lovely day.'

'Yes, but the lido won't be open, there'll be no loungers to sit on, no *ombrellone*.'

'I'll sit on my towel then. I'm sure I'll survive. And I've got plenty of food so you should come. Bring Raffaella.'

'She is too busy with her vinegars but I may stop by later.'

'OK, hopefully I'll see you then.'

Tosca was right and everything was closed, even the small café, although there were a few sun-silvered wooden benches left out beneath the pine trees. The crescent of beach was backed by cliffs and its sand dotted with pebbles. Choosing a spot, Stella laid out her towel and stripped down to her swimsuit, a cheerful red polka-dot one-piece that always made her feel like a 1950s bathing belle. For a while she sat looking at the waves and the seabirds swooping down. Then she smoothed on some sun cream and lay back to let her skin be toasted.

She was starting to doze when she heard voices. Sitting up, Stella saw a mother and child coming down the wooden steps to the beach. They were both dressed for a chillier day and the mother fussed as the little girl tried to remove her shoes and socks so she could paddle. Finally she relented and Stella watched them from beneath the brim of her red straw sunhat, the child running in and out of the waves, holding up her skirt and shrieking at the plumes of froth drenching her legs.

The mother called to her in Italian and the little girl shouted back, her voice full of fun. Stella didn't often let herself do this but, as they played, she superimposed her own face over the woman's and imagined the child was hers. They were on holiday, just the two of them. They had come to the beach for an hour and later on they were going to eat *gelato*. She was worried the water was too cold, but it looked like so much fun and she didn't have the heart to put an end to it.

There was a towel in her bag and when the child had had enough she would wrap her in it and hold her so close for warmth that she would feel her heart beating.

Stella looked away. Then she turned onto her stomach so all she could see was her own towel. There were mothers and children everywhere and you couldn't let that upset you. That was the deal she had made with herself. When it became obvious there would never be a baby she made a point of spending time with friends who had them, as if it would inoculate her from the sadness. She had to be realistic, she told Birdie, who protested she was torturing herself. And besides, she loved kids.

Closing her eyes, she rested her head on her hands. She could still hear them, the mother and her small daughter. She wondered what they thought of her lying there alone. People tended to make assumptions. Some of her friends thought she had chosen to put her career first, others that Ray hadn't been willing. She let them believe what they wanted because it didn't seem important.

Stella had left it too late, that was all. She hoped the sadness might go but it never did, not really. It only moved sideways and waited, until moments like this, when her guard was down, and it took a tilt at her.

Rolling over, Stella sat up and forced herself to look their way. She even smiled when the mother caught her eye. Sadness mustn't get the better of her.

Tosca provided a reprieve. She appeared at the top of the steps, eye-catching in tight white trousers and a striped top. In one hand was a fold-up chair, in the other a sun umbrella, and across her shoulders she had slung her handbag. The heels of her sandals sank into the sand as she struggled across it.

'Don't start telling me I'm late,' she called to Stella.

'We didn't agree on a time so how could you be?'

'That never seems to stop Raffaella complaining.'

Arranging things the way Tosca wanted took a few moments. They had to find a rock to hammer the bottom of the sun umbrella deep into the sand and then the fold-up chair was positioned in the tiny patch of shade it threw and a towel put down so her handbag wouldn't get sandy.

'So much effort just to be on a beach,' Tosca sighed, balancing carefully on the wobbly chair. 'I never really understand it.'

'It's beautiful here.'

'Yes, I suppose it is.' Tosca looked over at the mother and her child still paddling in the water. 'Those two must be freezing.'

'I thought I might go in for a swim, actually.'

'Then you are crazy. It will be ice water. You should wait for summer. July and August are the months for swimming. That's when it is so hot that throwing yourself into the sea is a relief.'

'I won't be here, though. Leo will be wanting Villa Rosa back by then.'

'Ah yes, Leo.' Tosca stretched out her legs so her calves were in the sun. 'I've learnt a few things about him.'

'Really?' Stella was curious. 'From who?'

'Yesterday in that vinegar place I was bored watching Raffaella flirting with the old man so I went back outside and found his daughter. We had a nice chat, she and I.'

'What did she say?'

'Leo Asti is a great guy. He designed their little garden and did such a wonderful job. She took me to have another look at it, told me the names of the plants, talked and talked.'

'The garden is lovely,' Stella agreed.

'Yes, but there is more. Leo and her father have become firm friends. Last summer they joined him for a few days at Villa Rosa. One of his cousins was there along with his family, but there was no sign of a girlfriend for Leo. Apparently he is single.'

'Don't I remember you saying he was with a blonde woman that time you met him?'

'Yes, there was one trailing after him but that doesn't mean they are together. As you can imagine, I could only find out so much from the girl without it seeming as though I was interrogating her. And she would keep talking about the garden.'

The mother and child were getting ready to leave. Stella watched as feet were dried and shoes put on. Hand in hand they walked up the wooden steps.

Tosca followed her line of vision. 'Have you ever asked Leo if he has kids?'

Stella shook her head. 'I didn't want to seem like I was prying. But he made it very clear it would only be him staying in my apartment so if there are kids they may be grown up.'

'For a man of his age it would be odd to be single and without any attachments; it would worry me,' Tosca mused.

'You are single and without attachments,' Stella pointed out.

'This is true.'

'Were you never married?'

'Married, no.' Tosca stared down the length of the beach. 'I specialised in being with other women's husbands.'

There was no coaxing her to say more. Stella tried but it didn't get her anywhere. Instead Tosca decided it might be hot enough to swim after all and she peeled off her clothes to reveal the tiniest gold mesh bikini. She had a boyish body with thighs free of dimples, skin smooth and honeyed and a belly that was amazingly flat. Paddling into the water, she winced at the chill, but kept going nevertheless. Stella followed, feeling rather lumpy in her swimsuit in comparison.

Once they were in over their shoulders it felt bracing but good. Tosca was a strong swimmer and Stella watched her striking out beyond the waves. Always more of a wallower herself, she stayed well within her depth, letting the water buffet her as she looked back at the now deserted beach. In summer it would be covered in holidaymakers, perhaps Leo among them, come for sunbathing and swimming. Who would he have with him? Stella wondered.

With a slow and stately breaststroke she swam towards the rocky cliffs, a wall of grey sandwiched by brilliant blue. It was so beautiful here. She tasted the salty water, heard the seagulls screeching overhead and tried to imprint the whole scene on her brain so she could bring it back in its entirety once she was home in London, returned to her own life. When she reached the rocks and turned, Tosca seemed to have disappeared. Treading water Stella felt a little anxious, her eyes sweeping the bay, looking for some sign of her. It was ten minutes before she reappeared, swimming around the point and making for the beach. She was standing at the tideline, water streaming from her hair and body, by the time Stella caught her up.

'If you're going to swim, you might as well really swim,' Tosca said, not quite managing to conceal that she was out of breath.

'I'm not very good,' Stella admitted.

'Really? Why not get better?' Tosca said, with her usual directness. 'It's not so difficult.'

'You're right, I should.'

'I'm always right,' she murmured. 'Hasn't Raffaella told you that?'

Once they had towelled themselves dry, Stella laid out their picnic. Tosca must have worked up an appetite because she tore into a hunk of bread thickly spread with soft herbed cheese.

'How far out did you go?' Stella asked.

'Far enough, until I started to feel tired; I haven't swum in a while.'

'I suppose in California you did lots of swimming?'

'I suppose I did.'

'So did you live in Los Angeles?'

Tosca gave a thin smile. 'I know what you're doing.'

'What do you mean?'

'You're fishing. You want to know about my life; Tosca the movie star. But none of it was what people think. And I'm finished with it now.'

'Right … OK.'

Tosca looked at her. 'This is my life now and I'm determined to make it work. I haven't forgotten about the speed-dating you know. You and Raffaella may laugh but I'm serious. I want to meet a nice guy before it's too late, one that might become a husband. In a place like this I'm unlikely to bump into him by accident.'

'Why stay here then? Why not live somewhere bigger like Rome or go back to America?'

'Money,' Tosca admitted. 'I have enough to live on but only because food is cheap here and I'm in the house that belongs to my family. When I think of the way I used to be, the clothes I bought, the credit cards I flashed around … I always expected more money to come from somewhere. I never thought ahead this far.'

Stella had always been a saver. She bought good clothes but at a staff discount, she ate in restaurants but never the more expensive ones. *Cautious* was the way she would describe herself when it came to money.

'Your life sounds a lot more exciting than mine has been,' she told Tosca.

'Exciting for a girl from Triento. But it's over and nothing will change that so I have to find a way to make this new life exciting … otherwise God knows I will shoot myself.'

Stella felt for her. 'Let's organise the speed-dating then.'

'Good, good. What about the drink with this boy from the linen shop who Raffaella says is far too young for me? This Roberto?'

'That too,' Stella agreed.

'And your romantic Leo … when he comes back for the summer I must see him again.'

Stella was taken aback. 'Leo?'

'Yes, he interests me.' Tosca carved herself another slice of cheese. 'Clearly I missed something the first time we met. I thought he was dull. I can't have been paying enough attention.'

Stella didn't much like the idea of Tosca being interested in Leo. She realised that was ridiculous – he didn't belong to her after all – but there was something about the way she kept referring to him as romantic, and the fact that she had bothered to question Elena at all – had been interested enough to want more details. Perhaps unreasonably Stella felt it was her place to be curious about him, not Tosca's.

Still sandy from the beach, a towel wrapped round her waist, an open bottle of cold beer gathering beads of moisture beside her, Stella sat beneath the bougainvillea in the garden of Villa Rosa and typed the words before she could change her mind.

Dear Leo, I'm sorry if this seems nosy but living in your house I'm growing curious about you. I keep imagining the place in summer and wondering who comes to visit you here. Do you have any children? There are no toys in the cupboards so I'd imagined not, but maybe they are much older?

You were right about the beach by the way. There was barely anyone there but once I got used to the chill the water was gorgeous. Tosca shamed me out there. You should have seen her move across the bay. I may never get that good but surely I can improve. I'm going to have to work on my fitness and my swimming skills. Stella.

Dear Stella, I have two grown-up children. Also I have a grandchild since my daughter Pia has a baby girl of her own now. My son Ricardo works in my landscaping business – he's looking after things while I'm here. Their mother and I broke up several years ago. She is a good person but we were so young when we married and were never suited. In those days if you got a girl pregnant then you stayed with her; there was no arguing. You've heard people talk about shotgun weddings? Well in Napoli sometimes there actually were shotguns!

When Pia came along we were a family. A couple of years later there was Ricardo too. I don't regret it certainly but things weren't perfect. I had my work to escape to but for my wife what we had together was everything and she wasn't happy.

Now she is remarried and it is better for her ... and for me too. To be tied to someone, to have your life tangled with theirs, it isn't always an easy thing. Maybe you know that? Have you been married? Do you have children? I'm here living in your apartment and I'm curious too! Leo.

Dear Leo, I'm divorced too actually. We wanted children but unfortunately it didn't happen. My husband has remarried but I'm still single which is fine. I like living on my own ...

Stella typed the words automatically. They were her stock response. And then she stopped, reread them and, pressing her finger on the delete key, cleared them one by one.

Dear Leo, my experience is very different from yours. I had a husband who loved me and I cared for him. We had a nice house, good jobs. But I wanted one last thing and that toppled the lot – a baby. I wanted one so much I couldn't think about anything else. And my husband had to watch as I shopped for bootees and tiny hats then sobbed when there was no baby to dress them in. Looking back ... I have nothing but regrets. That's not a good way to be, is it? So I'm divorced now; and childless, and jobless. My life is a clean slate. And I'm almost scared to write on it in case I do something else I'm sorry for. Stella.

Dear Stella, a life that is a clean slate could be scary or it could be exciting. That might sound like a cliché but I do believe it. What do you want, who do you wish to be? You get to decide and how many of us have a chance like that? I can see that you have had a lot of sadness in the past but right now I think that you're lucky in a way. Leo.

Hey Birdie, is it strange do you think that I've started having quite personal exchanges via email with a man I've never met? I'm finding myself telling Leo Asti all sorts of stuff. I feel as if on one level I know him quite well and on another not at all. How weird is that?
   Also how are you? Girlfriend? Job? Tell all. Stella.

Hi Stella, it's not weird. Everyone is having online flirtations these days. If anything you're behind the times.
   Ah yes, girlfriend, job, still have both, cautiously optimistic about one, in despair about the other. No prizes for guessing which is which! Birdie.

Knowing, not knowing

Stella went for a walk first thing, a brisk one round the coastal path, up and down steps carved into the cliffs then along narrow lanes past shabby houses with small flocks of dusty chickens and rows of vines.

Back at Villa Rosa she found a basket and filled it with produce picked from the garden: pea pods and herbs, buds of artichokes, bunches of spring onions. She planned to deliver it all to Raffaella once she had eaten breakfast in Triento.

The man who ran the corner bar greeted her like a regular. It was warm enough to sit outside and Stella found she could while away a surprising amount of time people-watching from her table.

This morning she ate her favourite pastry. It was shaped like a seashell with buttery crispy layers on the outside that you had to crunch through to get to the heart of sweetened ricotta, vanilla and zesty orange. The long walk had given her an appetite and she bit into it hungrily.

Triento seemed to be getting busier. At the next table were a group wearing sensible shoes, with their belongings in backpacks and what looked like a guidebook on their table. Eavesdropping, Stella realised they were German. So the tourists were beginning to arrive; she wasn't the only one any more and in a few weeks it would be summer and Leo would want his house back. Stella wasn't sure she would be ready by then to return to the clean slate of her life. Whatever Leo might say, it still seemed scary to her.

She saw Francesca cutting across the piazza, bare-legged

in a yellow gingham dress with a flouncy skirt, heading towards the linen shop.

'Good morning,' she called and raised a hand to wave.

'Stella, *buongiorno*, how are things?' Francesca called back, diverting her path to the bar. 'Are you going to be here for a while longer? I may join you. I'll be a few minutes late opening up the shop but what my mother-in-law doesn't see she can't complain about.'

'Angelica seems rather formidable,' remarked Stella.

Sinking into the seat opposite Francesca laughed bleakly. 'That's one way of describing her. The problem is she worked in the linen shop herself for years so of course she knows how everything should be done and tells me every chance she gets. Gennaro says to humour her and I try but it doesn't seem to make any difference.' She cast her eyes around the piazza. 'With my luck some busybody will spot me sitting here and tell her.'

'A few minutes isn't going to make much difference, is it?'

'Of course not, but she won't see it that way. Seven days a week that linen shop is open in the summer months. At least now there is Roberto to take over to give me a break, but God knows how long he will stick around this time.'

'Ah yes, Roberto. I spoke to Tosca and she's keen to meet him,' Stella told her.

'The movie star?' Francesca perked up. 'I am invited too, yes?'

'Of course, you and your husband should come. I thought we'd go to the new place that's opened. It's up by the statue. This evening if you like.'

'Gennaro won't want to come. He will be staring at his computer, that's all he ever does. But Roberto and I, yes definitely, and wherever you want to go is fine with us. How exciting!'

'You know, Tosca is just a normal person. She doesn't act like a celebrity.'

'She must have amazing stories though, about the famous people she's met?'

'If she does then she never shares them.'

'Really?' Francesca sounded disappointed. 'Surely if I asked her ... ?'

'You can try but I don't think she'll tell you.'

Francesca shrugged. 'Oh well, it's an evening out, isn't it, and a night when I won't have to cook and clean up after other people. Speaking of cooking, do you want another lesson? I could do this Sunday. It would be just like it was last time.'

Stella's eyes widened. 'Actually I'm busy,' she lied.

'Really? What with?'

'Er, you know.' Desperately she searched her mind. 'Sight-seeing.'

'Are you sure? It would be fun,' Francesca pressed her. 'We could make pasta this time, maybe a lasagne.'

'Sorry, I have plans.'

'Perhaps another time.'

Stella made a noise in the back of her throat, part cough, part grunt that Francesca obviously took as an agreement. She seemed more cheerful by the time she had drunk her coffee and was ready to head off to work.

'Have a good day then. Don't forget to tell the movie star we're looking forward to meeting her.'

Nothing on earth would persuade her to go back to the Russo house, thought Stella as she drove down to the harbour. She had taken a strong dislike both to the place and the old matriarch who ruled it. And besides, she wasn't going to be tricked again into paying for the privilege of helping Francesca cook her family's Sunday lunch, even if she did feel sorry for her working all the time then being expected to run the household too.

Stella managed to squeeze Leo's car into a tiny parking

space and, grabbing the basket of produce from the back seat, she walked the rest of the way to Raffaella's house, catching a view of the sea glinting between each tall building.

The smell of warm sugar and butter reached her as soon as she opened the front door and called out hello.

'What's cooking?' she asked, peeping round the kitchen door.

Raffaella was in disarray. She was wearing old pyjama bottoms and a belted black cardigan. Her hair was in a frizzy cloud round her head and her cheeks flushed pink. Every surface in the room seemed to be covered in vinegar bottles.

'Stella, good, I'm glad you came,' she said.

'How did you end up with so much vinegar? Surely there's more here than you bought the other day.'

'Antonio called me. He said there were some flavours that weren't out on display when we visited. Apparently he mentioned it to Tosca and she told him not to say anything. Can you believe that? Well yes, I expect you can. Anyway, Antonio very kindly drove over here and brought them to me.'

Stella couldn't help smiling. 'He came all this way just to give you more vinegar.'

'Possibly he had some other business in Triento. In fact, I'm sure he did. Anyway I have everything now; the whole range. This morning I'm using some of the sweeter ones to make desserts and I'm glad you've come to try them.'

'Oh ... I've only just had breakfast.'

'Please tell me you're not turning into Tosca and pretending you have no appetite.'

'I'm not,' Stella promised. 'Although I was at the beach with her yesterday and she does look incredible in a bikini. It made me feel as if I should firm up and lose a couple of kilos.'

'Better to enjoy good food than go round the place half naked,' responded Raffaella. 'And you won't be able to resist my desserts; no one besides Tosca ever can.'

Stella tasted a cinnamon-scented apple cake dusted with sugar and paddling in a shallow lake of warmed fig vinegar. A dense square of chocolate and nuts bathed in sour cherry. A pastry filled with toasted almonds, mounded with cream, a shot glass of gingerbread vinegar on the side.

'Now I'm really full,' she said, licking her spoon before putting it down.

'But it was good and it made you happy?'

Stella nodded.

'Even happier than being too thin? Because if so you should be sure to tell poor, hungry Tosca.'

'I don't think it would make any difference.'

'You are right, of course. Whatever we say she will go on living without all of this.' Raffaella gestured to the many plates of sweet things.

'Why have you made so much food anyway?' wondered Stella. 'Are you coming up with new dishes for the *trattoria*?'

'It's my habit, I suppose. When I find a new ingredient I want to test it to its limits, see exactly what it can be. And this vinegar with all its many flavours, it excites me. I cannot tell you how pleased I was to see Antonio bringing me more. I have told him that his next step should be to open a restaurant on the estate and I will help plan the menu.'

Stella smiled again. 'You seemed to get on well with him.'

'He is widowed just like me. We have a lot in common.' Raffaella glanced at her face. 'Oh stop it, you are as bad as Tosca. I'm not looking for love. Definitely not. It's the last thing I want at this point in my life.'

'In that case I have bad news. She hasn't forgotten about the speed-dating and I think we're really going to have to do it. On the beach she was talking about her struggle to make the best of life here. I felt really sorry for her.'

'She wants you to feel sorry for her. That's how she'll get you to do things.'

'Well it worked; I said we would.'

Leaning back against the kitchen counter dusted with flour and icing sugar and studded with pastry offcuts, Raffaella sighed. 'Speed-dating – what a waste of my time. I have buried two husbands; I don't need to outlive another man.'

'Two husbands? You were married before you met Ciro?'

Raffaella nodded. 'To a boy called Marcello Russo. Yes, he was from that Russo family, the ones who own the linen shop. In fact, I helped out there for a while, when we were living in the little apartment above. But then Marcello got sick and before too long he died. I was so young and it felt like my life was over. Ciro, he was my second chance and there couldn't have been a better one. With him I had a lifetime of love. Now he is gone I won't ask for more.'

'So you were part of the Russo family?' Stella was amazed. 'The old harridan, Angelica, what relation was she to you?'

Raffaella laughed. 'My sister-in-law, and she was a harridan even then.'

'And you lived in the linen shop?' Stella still couldn't get her head round the way everyone here seemed to be linked.

'We lived above it,' Raffaella corrected her. 'I loved that linen. And I loved Marcello, too. The rest of them I never liked at all.'

'Francesca is OK, isn't she? And Roberto seems charming enough.'

'They're greedy. Money is all they care about and even though they have enough, still they want more. If Roberto is interested in Tosca it's not because she was an actress in Hollywood, it's that he thinks she is rich. That one is always looking for the easy way, I think. He will lose interest once he realises she owns nothing of any value besides that small house.'

Stella could see how it might be true. 'I've arranged for him to meet her this evening. Do you think I should cancel?'

Raffaella turned to the bench and began balling up the

pastry offcuts. 'In a town as small as this there are many other ways to meet if they wish to. And they are not your responsibility.'

'I don't want to see Tosca get hurt.'

Raffaella was clattering about stacking dirty dishes now. 'What my friend needs is to make her own life instead of waiting for a man to come and build one for her.'

'It's not always so easy though, is it?' Stella was sympathetic.

'You've done it and so have I; she can too.'

'I'm not sure if I really have,' Stella confessed. 'Yes, I live on my own happily enough but if I'm honest there are things I miss – companionship and familiarity; someone to lean on when you need them, a person you can laugh with and say just about anything to.'

'I have friends and neighbours I can call on for all those things. I'm not lonely, whatever Tosca might think,' insisted Raffaella, filling the sink with water.

Stella found a tea towel. 'I didn't think I was lonely either. Now I'm beginning to wonder.'

They washed up the dishes together, standing to face the view of the sea, watching the sun playing over the waves and creating sparkles. Raffaella had made a mess with her vinegar experiments so they were kept busy scrubbing dough and batter from whisks and mixing bowls before it hardened.

Stella was thinking about Leo, how she was writing to him now as if he were someone she was close to and how strange that seemed, whatever Birdie said. She was living in his house, sleeping on his linen, eating from his plates and there was an intimacy to that, but in actual fact she didn't know him. It started her fretting again. Who was this person she was telling so much about her life to? Was she being unwise?

As soon as she got back to Villa Rosa, she grabbed her laptop.

Hi Birdie, you say it's quite normal these days for people to get to know each other online but to me it seems risky. I mean, there is Leo living in my apartment and all I know is what he tells me. He seems like a great guy – the few people I've met who know him haven't had a bad thing to say – still, how can I know for sure from words on a screen? Living here surrounded by his things it's like I'm circling him from a distance. I look at his pictures on the walls, the books on his shelves, even the glassware in his cupboards and try to work out what they say about him. What sort of person owns a house like this and so carefully restores it and buys art by an artist who lived here and spends time creating a scrapbook to keep me entertained? Is he too good to be true? I can't stop wondering. Stella.

Dear Stella, thanks so much for asking your friend Birdie to get in touch with me. She said you were concerned I might be lonely here in London and actually I have been a little. So we're going to meet for a coffee or a glass of wine some time, maybe even see a movie. I'm looking forward to it. I'll have to return the favour and ask a friend of mine to come and look you up. Leo.

Nicky Bird, you bad girl, what are you up to? Stella.

Stella ended her afternoon by swimming in the sea. The beach was empty, she was entirely on her own, and this time she went out a little further, until she could stretch her legs as far as possible and her feet no longer brushed the sandy bottom.

Later, tiptoeing over the pebbles and briskly towelling herself dry she thought of what she was going to say to her interfering friend Birdie the next time they spoke. This was exactly the kind of thing she would do of course and

Stella wasn't really sorry; not if this was a way to find out something more about him; not if he really had been feeling lonely.

Dear Leo, Birdie is my best friend and she's a lot of fun. Actually we met through our husbands and have kept each other even though we no longer have either of them. Anyway, she knows all the best places to go and I'm sure you'll have a good time.

Sorry to hear you've been lonely. Big cities do that, I suppose – easier to be solitary here than a place where you are surrounded by lots of people.

I'm about to go and meet Tosca for dinner at that trattoria your friends are running up by the statue. I've done a bit of matchmaking for her but am concerned it's going to end in disaster. No getting out of it now though. I'll let you know how we go. Stella.

The restaurant was empty when they arrived and Stella detected a touch of desperation about Benedetto in the over-cheerful way he ushered them in and the beaming smile he gave when he heard there were more people coming.

'Excellent, excellent, I will go and tell Maria. She will be pleased to know you've returned for more of her food.'

Stella watched as he headed towards the kitchen. 'This place isn't going to succeed, is it?' she said in a low voice to Tosca.

'If Raffaella thinks it's doomed then I wouldn't hold out much hope.'

'Such a shame – the food is good and they are trying so hard.'

'Didn't I have a solution to suit everyone? Raffaella could still do it; offer them a lease on her place. But she never listens to my advice,' complained Tosca.

Stella hid a smile. If only the two of them could see how

similar they were in so many ways. There were differences, of course. Raffaella would never have spent the time finessing her appearance that Tosca had dedicated to it this evening. She had tonged soft curls into her hair and done something complicated with her eye make-up. Her fingernails were polished in a dramatic dark red and Stella could tell the dress she was wearing had been carefully chosen. A fine jersey, it covered her arms and was cut high at the neck but clung to her curves. A gold bracelet clasped one of her slender wrists and more gold dropped from her ears.

'Let's order the best bubbles they have,' Tosca suggested.

'Too flashy,' said Stella, wary of creating the wrong impression. 'And anyway I'm craving a cold beer.'

'Beer.' Tosca wrinkled her nose. 'That has no style. I'm starting with a glass of good Prosecco.'

Francesca and Roberto arrived not long after their drinks had been delivered to the table, Roberto insisting on ordering more bubbles. Taking a seat next to Tosca, he proposed a toast.

'To new friends,' he said.

Stella raised her beer glass for the obligatory clinking. 'New friends,' she echoed.

The food was as great as she remembered. Small dishes of antipasti, stuffed fried olives and grilled prawns topped with a crust of parsley and toasted breadcrumbs, offered a harmony of flavours. Stella was relieved. She was the one who had organised the evening so felt responsible for it going well. Bringing new people together was always risky. They might like or loathe each other, discover things in common or find conversation a struggle. Stella didn't know any of them well enough to guess how the night would turn out but if what they ate was delicious that was a good start.

Everyone had dressed up much more than she'd expected. Francesca was wearing black velvet pants and a top with an overload of blingy silver beads stitched on in flower patterns.

Roberto was in black, too. His jacket had a satin sheen to it. In her understated petrol-blue wrap dress, a plain silver bangle on one wrist and her coppery hair pulled into a top-knot, Stella felt marked as the outsider.

They spoke in English so as not to exclude her. To begin with Francesca seemed shy of Tosca but it wasn't long before she had engineered the courage to begin asking questions. She wanted to hear stories of Hollywood, of parties, film sets and famous people but, as Stella had suspected, they weren't forthcoming. Tosca deflected her skilfully, with a flippant remark or a change of subject, or simply by choosing not to hear whatever had been said.

Increasingly she directed her words towards Roberto, until their heads were half-turned towards each other, their gazes meeting and the food left uneaten on their plates. When Stella listened in, what they were talking about was commonplace: movies they had seen or music they enjoyed. It was the way they were talking that was highly charged. Almost every word seemed a flirtation.

What she couldn't tell was if Tosca was truly interested in this man or if it was all play to her, the to and fro of words, the exchange of glances. She was enjoying herself; that much was obvious. And Roberto appeared flattered by her attention.

'Why haven't I ever seen you in the village?' he was asking now.

'I'm up there from time to time. You just haven't noticed me,' Tosca told him.

'I find that impossible to believe.'

'You must be very busy in your linen shop,' she countered.

'Not that busy.'

'Well next time I'm passing I'll stop by to say hello,' she promised. 'Perhaps you might even have time for us to have a coffee together.'

'I'm quite certain I will.'

Stella nibbled on an olive as she watched them. Perhaps Roberto really was too young for Tosca, but neither seemed to care, not right then anyway, with the light softened by candles and the mood lifted by a second bottle of bubbles.

Francesca was watching too, eyebrows raised, her expression amused. 'My brother-in-law seems to have met his match,' she remarked to Stella.

'It seems like it,' Stella agreed.

'Roberto is the extrovert of the family. My Gennaro is the quiet, more reliable one. Everyone has always said they couldn't be more different, the two Russo boys.'

Her words jogged Stella's memory. 'I hadn't realised until today that Raffaella used to be a Russo, too.'

Francesca nodded, dabbing at her mouth with a napkin. 'Yes, Gennaro told me that. No one in our family really talks much of those days any more but I know Angelica and Raffaella aren't friends. Perhaps there was competition between them once. Old people like to hold onto their feuds, don't they?'

Stella never thought of Raffaella as properly old. Even though her hair was entirely grey and her skin lined there was something so youthful about her spirit.

'Gennaro said something else that's interesting. Did you know that Raffaella got arrested when she was younger?' Francesca continued.

'She what?' asked Stella, as Tosca darted a glance over.

'Yes, she was accused of sabotaging the statue while it was being built. Gennaro heard that she and her father both spent time in the police cells.'

Tosca interrupted, her tone brusque. 'Raffaella didn't damage anything. Don't spread old gossip when you weren't there and you don't know what happened.'

Francesca looked startled. 'But that's what people say,' she argued, 'that the fishermen were against the statue and they sabotaged it and that she was involved somehow.'

'And perhaps it is true but now it's in the past and the statue is here, safe and sound, so why should we care?' Tosca replied and then said something in Italian that caused Francesca to lower her eyes to her empty plate.

'I'm sorry,' she said.

'Good.' Tosca's voice softened. 'Those old stories, they don't need to be told any more.'

Stella wanted to know more, of course. She was fascinated by these two older women who'd had lives that seemed immeasurably more colourful than hers. The more she thought about all the years that had gone by, the more Stella wondered how she had filled them. With cups of tea and TV shows? With running an office efficiently? With hoovering beneath the sofa? There were vast tracts of time she didn't really remember.

This time, though, right now in Triento, she didn't think she was in any danger of forgetting. It was a burst of pure pigment on a canvas of grey. Why hadn't she realised sooner that she didn't have to live her life on repeat? When her marriage had failed and her hopes of being a mother had been blasted away she should have tried to change things then. Instead she had kept creeping along, trying to return to normality.

Stella was sick of normal now. She wished she'd had a life that people found interesting enough to gossip about; that she could look back on her past and see more than habit and sadness. She would never be a film star or an outrageous flirt like Tosca ... and hopefully would never get herself arrested as Raffaella apparently had ... but surely it was possible for things to be a little bit exciting?

More food arrived: mussels in a peppery broth, thinly sliced raw beef with a dressing of goat's cheese whipped up with oil and vinegar, a dish of yellow chicory and mustardy mayonnaise, and then a risotto with sweet fennel and creamy ricotta. Stella ate it in a different way, savouring each forkful, thinking about what Maria might have done to bring out the flavours so they seemed to fill her mouth and linger on her tongue, savoury and rich.

'God, that was amazing,' she said when she'd finished. 'We need to tell people about this place.'

'I noticed a flyer for it the other day but I'd never have bothered coming all the way up here if you hadn't suggested it,' Roberto told her.

Stella turned to Tosca. 'Perhaps we should hold our speed-dating here,' she suggested.

'Speed-dating?' Roberto sounded intrigued.

'Just a little social evening I'm planning,' Tosca told him. 'Come along if you like. I'll let you know when I decide on the date.'

'I've read about speed-dating but I don't think we've ever had anything like it round here,' said Francesca.

'Well then, perhaps it's time we did,' Tosca replied crisply.

Stella finished with a dessert because it seemed a shame not to. As she dug her spoon into a *semifreddo* flavoured with vanilla and laced with chocolate and candied fruit, she thought about all the sugar consumed at Raffaella's that morning and felt a prickle of guilt, but it faded with the first bite. Francesca and Roberto drank some bitter liqueur they said was made with artichokes and good for the digestion, and Tosca contented herself with an espresso.

'What a perfect evening.' Roberto seemed to be talking only to Tosca again. 'We must do it again.'

'Absolutely.' Tosca smiled at him. 'And very soon.'

Dear Leo, I don't know why I was worried about Tosca – she's an unstoppable force. The man that I matchmaded her with is the one to be concerned about. I hope he can handle her!

We had another perfect meal in your friend's res-taurant (very quiet up there so not sure how well things are going). Anyway I'm fairly confident that by the time we said goodnight Tosca had arranged another date. She looked very satisfied, and I don't think it was the food.

It's warm tonight at Villa Rosa. I sat outside when I got home and thought about things for a bit. What was on my mind is that phrase people are always using – 'you've got to move forward with your life'. I've heard it from friends several times, after my marriage ended and when I lost my job. It made me roll my eyes. 'Move forward, what senseless talk,' is what I would think, 'we're all moving forward: it's the only direction we can go in.'

But perhaps I wasn't really – or if I was it was very slowly. I want to now, though; I'm not sure which direction I'll take but hopefully, if I keep on thinking, it will come to me. Stella.

PS – You should taste the things that Raffaella can do with vinegar.

Birdie, hey! You haven't got back to me. What do you think you're doing asking my silver fox out on a date? Stella.

Stella, just another of my genius plans. Don't worry, I'll report back afterwards with all the details. Birdie.

Birdie, well hurry up then. I keep sending him these emails and his replies are always interesting. He never trots out the usual things, never says what I might expect. I really want to know what you think of him. Stella.

The visitors

The day didn't go as planned. Stella had intended to pick another outing from the scrapbook but when she texted Raffaella and Tosca both said they were busy so she decided to wait till they were free. A quiet, solitary time would be nice enough. She spent the morning wrapped in a sarong and lazing on the terrace beneath the bougainvillea with one of the novels she had taken from Leo's shelves. It was light reading and she closed her eyes from time to time, lulled into doziness.

'Hello? Is anyone home?' There was an English voice, coming from just beyond the gates.

Stella's eyes snapped open and she sat up. 'Who's there?'

She heard the clang of metal and turned to see a woman, basket in hand. She was younger than Stella, and wearing clothes that were simple yet chic; bright blue capri pants and a striped top, a silk scarf knotted at her neck.

'So sorry to disturb you; I'm Rosie Santi, a friend of Leo's – he suggested I should drop by.'

'Oh hello. Come on in.' Stella was fairly sure she hadn't bothered to brush her hair that morning and knew she looked crumpled in comparison. 'Leo did mention that he might get a friend to look me up.'

'I should have got in touch first,' Rosie apologised. 'It's just we never do round here. We're poppers-in.'

'You're a Londoner,' guessed Stella.

'That's right, but I'm married to a local and I've lived here for years. We've got an olive estate a little way out of

Triento.' She held up the basket. 'Actually I've brought you some of our oil.'

As Stella made coffee and found a few biscotti, Rosie chatted away, peppering her with questions then barely giving her a chance to reply.

'Sorry, I don't usually go on like this. I think I'm over-excited at meeting another English person. It's been ages.'

'It must be a busy life running an olive estate.' To Stella it sounded rather glamorous.

'My husband Enzo does most of the hard work but I help out where I can and look after our son. Lately my mother-in-law has been sick so it's been difficult to get away. I haven't been to London for ages. I miss it, especially the shopping – sometimes Liberty comes to me in my dreams.'

Stella laughed. 'I'm not missing it at all, to be honest. Not even Liberty.'

'Ah well, Villa Rosa is a special place, isn't it? Actually I holidayed here once, well before Leo owned it. The house was pretty run-down back then and the garden was a jungle. It's been good to see him rescue it before things slipped back too far.'

'How long have you known Leo?' Stella asked it casually, but this was her first real chance to talk to one of his friends and she was bursting to know everything Rosie could tell her about him.

'A while now. I think he was midway through the renovations when we met. He came to the estate for an olive oil tasting – I do tours over summer when there isn't much else happening. We got talking and because I knew this house I was keen to see what he was doing. Actually I helped him pick out the colours for inside and choose where to hang the paintings.'

'You did a lovely job.'

'It made me happy to. It's one of those houses people have come and gone from over the years and it's lain empty too much. A rich family built it apparently, but they had lots of other holiday houses and hardly ever came here.'

Stella didn't especially want to hear the history of Villa Rosa, but wasn't sure how to steer the conversation back to Leo.

'I suppose it's empty a lot nowadays too,' Rosie continued. 'That's why it's so good that he is doing this home-swap thing with you. This house needs love.'

What is he really like? is what Stella wanted to ask. Is he funny, the loud one in a group or more reserved? Is he generous? A typical Italian, passionate, moody even? What is he like to have as a friend?

'I've never actually met Leo,' Stella said. 'All our contact has been via email.'

'Not even a phone call?'

Stella shook her head.

'I suppose everything happens online or by text these days, doesn't it? My phone hardly ever rings.' Rosie frowned. 'I can't say I like it but that's probably a sign I'm getting old.'

'We've got to know each other over email and if I called him now it might be like being strangers again, back at the very beginning,' Stella told her. 'I think that's what has been putting me off.'

Rosie gave her a sideways look. 'Have you been emailing each other a lot then?'

'Pretty much every day,' Stella admitted.

'Is that usual with these house swaps?'

'I've no idea what is usual; this is my first one. I hadn't even thought about it.'

'What sort of things do you write about?' She sounded fascinated. 'Sorry, I'm being completely nosy, aren't I? You can tell me to mind my own business; I won't be offended.'

'No, that's OK. Mostly we say what we've been doing or thinking or feeling; just the usual things that friends talk about. Does that seem odd?'

'Actually no, it seems quite like Leo.'

Stella gave up trying to hedge around the issue; if Rosie could be blunt then so could she. 'What is he like exactly?' she asked.

Rosie smiled. 'Leo? He's one of the good guys.'

She might have got more out of her but didn't have a chance. There was the sound of a car horn hooting, then a door slamming and a few seconds later Francesca appeared, out of breath and tear-stained, dressed in pink jeans and a sloppy grey top, and straining to carry a large suitcase.

'Oh thank God this is the right place,' she said shakily. 'I've been driving all over the coast in a taxi looking for it half the morning.'

'What's happened?' Stella was alarmed by the state she was in.

'I've left my husband,' Francesca declared and then, dropping her suitcase, put her hands over her face and let out a wail.

So much for her solitary, peaceful day, thought Stella, as she waved off Rosie amid promises to meet again soon. Francesca was in the spare bedroom, a mound under the covers, waiting to be brought a cup of tea. She had been crying too much to talk properly and Stella was hoping a rest might calm her.

Ten minutes later when Stella appeared with the tea and the rest of the biscotti, Francesca's sobs had become snuffles. She managed to sit up in bed and take the hot drink in her trembling hands.

'What's happened?' Stella asked. 'Do you want to talk about it?'

'Can I stay here with you for a while?' Her voice was hoarse.

'Why, Francesca, what has your husband done?'

'He's done nothing, that's the whole problem.' Cupping

the mug in both hands, Francesca took a tentative sip then frowned. 'I don't usually drink tea.'

'We English think it's good in a crisis and this seems like one to me.'

'Yes, it is,' she agreed. 'I've felt this way for a long time but last night we had our worst argument. All he does is work. He says it's for our future but what about right now? My life is so small, only the shop and the house every single day, and I want to travel and do interesting things like you. But Gennaro says that now I'm in my thirties it's time to start a family.'

'Don't you want children?' Stella asked, hoping she wasn't sounding judgemental.

'Yes, but if babies start coming now then I really will be trapped. It would be different if we had our own place but he refuses because his mother needs us and Roberto can't be trusted to stay around. Nothing I say will change Gennaro's mind.' Francesca was starting to cry again. 'I've stayed there so long hoping something might change and I can't stand it any more, I just can't.'

'What about your family – couldn't you go to them?' Stella gave her a tissue.

'I know what they'll say; I married him and I have to make it work. They'll tell me to go back.' Francesca dabbed at her face but the tissue was no match for the tears coursing down her cheeks. 'And my friends are all Gennaro's friends too, so they won't want to come between us. I can't afford a hotel and I knew you had this house all to yourself. If I could stay here for a little ...'

Stella didn't want to share Villa Rosa with Francesca but felt like there wasn't much choice; she could hardly throw her out on the streets. 'I'll have to check with Leo Asti; this is his house after all.'

Francesca managed the tiniest of smiles. 'Leo Asti; he is the older man who likes to buy my tea towels, the Neapolitan. He seems very nice. I'm sure he won't mind.'

'It can only be for a short time,' Stella warned her. 'I don't really know how long I have here myself.'

'A few weeks at the most,' she promised.

Stella's heart sank. 'Perhaps not that long ...'

'Please, please,' Francesca begged. 'I don't have much money but I'll contribute what I can. They pay me hardly anything you know for working in that shop. I'm meant to be doing it for the good of the family.'

It was impossible not to feel sympathy yet still Stella couldn't help wishing Francesca had missed Villa Rosa and washed up somewhere else to become another person's problem. Now she was here, she supposed she really had to help.

'Do you have any sort of plan?' she asked.

'Yes, of course, I'm going to go to Rome and get a job in a shop. I'm a good saleswoman so I'm sure I'll do well. When I've saved enough money I'll leave Italy and head off to see the world. Perhaps I'll come and visit you in London.'

'And what about your husband?'

Tears welled in Francesca's eyes. 'He's a sweet man. I'll miss him so much.'

Stella had coaxed Francesca out of bed and convinced her they should clear their heads with a walk when she heard the sound of another car approaching. This time it was Tosca, dressed in the smart Milly Munro suit she had been wearing the first time Stella saw her.

Seeing Francesca, she raised her eyebrows. 'Clever move, he'll never think to look for you here,' she said.

Francesca gave her a wary look. 'How do you know he's looking for me?'

'I've just had lunch with Roberto. He told me Gennaro is frantic, that he's been going from place to place all morning. It's all-out war at your house apparently. His mother isn't happy at all. She wants you back where you belong.'

'I'm not going,' Francesca said stubbornly.

Tosca half-shrugged a shoulder. 'They all want you back, Roberto too. He says he'll miss you.'

'Only because he'll have to run the shop if I'm not there.'

'That might be true,' Tosca conceded. 'He didn't seem very happy about it. In fact, he had to cut our lunch short, which was unfortunate.'

'Francesca and I were about to go for a walk round the coast path,' Stella told her. 'Want to join us?'

Tosca gestured towards her shoes, spiky high heels not suited to anything but teetering a few paces. 'Surely what is needed right now isn't walking, it's drinking.'

'Stella gave me a cup of tea,' Francesca said.

'We can do better than that.'

Tosca filled tall tumblers with ice, cucumber, mint, a hit of gin from a bottle she found at the back of Leo's kitchen cupboards and lots of sparkling water. Sipping their drinks out on the terrace, basking in the warmth of the late afternoon sun, they listened to Francesca complain about the unfairness of life and aim barbs at her mother-in-law.

'In the beginning I tried so hard to please her but she doesn't want to be pleased. She looks for flaws in everything because then she can criticise and that's what she loves most. The coffee I make is too strong, the pasta sauce too salty, I don't know how to clean a floor without leaving streaks, or how to choose a good piece of meat at the butcher's. Can you imagine living with it day after day?'

'If she's that bad I'm surprised you've put up with her so long,' said Tosca.

'I wanted to walk away but I didn't know where to go.' Francesca took a gulp of her gin. 'I'm so exhausted from doing so much for everyone that I can barely think. That's why it's such a blessing Stella is letting me stay for a while. It will give me a chance to recover before I begin on my new life.'

Seeing how Francesca was powering through her drink, Stella thought it might be wise to find something for her to nibble on. Back in the kitchen she loaded a plate with hunks of caciocavallo cheese, pieces of peppery salami and a mound of chilli-drenched olives. As she was slicing up a loaf of crusty bread, Tosca swept in clutching the gin glasses.

'I'm going to refresh these,' she told Stella, and set about topping them up. Lowering her voice, she added, 'Don't worry, she won't be here for too long.'

'Do you think so? I'm not sure.' Stella stared out at Francesca, who had reclined her chair and was settled back in it, eyes closed against the sun.

'She is giving her husband a fright,' Tosca told her. 'By the time he finds her he will be willing to listen to whatever it is she wants.'

It was the linen shop that Francesca wanted to gripe about when they returned with the food and drinks. Customers who wasted her time because they couldn't make up their minds, stacks of fabric that needed folding and refolding, how boring it was and how much she had grown to hate everything about the place, even the way it smelt.

'You can't mean that,' Stella said. 'The smell is one of the loveliest things about that shop. And the linen is so beautiful; some pieces are like art.'

'You should work there if you like it so much,' Francesca said.

'I would very happily if I could speak Italian.'

Francesca sat up, clapping her hands in excitement. 'That's what I can do to make myself useful while I'm here; I'll teach you. Wouldn't that be good? No charge, of course. We'll have a lesson every day and then we'll talk in Italian as much as possible. I'm sure you'll start to pick things up very quickly.'

'Really there's no need—' began Stella, who wasn't excited by the prospect.

'I think it's an excellent idea,' interrupted Tosca. 'We've all been speaking English for you and it's made you lazy. But you should make an effort, even if you only pick up a little. After all, you're not really a tourist; you're living here.'

'OK then,' agreed Stella, feeling steamrollered. 'We'll give it a go.'

'Let's start right now,' said Francesca happily.

While Stella was learning a few first phrases, Tosca occupied herself with her phone. She was texting back and forth with someone and every now and then she smiled. Halfway through her second gin some of the care had gone from the way she arranged herself. She had kicked off her heels and hung her jacket on the back of her chair; her lipstick had worn off; she looked relaxed and softer. The texts were making her laugh now. Stella assumed they were coming from Roberto and wondered how fast things were progressing between them.

After a very long half-hour Francesca decided they had spoken enough Italian. She stood up for a lazy stretch, gazing out at the view. 'This feels like being on holiday. Shall I make us more drinks?'

'Not for me,' said Stella. 'I need to head off and buy food. There's nothing in the house for dinner.'

Tosca frowned. 'Imagine the freedom we would feel if there wasn't this tyranny of meals.'

'Freedom, yes, but also hunger,' replied Stella. 'We need more in our stomachs than a bit of cheese and salami.'

'There's no need to go out. I'll get Raffaella to bring us something. She lives to fill people's stomachs. And besides, I'm sure she's been busy all day cooking things with her new boyfriend's vinegar.'

Stella laughed. 'Don't call him that to her face,' she advised Tosca.

'He will be, though, you wait and see. I'm often right about these things.' Tosca began tapping on her phone again. 'I'm certainly right that she'll be happy to feed us.'

Villa Rosa's fourth visitor of the day arrived in a car that had trays of food piled on the back seat and baskets of it in the boot. As they unpacked, Raffaella listed the dishes that she had brought. Baked courgettes slippery with melted mozzarella and wearing a splash of a herby vinegar, a leg of lamb cooked until the meat was shredding and basted in something spicy, radicchio that had been grilled and marinated, baby onions braised with garlic and saffron vinegar.

'A feast,' Stella marvelled.

'Thank God I texted you. Who would have eaten all of this otherwise?' asked Tosca.

Raffaella tossed her head. 'I have a fridge you know ... and an appetite. I'm sure I'd have managed.'

Before they ate, she wanted a tour of the house to see what changes Leo had made. She seemed to approve, although she deemed the chandelier in the hallway too flashy and nothing but a dust-collector.

It was the outdoor fireplace Raffaella seemed most entranced by. 'See how it has this grill that you can lower if you want to blister some red peppers over the flame, and it is big enough to throw out real heat if you stoke it up. I would like one of these at my place. Let's light it and eat our dinner out here,' she suggested.

'I'm not sure there is any wood,' Stella said.

'Of course there is. It will be where it was always kept, round the back of the house, sheltered from the weather.'

Sure enough they found a neat stack of logs beneath the eaves. Raffaella took charge, showing them how to lay the fire with layers of kindling to make sure the flames caught quickly.

Afterwards when she thought about that night it would be the faces by firelight Stella remembered. Tosca looked golden, a glittering, fabulous creature, and Francesca pink-cheeked and excited, but it was Raffaella who was most transformed. It was as if the flames returned to her some of what she used to have, a fiery, gypsy-blooded sort of beauty. She was all glittering dark eyes and strong cheekbones and where the shadows fell they seemed to sculpt away the years. Suddenly Stella could imagine her being wild enough to sabotage the construction of a statue and too rebellious to care if she were arrested for it. She could imagine so much of this incredible woman.

'Someone should tell a story,' declared Francesca. 'Or sing. That's what you're meant to do when you're sitting round a fire like this.'

'Sorry but I have no good stories,' said Stella.

'And I have no songs,' said Raffaella.

All three of them looked towards Tosca and she shook her head. 'Oh no.'

'Don't you have plenty of both?' asked Francesca.

'Too many; more than anyone needs, stories I'd prefer to forget.'

'Tell them all to the fire then,' Raffaella said softly. 'Let them burn up and turn to smoke. Let the words out. You have to sooner or later surely, so why not now?'

'I don't know ... maybe I will ... if I can.' Tosca stared at the flames. 'If you pour me another drink and promise never to say another word about any of it after tonight, then yes I have a story for you.'

The story of Tosca

It all started with the magazines – pictures of beauty queens and film stars; I couldn't get enough of them. Mamma told me I was a dreamer but then she found out there was money to be made and changed her mind.

It was a tough year for fishermen, lots of storms and the boats having to turn back so many times. You remember that year, Raffaella? All of us suffered. When I couldn't afford to buy magazines then I would steal them; I wasn't going to give them up. Eventually Mamma found out and was furious. She confiscated every single one. For an entire week I wasn't allowed to leave the house. And then the next thing I knew we were packing a suitcase and heading to Rome. Mamma had read one of my magazines and seen an advertisement for a beauty contest with prize money on offer. She decided I was going to win it.

We stayed in the apartment of a cousin who lived in Testaccio near to the slaughterhouse. Mamma and I slept together on a single mattress she put down on the floor of her dining room. Every day was filled with preparations. They patted creams on my skin and oiled my hair; Mamma's cousin made me an evening gown and we borrowed a swimsuit from one of the neighbours. Even I believed I was going to win this contest. I was very excited.

Unfortunately there were lots of beautiful girls and I only managed third place. My prize was a garland of flowers and no money. Mamma was disappointed and told me we would have to go home. But as we were leaving the contest a man stopped us and said he wanted to give me work. And that's how I ended up being a model for the *fumetti*, the photo-romance magazines that were so popular back then. I would pose in a scene with a good-looking boy and it felt like being an actress. I loved to see myself in those magazines, pretending to be scared or happy or in love, a speech bubble above my head.

After a while Mamma left Rome and I stayed on with her cousin, earning enough money to send a little back home. When I wasn't posing for the *fumetti* I was busy looking after the children and helping with the housework. I kept entering the beauty contests though; and I got cleverer with my hair and make-up until at last I won one. The prize included a trip to the Venice Film Festival. Can you imagine how thrilled I was? Movie stars, glamour, red carpets; it was everything I'd dreamed of.

Mamma's cousin tried to crush my dreams. She said it was impossible, there was no one to chaperone me, she was far too busy, so I couldn't go to Venice and would have to turn down that part of the prize. She thought I was a meek little girl who would do as I was told. Not for a moment did she expect me to pack the few things I owned and steal away at dawn before the household was awake. I knew I'd never be welcomed back but I didn't care. My life was going to change in Venice. There would be no need to go back anyway.

I was so young. All I had was a pretty face and far too much faith in myself. I attended all the screenings and parties I was invited to, talked to everyone, lied about my age and my experience, made sure they remembered my name.

There was one film producer that seemed to be every-where, an older man, not handsome, but clearly important. Filippo Olivieri was his name. I had never heard of him but I saw how he was treated, made note of so much deference and such respect, and was determined to speak with him.

He must have seen me for exactly what I was, a pushy young girl who had worn the same gown to every occasion and was surviving on canapés. The first thing he gave me was a warning: be careful whom you trust in this industry, stay cautious.

Filippo invited me to a gala dinner, bought me a new gown and borrowed some diamonds for me to wear. On his arm I walked down the red carpet and posed for the paparazzi. Everything that night seemed to glitter, even me. It seemed obvious this was my world, where I belonged, and I had to find a way to stay in it.

That night I went back to Filippo's hotel suite. He was gentle with me, very kind. He told me I needed a protector. And then he offered me a small role in a movie he was about to make, something to cut my teeth on and see how I managed.

That first film was a comedy, a silly story about bungling criminals that became a huge success. Filippo told me I'd done very well. He gave me a bigger role in his next production and after that it was my face in the magazines and they were starting to call me 'Italy's sweetheart'.

Filippo signed me up for several more films. My contract covered every small detail: how I wore my hair, the way I dressed, where I lived, the image I was to present to the world. No one was supposed to know that we were lovers, he and I, because of course he had a wife and several children. I had to be so careful what I said, even to my friends. But Filippo rewarded me by living up to his promise and he was my protector, in control of everything.

When he travelled to Hollywood to make a film I went with him. We would both be big stars, he told me, and I believed him because everything else had happened just as he said. Except this film was a complete flop and after that no one there would touch him.

Perhaps his wife had always known about us. We were

discreet but she must have somehow. While Filippo was at such a low point she seized her chance. Unless he dropped me there and then he would lose everything – his family and his career; his children would be strangers. Even when he came to say goodbye he was nervous she might find out.

I suppose I could have caused a scene, fought to keep him, but I knew I'd never loved him and thought his wife probably did. Besides, I didn't want to follow him back to Italy.

It wasn't difficult to find another man to be my protector. This one wasn't as soft-hearted as Filippo. He didn't treat me so well. But I was in Hollywood and soon I would have my big break and be able to walk away from him; I was sure of it.

There were small parts in films, but never any major roles, never work that tested me. I took acting classes and improved my English. I dropped one man and picked up another.

I moved around the edges of the world I wanted to belong in but I wasn't unhappy. Better to be there than in my old life, a fisherman's daughter waiting for someone to marry her – at least that's what I thought. There were parties, lunches, weekends spent drinking cocktails besides someone's pool and lots of men, some married and some not. Always I had faith in my talent as an actress. Success would find me if I waited for it long enough. I had come so close. I was nearly there.

Years went by like that. I wasn't one of the young ones any more but the man I was with by then was generous with his money and seemed to care for me. I still called myself an actress long after I'd become something else entirely. A woman who made a man's life smoother, who presided over his parties and introduced the right people to each other, who ran his house, chose his clothes, listened to him and looked good. That was my job and I was well rewarded.

Inside me there was still some ambition but it seemed better to forget it and enjoy what I had. When the offer came in I almost said no. A play in an off-Broadway theatre, a leading role with a director who remembered me from some film or other and was sure I'd be perfect. I was flattered. And then the man I was with said, 'Go to New York, follow your dream,' and so I did.

The rehearsals for that play were the happiest time of my life. I loved being on stage, acting in a bigger way than you can in front of a movie camera, performing with my whole body. I felt exactly the same as when I ran away from Venice; everything was changing, dreams were coming true.

But the day the play was meant to open I couldn't get out of bed. I wasn't sick, or if I was then it was only inside my head. They call it stage fright but that doesn't begin to describe the way I felt. It was a horror, a bleak, awful certainty of failure. If I got up before an audience my body would seize, the words dry up inside my mouth or come out in a whisper. The scenes that played through my mind that day: the expressions on the faces of the audience, the director in the wings and me on the stage, frozen. I wanted so much to be a fine actress, a real star, but instead I stayed in my room, curtains drawn and refused to answer the phone.

They sent on the understudy that night, and the next and the one after. The story put out was that I'd been taken ill very suddenly. After all those years I'd had my chance and I'd failed. It was over for me.

Only then did I realise how much I'd been living on hope. There must have always been a part of me believing I would make it. With that gone I had nothing.

I did the only thing I could, went back to Los Angeles and took up the threads of my old life, pretending I hadn't failed but only been unlucky. I'm very good at putting on a front so some people may have believed me, but there was gossip behind my back, I'm sure of it; people laughing, enjoying my disaster, turning it into just another story to tell.

I carried on in the face of it all, still acting, if that's what you call the small parts in TV series and movies. I was the woman murdered in the first few moments, a face in a crowd scene, a waitress in a diner, a patient in the next bed. I moved from role to role like I did from man to man, each one seeming more shallow than the last, none of them satisfying me.

And then Papa became ill and called me home to look after him. I was glad to come. I missed the girl I used to be, full of dreams and confidence. I thought I might find some small trace of her here.

I hoped for another chance, that the life I might have had if I'd never left Triento might still be here waiting for me. Perhaps I'm being naive and it's too late, but I have to try; I don't know what else to do.

For a few moments there was only the sound of the flames catching at the wood, crackling and hissing, and the quiet breathing of the four women sitting round it.

Francesca was the first to speak. 'At least you tried,' she said. 'You went to Hollywood, you had an adventure, you saw and did things ...'

Raffaella hushed her. 'Tosca's stories are in the fire now. They're burning and turning to smoke, rising up and away, disappearing. No need to speak of them again. *Va bene?*'

Fare una passeggiata (to go for a walk)

Dear Leo, so much has happened since I last wrote I'm not quite sure where to start. I suppose the first thing I should tell you is that I have a guest at Villa Rosa. Francesca Russo is staying here. She's left her husband and has nowhere else to go. Actually I think the person she has really run away from is her mother-in-law and I can hardly blame her. Still, I'm hoping she'll sort things out soon and go home. Tosca seems to think she will.

Ah yes, Tosca. We had an extraordinary time last night. She talked to us about her past – her childhood, America, all of it. We'd drunk a lot of your gin (I owe you a bottle) and then some wine and we were sitting in the darkness around your outdoor fireplace when she started talking and couldn't seem to stop. I think it may have been a relief for her. I hope so. But afterwards she was so quiet, deflated almost, as if all the energy had flowed out of her along with her story.

Tosca is a different woman than I thought; much more complicated, much sadder. I wish there was something I could do to help her but I suspect she's not a person who can be easily helped; besides, my own life isn't exactly sorted.

Anyway, I hope it's OK about Francesca. She seems to think you'll be delighted to have her here! Stella.

Hi Stella, you're welcome to have whatever guests you wish to stay. You must treat the place as your own. All the same, I hope you're not going to get caught up in someone else's marriage problems. That would be very boring and not at all relaxing.

While you were listening to Tosca's stories last night I was hearing some of your friend Birdie's. We had dinner in a wine bar in Soho and then drinks afterwards at a private club upstairs. You're right, she is a lot of fun – I didn't get back home till late and I'm having a slow start this morning. I've drunk two cups of coffee sitting out in your courtyard. I may need to stop for another on my way to work.

The sun is trying to shine today but there isn't much warmth in it. I've realised that I'm missing Italy. On my way to meet Birdie I went into a little delicatessen on Dean Street and just breathed the air. The savoury smell of hard cheeses, cured meats and freshly made pesto, all intermingling; that's the closest I've felt to home since I've been here.

I don't want to rush this project, not when it's starting to take shape at last. But we need to move things along a little faster. I want to come home!

Oh and don't worry about replacing the gin. That bottle must have been a gift from someone. I didn't even know I had it. Leo.

Hi Birdie, so you went out with Leo? He says he had fun. What's he like? Did you get on with him? Tell me everything. Stella.

Francesca was taking her duties as a language teacher seriously. When Stella came downstairs that morning she was already busy covering everything in labels. She had found some paper and sticky tape, and neatly written down the Italian word for every household item, from the fridge to the dining table.

'This is how we will improve your vocabulary,' she said. 'From now on you don't say table you say, *il tavolo*; and instead of fork you say *la forchetta*. It's the best way to remember.'

Stella yawned. 'Are you always this perky first thing?'

'Of course.' Francesca must have missed the irony in her tone. 'I've already thought of some ways to help you remember irregular verbs. We can start now if you like.'

'OK, after I've had some coffee, and only for an hour or so.'

'Not coffee, *il caffe*.' Francesca pointed to the label she had stuck on the jar. 'You'll have to get into the habit or it won't work.'

Stella managed to stifle a sigh. 'Yes, of course – *il caffe*. Once I've had a cup I might be able to concentrate a little better.'

'A cup ... *una tazza*,' Francesca said brightly.

How she could talk. She chattered away as Stella was grinding coffee beans and filling the moka pot. Most of what she said seemed barely worth listening to, gossip about people in town, stuff about her mother-in-law, stories that ran together so that Stella felt disoriented by them. She missed her usual quiet mornings. Leo was right; having Francesca here was unlikely to be relaxing.

Stella interrupted her mid-flow. 'What would you like to do after we've had our Italian lesson? I was thinking about an outing.'

'Oh no, I'd rather stay here,' Francesca said quickly. 'That would suit me better.'

'You don't want to risk bumping into your husband?' Stella guessed.

'It's peaceful here. I like it.' Francesca accepted a cup of coffee. 'I might read a book or lie in the sun. It's a long time since I've had a day to please myself.'

They went and sat outside. There were still some empty

wine glasses left abandoned by the fireplace and its ashes continued to smoulder, although not enough to throw out any heat.

'That was an interesting evening,' remarked Francesca. 'What a story.'

'We aren't talking about it, remember? Tosca is a very private person. She wouldn't like to be gossiped about.'

'I wasn't going to.' Francesca was indignant. 'I'm very private too. In fact, if you don't mind I'd really prefer it if you didn't mention to anyone in town that I'm staying here. I don't want people gossiping either.'

'Your husband will be worried, you know.'

'Good, let him worry. It won't do him any harm to think about something other than work for a while.'

Stella managed forty-five minutes of repeating Italian verbs before she ran out of patience. It was a waste of time anyway. Leo was already talking about coming home and she would have to be clear of Villa Rosa by the time he did. Once in London she needed to take her life in her hands and decide what to do with it. There would be no more excuses to procrastinate, and most likely no chance to come back here.

As soon as she was free she checked her emails. Still no reply from Birdie; how frustrating. Stella kept wondering what she and Leo had talked about, which stories had been told and whether they had got on as well as he seemed to think. Surely Birdie would tell her. Brutal honesty had always been her thing. Never had she bothered to hide what she really thought of Ray, for instance. Some people might have taken offence but Stella rather admired her for speaking her mind.

Birdie had known Ray for much longer, of course. He was a schoolfriend of her husband Johnny and had been the best man at their wedding. She thought he was unbearably finicky. Those were the exact words she'd used the very first time Stella had met her. It had been at a dinner party – one of those drawn-out evenings where the host has tried too hard and all anyone talks about is house prices.

'We're hoping you girls are going to be great mates,' Ray had said when he introduced her to Birdie. At first Stella hadn't been sold on the idea. Birdie didn't seem especially friendly. Then halfway through the evening she had headed outside for a cigarette and suggested Stella join her.

'Actually I don't smoke.'

'Come and talk to me then, keep me company.'

It was raining and they had stood in the porch while Birdie got through three cigarettes in a row. 'So you're Ray's new girlfriend? Do you know, I've always assumed he's gay.'

'Why would you think that?' Stella had asked.

'He's unbearably finicky. That last woman he was seeing, he used to pick out her clothes and dress her like she was a little doll. He was always fussing round her. Does he do that to you?'

It was true that Ray always had an opinion about what she was wearing but Stella rather liked that. 'He's interested in clothes; that doesn't make him gay.'

'Interested in clothes? Obsessed, you mean. The drama we had over the suit he was going to wear when he was Johnny's best man. The fabric, the cut, the colour – he must have called to talk about it a hundred times. There was only one bridezilla at my wedding and it was him.'

Despite herself, Stella had laughed. 'I can imagine that, actually. I bet he looked good in the end though.'

Birdie had laughed too. 'Oh yes, he looked marvellous. I'll show you the photos some time. He's in a lot of them.'

After that it had seemed natural for them to pair up at parties and dinners. Birdie always made things less boring. She had nicknames for everyone; sometimes they were mean, but they were always funny.

Later Stella realised she couldn't have been very happy at that point; because of course she was the gay one, not Ray, but she hadn't admitted it, possibly even to herself. Things must have been tough when eventually she left Johnny. There was lots of talk and people were far meaner about her than she had ever been about them.

Stella had stuck by her; so had Ray actually. Of course by then they'd had issues of their own. They were caught up in fertility treatment with its cycle of hope and despair. To Stella it had often seemed like Birdie was the one person it was OK to say absolutely anything to.

Now she wasn't replying to her emails. Stella tried calling her but there was no answer. Infuriating. She sent her a text instead: *Hey! Remember me? I'm still waiting to hear all about your evening with my house-swapper.*

She hoped Birdie wasn't teasing her, stringing her along. That would be quite like her too, and while often her mischief was amusing, this time Stella didn't have the patience. She wanted Leo to take shape, for the blurred lines of his character to come into sharper focus, and at this point only Birdie could help her. She trusted her friend's opinion. And when it came to this man who was living in her apartment, eating his meals from her dishes, sleeping in her bed, wrapping his damp body in her towels, Stella didn't want to wait much longer.

With no desire to spend a whole, long day at Villa Rosa in Francesca's company, Stella decided to turn to the scrapbook for inspiration. She hadn't picked it up since the outing to the vinegar estate and it took a while to find it, half shoved under her bed, the familiar plain cover looking a little dusty. Carefully she opened the book to a page near the end and found Leo's words waiting for her.

Dear Stella, all women like to look around shops, don't they? And to go for a passeggiata *along a busy street, perhaps stopping for a coffee or an* aperitivo?

I'm hoping you enjoy those things because today I'm suggesting you go south to a Calabrian town that is rather elegant considering how small it is. There are wide boulevards and pavement cafés and shops filled with ridiculously expensive designer items. I'm not sure who buys them – not me certainly – but if I'm in the mood then I do enjoy browsing.

Don't spend too much. Or if you do then please don't blame me! Leo.

Stella did quite like shopping. To stroll around looking at beautiful things and flirt with the idea of owning them was a pleasant way to pass a day, particularly in a foreign place. She sent texts to both Tosca and Raffaella, hoping they might want to join her. There was no word back from Tosca but ten minutes later Raffaella called.

'Shopping?' she said. 'I'm disappointed. After the vinegar estate I was hoping for something more interesting from your friend Leo.'

'This was on a page right near the end of the scrapbook,' Stella told her. 'Perhaps he was running out of ideas by then. But it will be fun. Won't you come?'

'I don't know. Shopping isn't my thing. Tosca is a better companion for that.'

'I've tried her but she isn't replying.'

'No, I don't expect she would. After last night she may want some time alone. She'll come round soon though, I hope. We'll give her a day or so.'

'Is there anything we can do?'

'I don't think so. Not right now. She needed to talk and now what she needs is to be silent.'

'Her story wasn't what I expected ... sorry, I know we promised not to discuss it.'

'She failed and can't forgive herself,' said Raffaella. 'That's the important part. All the rest we can forget.'

'Poor Tosca.'

'Oh, she would hate to hear you saying that about her right now.'

Stella could understand. 'Yes, I expect she would.'

'Now about this shopping trip,' said Raffaella, 'maybe I might manage an hour or so. I remember a place down there where the food was always fairly good. We can have lunch afterwards.'

'That would be lovely. I'll get myself ready.'

Stella put on a silk Milly Munro frock with a striking mosaic print that hadn't left the wardrobe so far because there had been no occasion to wear it. Raffaella hadn't bothered to make the same effort. She was in the dowdy black outfit she often wore, her hair caught up in a careless bun, her face free of make-up.

With Stella at the wheel, they followed Leo's directions to the elegant Calabrian town with the wide boulevards. He had sent her there before, Stella realised. This was the place with the church in the tufa rock cave and she had always intended to return and explore it a little further.

The main street was shaded by tall trees and lined with boutiques and jewellery stores. Once they had parked, they drifted from one to the other, gazing through windows and flicking through clothes rails.

For all she had complained about shopping Raffaella seemed to enjoy it hugely. She scoffed at the prices of designer handbags, was fascinated by the follies of the latest fashions and difficult to dislodge from a place that sold kitchenware. 'I could spend a fortune in here,' she admitted. 'Not that I really need any of this, but it is so stylish.'

'What about a new outfit?' Stella suggested. 'Perhaps that's something you do need? I could help you choose it.'

'I don't think so. When I was younger I loved pretty

clothes but now what is the point? I'm an old woman who never goes anywhere.'

'You might go to London at some stage to visit your sons; and come to see me when I'm back there. I'd like that.'

'Yes, maybe. But I don't need special clothes. No one is going to be looking at me, are they? I'm fine in my usual things.'

'Invest in one really nice dress,' suggested Stella, who was sure it wouldn't take much more than that to polish up Raffaella's beauty to a high shine.

The final boutique they visited was reasonably priced and featured clothes to skim the soft curves of older bodies, to drape rounded bellies and conceal arms that might have lost some of their firmness. Stella looked through the racks, dismissing most of what she found as too pedestrian. Her eye was caught by one dress in a vibrant red. It looked perfect and, taking it from the rail, she held it up for Raffaella to see.

'I think you should try this on.'

Raffaella made a face. 'Not my style.'

'It would look great on you. Just give it a go; it'll only take five minutes. And you haven't tried anything else.'

Raffaella gave a stagy sigh but she took the dress from her and disappeared into the changing room with it. Emerging a few minutes later, she stood before the full-length mirror. 'Too much bare skin,' she said, touching her chest.

'I can fix that,' Stella promised, and from a display of co-lourful scarves she pulled out one in a lively shade of orange to fold around her neck.

'Too bright,' declared Raffaella, starting to take it off.

'No, no,' the sales assistant stopped her, eyes wide, hands in the air. 'You look sexy, so sexy.'

'You do,' Stella agreed. 'Don't sigh like that. Look at yourself properly.'

Raffaella glanced sideways at her reflection and shook her

head. 'No, not sexy, only trying to be something I'm not.'

Stella took her shoulders and turned her square on to the mirror. 'You're wrong. I wish Tosca were here because she would back me up. This *is* who you are. Actually it's the first time I've ever seen you in clothes that reflect your character. Now you're vibrant inside and out.'

'Women my age shouldn't even try to be sexy,' Raffaella argued.

'My old boss Milly Munro wouldn't have agreed with you. Dress well, look good, feel great, was one of her mottos.'

'Perhaps that's true for lots of women but I don't need to fuss with the way I look to feel good about myself.'

'But the red and orange bring you alive, they're your colours.'

'So sexy,' the sales assistant murmured again.

Raffaella's hands were on her hips and she was glowering at her reflection. 'Fine, I'll buy them, if only to make you both stop this nonsense.'

'A bangle might be nice.' Stella turned to the assistant. 'Do you have one in the same orange as the scarf by any chance?'

'Enough,' cried Raffaella. 'I'll take this and I'm finished. Then we go to eat.'

'OK, but don't change back into your other dress. Leave that one on.' Stella was pleased to have won the battle. 'You are so gorgeous in it.'

Raffaella always carried herself well. Her back was straight, her shoulders strong, her stride a long one. Now she blazed with colour and heads turned as they walked down the boulevard – mostly women's heads, not men's, but that was fine. In Stella's experience they were the best appreciators of another woman's beauty.

The restaurant she had chosen had a large outdoor area. There were fairy lights tangled through the trees and at night it must be a buzzy place but right then only two other tables were occupied. Stella recognised the couple at the closest one.

'Look, it's Benedetto and Maria, Leo's friends from the café up by the statue. We should say hello.'

The couple were sharing a dish of prawns and deep in conversation so hadn't noticed their arrival. They looked up at the sound of Stella's voice.

'Ladies, you both look so elegant today,' exclaimed Benedetto. 'Is this a special occasion?'

'Just a day out shopping,' Stella said.

'Well then, you must join us,' he insisted. 'Please do.'

'Are you sure?' Stella turned to Maria. 'We don't want to intrude on your lunch.'

'We would welcome your company,' she promised. 'Benedetto and I are always together, at home and at work. We have no friends in Triento, only each other.'

'You must miss your family,' said Raffaella, pulling out a chair and sitting down.

'Yes, we do,' Maria agreed. 'Our daughter is pregnant so we'll have a grandchild soon and it will be even harder. But we're hoping they'll join us when things get better.'

'How is business?' Raffaella asked.

The couple exchanged glances. 'It will get better,' Benedetto said.

'It has to,' added Maria.

'What if it doesn't?'

'It will.' Benedetto sounded certain. 'We've been eating at other restaurants nearby, mostly in Triento, but today we've come further afield. Our place compares well. Our menu is more interesting, we take more care with our ingredients, our food is good; we just have to let people know.'

Leaning forward, Raffaella rested her elbows on the table. 'That bar beside the statue has never stayed in anyone's hands for long. I've been asking around. What people tell me is that the old couple who had it before you barely eked out a living, even in the summer, and all they served was snacks and drinks, not food that is ambitious.'

'So you think we should give up and go back to Scampia?' Maria's tone was touchy. 'Back to the slums where we belong? Is that it?'

Putting a hand on her arm, Benedetto said, 'The *signora* doesn't understand, *cara*. This is our dream, what we have always wanted, and we'll work hard for it. Of course we won't give up.'

'Just tell me one thing: are you locked into your lease on that place?' asked Raffaella.

'No,' Benedetto admitted. 'A longer lease was too much to pay. We are taking it month by month for now.'

Raffaella looked down at her knees, smoothing out a wrinkle in the bright red fabric. 'What if you could do the same thing that you are doing there but somewhere better?'

'Unfortunately we don't have that option.'

'What if you did?'

'Then we would consider it,' Benedetto told her. 'We'd be crazy not to.'

Raffaella stared at him wordlessly for a moment then shifted her gaze to Maria. 'We should talk. Come and see me. I can't promise anything ... not yet. But we can talk.'

'We would appreciate any help you could give us, *signora*,' Maria said softly.

Benedetto nodded. 'Any help at all.'

After that the conversation quickly turned to food. Raffaella tried the prawn dish and discussed at length with Maria how it might be improved. More food was ordered and each plate arriving on the table came in for the same scrutiny. Both women seemed to be able to tell from a single mouthful what ingredients had been used for flavouring, what might be out of balance, too salty, too sour or sweet. They had opinions on everything from texture to appearance, strong opinions and several times voices were raised.

Stella was reminded of meetings at Milly Munro's with all the staff encouraged to be vocal about designs for the latest collection. This was the same passion, the same creative spirit; it made her smile to listen to them.

'Who taught you to cook?' she asked Maria.

'The women in my family have all been cooks – Mamma, my aunts, Nonna, so I learnt from them. I'm still learning, of course. That is the great thing about food, there is always something new.'

'My mother used to say that,' Raffaella told her.

Maria smiled. 'Mine too.'

Later as they drove the twists and turns of the road back to Triento, Raffaella gazed out of the passenger window, her head resting on the glass, and said very little. Stella hoped she wasn't regretting her offer to help Leo's friends. Before leaving she had given them the address of her *trattoria* and agreed a time for them to visit. She had hinted that she might have the perfect solution; now, though, she seemed to be brooding, and when Stella tried to rouse her, Raffaella's replies were short and to the point.

'What's wrong?' Stella asked eventually.

'Nothing.'

'Well, what are you thinking about then?'

'I'm thinking about all the time those two have ahead of them to cook and work together. If Ciro was still alive that's what we'd be doing ... although maybe it was the work that finished him. I've often wondered about that.'

'What happened?' asked Stella.

'A heart attack, very sudden; he had been fine right up until that day. Ciro was always the healthy one. I never imagined losing him. I wasn't prepared ... I'm still not.' Raffaella paused and added, 'He was in the shower. I heard him fall.'

'God, how awful.'

'I begged him not to leave me; I begged him. But he did.' Stella didn't want to take her eyes from the road but she could tell from the way her voice had changed that Raffaella was crying. 'That was almost three years ago but the way I feel it might have been yesterday.'

'Loss is like that,' said Stella, who knew, then suddenly she realised something. 'Oh no, that's why you always wear black, isn't it? It's for Ciro?'

'It was the old tradition. When I was a girl and lost my first husband I resented it. This time it felt right to have all the colour go.'

'And I made you buy that dress ... and the scarf.' Stella bit her lip. 'How tactless of me. I'm so sorry. I had no idea.'

'You made me buy a dress the colour of rubies and Ciro would thank you. He hated me to be unhappy. He was a gentle man but if someone upset me it made him so angry. To see me in black year after year wouldn't have pleased him.'

Stella felt guilty about pushing her friend into something she hadn't been ready for. 'Wearing black is fine if it makes you feel better.'

'Nothing makes me feel better. When it happened I wanted to disappear from the world. I still fight that feeling every day. Grief shouldn't set me apart from other people; after all, most of us have known some, and yet it seems to me that it does. So I wear black, to mark myself as a widow, the way all the old women did when I was young. They went further, of course: black gloves, earrings, hats, scarves. The young men had black armbands as a sign of respect. Grief was a visible thing then. Now we are supposed to deal with it in private, come to terms, move on, and I'm struggling with that.'

They were nearing Villa Rosa now. Stella wished she had something to say, some wisdom to make things easier or better.

'What would Ciro have wanted you to do?' she asked.

'I don't really know. Even though we were getting older we never spoke about it. Perhaps if one of us had been sick ... if we'd seen what was coming. All I can think is Ciro would have wanted whatever made me happy. The trouble is I'm not sure if I can be.'

Stella steered the car through the gates of Villa Rosa, parking beneath the shade of a tree. 'Will you come in and have a drink?'

'Thank you but I need to go home.' Raffaella opened the door. 'I'm sorry if I haven't always been the best company today. Next time I'll be brighter, I promise.'

She was away and into her own car, starting the engine and backing out of the gates. There was the wave of a hand and the flutter of an orange scarf at the window as Raffaella took off, leaving behind a cloud of exhaust fumes as she roared up the hill.

Stella stood for a moment by the gates of Villa Rosa thinking about her and Tosca. Their company had been so welcome when she arrived in Triento. She had enjoyed being included in their friendship, enjoyed the lunches and outings; it had all been so much fun. Now things were deepening and complicating. She was learning there was so much more to these two new friends of hers; that they were easily as lost as she was; as uncertain about the next steps they should take; as deep-down sad. Stella winced as she thought about how she had gone and blundered in, trying to help with clothes, with cheerful colours and the right accessories. She shook her head at her naivety.

Stella might have preferred to slip inside unseen but Francesca was hovering out on the terrace, pacing back and forth, impatient and full of things to say.

'There you are.' She sounded almost accusing. 'I thought you'd never get back. You've missed all the action.'

'What do you mean?' Stella was thinking about taking a long shower and then retiring to bed with a book.

'The house next door – people have arrived, a man and his son. They were dropped off by the taxi.'

'Holidaymakers, I expect,' said Stella. 'Leo told me the house gets rented out sometimes.'

'Yes that's right, I talked to them. They're here for a couple of weeks. I said we would have them over for dinner. I could cook it if you like.'

'Not tonight?'

'No, of course not, they'll be tired from their journey, but another time.'

'Sure,' Stella agreed, her mind still very much on Raffaella.

'You should go over and introduce yourself in the morning,' Francesca said. 'They are English and seem very nice. The man is quite good-looking although he's pretty old … well your age probably … and he told me he's a divorcee. They're here for two weeks and they seemed to think they could do without a car but I told them there's no way they can walk into Triento from here. It's too far; besides, the road is so narrow and busy it would be dangerous.'

'Mm,' murmured Stella.

'I gave them the number of the rental place and said to get a car, not a scooter, but you might want to talk to them when you go over in the morning.'

'Fine,' said Stella wearily. 'Right now I'm going to take a shower and then I may crash out.'

'What about dinner? I was going to make a risotto with some vegetables I picked from the garden. And I found a bottle of wine I thought we could share.' Francesca sounded eager.

'Have you labelled the bottle with its Italian word?' Stella asked.

'Yes, I've labelled almost everything. I'm earning my keep.'

Stella hid a smile. 'OK then, I'll have a shower and check my emails then we'll open the wine.'

'*Una bottiglia di vino*,' Francesca called after her as Stella turned and headed towards the house.

Hi Stella, hah, I knew you'd be desperate to hear from me! In fact I told Leo you would be. So let me start at the beginning. I took him to Andrew Edmunds wine bar in Soho because it is tucked away and not one of those see-and-be-seen places. Afterwards I was planning to head to the Academy Club for a drink so I invited him along. I think he liked it. You get such an eclectic bunch of people up there and we found ourselves at the long table chatting with an artist and some old guy who is an expert on local history – Leo talked to him for ages, actually. I think they were planning some sort of guerrilla gardening escapade in Soho Square but possibly that was just all the wine they'd drunk doing the talking.

Anyway he's not your type at all, I'm afraid. He couldn't be more different from Ray. We're talking faded blue jeans, roughened hands and possibly even a bit of soil under the fingernails. He looks like what he is, someone who spends a lot of time scrabbling in the earth and doesn't give much thought to his appearance.

He's crazy about that house you're staying in, by the way. He talked about it a lot and showed me about a hundred pictures on his phone. But he's also one of those guys who asks questions then really listens to the reply – again not at all like your ex-husband, who I always thought only asked questions to make himself seem more intelligent. So I liked Leo. And I'm sure he's looking after your flat; he certainly didn't seem the type to trash it.

I'll try to catch up with him again if I can. But actually

I'm going to be away for a bit. I'm heading to Scotland with the woman I've been seeing – we're going to an island she says is the best place on earth. We've hired a cottage and we'll drink whisky and walk on the beaches and go fishing. Sorry, but that means I won't be able to get over and see you. I feel bad. You're OK there, aren't you? Not so lonely now? I really like her. She is definitely my type. And when she brought up the idea of Scotland I couldn't say no. Don't hate me! Birdie.

Hi Birdie, so things are getting serious? I need a photograph immediately. And tell me some stuff about her. How old? What does she do? What is her name?

No need to worry about letting me down. Everything is good here. I know why Leo loves it so much. I'm going to find Villa Rosa difficult to leave when the time comes.

Oh and what do you mean, he's not my type? Who do you think is exactly? I'm not looking for another Ray, you know. One was enough. I didn't think I was looking for anyone at all but now I've changed my mind. It would be good to have a partner to walk on a beach with, to feel as if I were joined up instead of on my own. It's a matter of meeting the right person though, isn't it?

I think I'd started to hope it might be Leo. A nice fantasy, but really, what are the chances? Even if I did get to meet him, as you say he might not be my type at all – and I might not be his.

Perhaps when I get back to London I'll do the online dating thing. In the meantime there is always Tosca's speed-dating if that ever comes off – there's a lot of talk but nothing seems to be happening. Oh and there's a new arrival in the neighbourhood, a man staying in the house next door who according to my new friend

Francesca is good-looking and single. I fear Francesca fancies herself as a bit of a matchmaker.

Have fun in Scotland. Stay in touch. And don't forget to send me a picture of this woman who really is your type. Love Stella.

Arrivals and disappearances

Stella had set her alarm to be sure to wake up early and escape the house before Francesca could trap her into another Italian lesson. She truly had labelled every single thing in sight, even the bathroom fittings, and over dinner last night had been slightly manic. Stella supposed she was used to the comings and goings of the linen shop and wasn't enjoying the solitude as much as she thought she might.

Slipping on her walking shoes, Stella crept downstairs, opened the front door as quietly as she could and closed it softly behind her. It was a beautiful morning, the last streaks of pink fading from the sky and the blue growing brighter and clearer. Stella set off around the coastal path at a brisk pace, continuing on further than the last time, clambering over rocks in places where the path petered away and skirting the walls that divided it from people's gardens. There were plenty of other summer houses here but none as special as Villa Rosa, at least in Stella's opinion.

As she walked, she recalled Birdie's email. She tried to imagine the man it portrayed: a little scruffy perhaps, but lively, deep in conversation with strangers, curious, interested. She recalled the photographs she had seen of Leo and tried to place him where he and Birdie had spent the evening; the candlelit wine bar, then the louche drinking club upstairs. She had gone to both with Birdie numerous times and it was curious to think Leo had been there too now.

He was not her type, Birdie had insisted and she might be right. All the men Stella had dated in the past had been well scrubbed, the type to iron a crease into their jeans and care about the fit of a jacket. Her father was like that too; dapper, many people called him – he always looked immaculate right to the end, even after her mother had died, and after he himself was far from well. Whenever she thought about her father, she remembered the fresh citrusy smell of the cologne he dabbed on every morning. Stella thought about him a lot; she missed him. When Raffaella spoke of grief, and the way it marked a person, he had been at the forefront of her mind.

Stella was in a rhythm with her walking now and might have kept going, except she remembered Francesca, lonely at Villa Rosa. Taking pity on her, she turned to retrace her steps.

Stepping up through the terraced gardens of Villa Rosa, she decided to take a detour through the bottom set of gates and go past the house next door. Sure enough there were signs of life. Shutters and windows had been thrown open and she could hear music. Thinking Francesca was right and she ought to introduce herself, Stella headed up the pathway and knocked on the door.

'Hello,' she called out.

'Well, good morning.' A man was looking down at her from the balcony above. 'You must be Stella? I'm Neil, nice to meet you. Hang on, I'll come down and let you in.'

As he opened the door she saw he was very tall, around her age, with cropped brown hair, bright blue eyes and skin that looked like it would tan easily. He was dressed in crisp white shorts and had a just-showered smell about him.

'Come in,' he said. 'I was about to make coffee. Would you like one?'

The house seemed a typical holiday rental, white walls, plain furniture and very little character beyond a few bright ceramic plates hanging on the wall.

'Yes please, I got up early and haven't had any yet.' Stella was aware she was pink-cheeked and perspiring from her walk, poorly dressed in a faded old T-shirt and a pair of Lycra shorts she had picked up from the floor that morning.

'Are you hungry?' Neil asked. 'I can offer you some of these dry toast biscuit things and jam. They were in the welcome basket along with the coffee, but there's not much else I'm afraid. I was under the impression this place was closer to town. I'd planned to walk in every morning and eat breakfast at a local café but it doesn't seem like that's going to happen.'

'It's not that far to drive,' Stella told him. 'I can give you a lift in later if you like. But if you're here for a while then you really need to hire a car.'

'Your friend Francesca said the same. She's been very helpful, came over this morning and rang the rental place for me. Oh and she said you'd like us to come over for dinner tonight, which is lovely, thank you.'

Not for the first time, Stella felt railroaded by Francesca but she could hardly take back the invitation. Through a slightly forced smile she said, 'How many of you are there? Is it just you and your son?'

'Yes, Otis is still in bed. Teenagers, you know.'

Stella nodded, as if she did.

'He's a good kid. We're having a boys' holiday, a bit of bonding, you know.'

'Why choose this place?' Stella asked.

'Oh, I've always had a thing about Italy. Love the food, the people, the culture, everything. Someone told me this is the new Amalfi Coast. It was Otis who went online and found the house. It's got Wi-Fi and a swimming pool out the back; that's pretty much all he needs to stay happy. What about you? What brought you here?'

Stella explained about the home swap as the smell of coffee filtered through the kitchen. She started to tell him about Triento, the best bar and the places to shop for food, but it seemed Francesca had filled him in already.

'Your friend knows the village really well. She's not house-swapping too I take it?'

'No, she's local; it's a bit of a long story.'

'She seems very enthusiastic about having us over for dinner. You just missed her actually – she went off to make a shopping list. You must let me know what we can bring.'

'Oh, I expect Francesca will tell you,' said Stella drily. 'Come over when your son has got up and I'll drive you to town.'

'Are you sure it's not a bother? I do need to head in to pick up the rental car but we can always get a taxi.'

'I'm going there myself so it's no trouble at all.'

'Great, thanks.' His eyes met hers and he smiled. 'Let's go out by the pool and we'll drink our coffee.'

The pool was really only a small rectangle of blue water, hidden from the road by a high wall, and surrounded by a few cactus-like plants. Neil set the coffee things on a small table on the terrace beside it.

'Sit down, tell me about yourself.'

Sipping on her coffee, Stella ran through the bare details, where she lived and the job she'd had until recently. 'So what do you do?' she asked once she had finished.

'I'm sort of in the fashion industry too, actually – but eyewear, not clothes. I have a company that designs and makes spectacle frames.'

Neil poured a second cup of coffee and told her more, how his marriage had broken up and his son had struggled but was back on track, how work had been crazy busy and he was ready for this break, how he was thrilled to discover them as neighbours because, much as he loved Otis, it would be good to have some adult company while they were here. Stella thought there was something very warm and open about him, although maybe that was down to the way his clear blue eyes kept meeting hers and seemed to sparkle.

'I should go,' she said. 'I haven't even had a shower yet and I went for a long, hot walk so I need one.'

'I'll see if I can dislodge Otis from bed and come over in half an hour or so. Is that OK?'

'Yes, perfect,' Stella said. 'See you soon.'

Stella found herself considering what she ought to wear. Her yellow sundress? A pair of navy linen pants and a little broderie anglaise cotton top? Something light and silky? She wondered if half an hour was long enough to do something with her sweaty hair.

Back at Villa Rosa, she found Francesca at the kitchen table planning the night's menu. The list she was making seemed long and her brow was furrowed in concentration.

'Oh don't worry, I'll do all the cooking,' she said, realising Stella was reading over her shoulder. 'I just need you to pick up a few things in the village.'

'That looks like more than a few things. Are you sure you're not being over-ambitious?'

'It's a dinner party. We have to do things properly,' Francesca insisted. 'So did you go and say hello to our new neighbour yet?'

'Yes, he seems nice. Actually he's coming over in a little while. I'm taking him to pick up his rental car.'

'Really?' Francesca looked her up and down. 'Shouldn't you go and change then? Put on a nice dress?'

'Only if you tell me the Italian word for it,' Stella teased.

Francesca screwed up her face. 'Very funny.'

But Stella did put on a nice dress. It was an old one that made her waist seem narrower; one Ray had always liked her in. She fussed about with her hair and make-up and when she went back downstairs Neil and his son were already there, sitting out beneath the bougainvillea and admiring the view.

'This place is sensational.' Neil turned to her. 'I was

pleased with ours till I saw yours and now I've got holiday-house envy.'

He introduced her to his son, a gangly boy who glanced up from his smartphone for a moment to give her a smile that was very like his father's.

'Shall we head up to the village?' said Stella. 'If no one's had a proper breakfast I thought we could go to my favourite bar for a big creamy pastry before you find the rental car place.'

'Now you're talking, eh, Otis?' said Neil.

Stella drove the winding coast road to Triento, Neil in the passenger seat beside her, making easy conversation. By the time they reached the edge of the village, they'd made a couple of connections, people they both knew through work, and were exclaiming about the coincidence.

At the bar Neil took Otis to choose the pastries, returning with two loaded plates. 'Teenage boys have an appetite,' he told her. 'Do you have any kids?'

Stella shook her head. 'No, none.'

'Well, try not to be shocked when you see how much food disappears into the mouth of this one.'

It turned out Neil was a people-watcher just like her. Together they played a game. Whether it was an old man, a young boy or a middle-aged woman walking past they speculated about what each one did and how their lives might be. This man was so neat and tidy he must be a former soldier; that person had a red nose and looked like a drinker; another, from the set of her mouth, seemed like life had disappointed her. From time to time Otis joined in, although his suggestions were cheekier.

'Busy little spot, isn't it?' Neil sat back and surveyed the piazza. 'Just think, while I'm stuck at my desk day after day all this life is going on without me. God, that sounds totally self-centred, doesn't it?'

'No, I understand what you mean,' Stella told him. 'We

all get trapped in our own small worlds, don't we? That's one of the reasons I'm loving this house swap. It's a chance to escape myself for a while.'

Neil looked thoughtful 'What if you lose yourself completely?'

Stella laughed. 'I'm sure that won't happen.'

'But you might not want to go back to your own small world. What then?'

'I don't think I'll have much choice in the matter.'

'Could you do it, though?' asked Neil. 'Live in a village like this? I think I'd get bored pretty quickly.'

'I don't know if Triento is less interesting than London. There may not be any theatres and fewer restaurants but there seems to be as much going on under the surface. Also I think it's easier to get to know people here than in a big city.' Just then Stella spotted Leo's friend Rosie walking across the piazza with a skinny, dark boy who must be her son. She waved to attract her attention. 'In fact, here's someone now that I know a little.'

Rosie waved back when she saw her. She came over and stopped for a chat. As at their last meeting she looked coolly chic, this time in a belted dress in the softest of creams with short sleeves and a scooped neckline. Stella considered asking where she bought her clothes since she hadn't seen anything quite like them on sale in or around Triento.

They talked about the things that people who hardly know each other tend to fall back on: how warm it was, how much hotter it was expected to get and when the lido at the local beach would open properly with deckchairs and sun umbrellas available for hire. Rosie asked after Stella's unexpected houseguest and laughed when she heard Francesca was showing no sign of leaving.

'Fortunately Leo doesn't seem to mind,' said Stella.

'I'm sure he doesn't, but the important thing is, do you?'

'Ideally I'd prefer to have the place to myself,' Stella

admitted. 'Francesca's trying to make herself useful though and I suppose eventually she'll get bored and go home.'

'When she made her appearance so dramatically the other day I quite forgot the main reason I'd come,' Rosie told her. 'Sunday lunch at my place: it's a bit of a tradition, crowds of people, very casual. You must bring your friends.' She smiled at Neil and Otis. 'And your houseguest too if she wants. Just let me know the numbers so I don't descend into total chaos.'

'That would be great,' said Stella. 'I'd love to see your olive farm.'

'We'll give you the grand tour,' she promised. 'Everybody gets it.'

Once Rosie had said her goodbyes and headed off, Stella explained Francesca's history, making Neil laugh with her descriptions of the Russo family. She pointed out their linen shop, which this morning had a tall rack of colourful tablecloths fluttering outside its open door. When he seemed curious to take a look inside she offered to join him, thinking Roberto would be working and she could ask whether he had seen anything of Tosca.

But it was his mother Angelica's frown that greeted them as they walked through the door. 'Oh it's you,' she said, coolly, on seeing Stella. 'Have you come to buy or just waste my time?'

Neil was clearly taken aback by her unfriendly tone. 'We were just going to have a browse, if that's OK?'

'Everyone wants to browse here,' Angelica said sourly. 'And then they think they can look on the internet and find it cheaper, but they won't. These are exclusive fabrics, not mass-produced in China. I get so tired of telling people that. No one listens.'

'I expected Roberto to be working here today,' said Stella. 'Is he around?'

'No, my eldest son is away at the moment. So is my

daughter-in-law Francesca. But I worked behind this counter before either of them. It is good for me to come back occasionally and make sure all is as it should be.'

Neil was looking round the shelves, his son trailing behind him. Stella watched his expression as he sorted through the quilts, the embroidered cloths, fine linen napkins and pillow-slips. He seemed to understand the quality of what he was looking at.

'Her stuff is beautiful,' he said when they were back outside. 'I'd love to buy a quilt but I'm not sure I want to put my money in the pockets of that old witch.'

Stella giggled. 'That old witch is Francesca's mother-in-law, the one I was telling you about.'

'Of course it is. I should have realised. No wonder Francesca has gone into hiding to get away from her.'

Stella laughed. 'I suppose she must have some redeeming qualities but I can't imagine what they are. I wonder where her son Roberto is. I expected to find him there.'

'Perhaps he fled too,' suggested Neil.

'Well I hope he doesn't turn up at Villa Rosa. Things really would start getting too crowded.'

Once she had helped Neil locate the car rental office, Stella went for a wander. She was looking for a shop that sold the kind of outfits Rosie wore, stylish but relaxed. However, everything here seemed designed as fodder for the tourists: coral necklaces, woven bags, things studded with pebbles and shells. And yesterday in Calabria most of the shops had displayed showier items, tops with an extra hit of bling that really wasn't needed, skirts with impractical splits, gauzy transparent dresses. For someone her age, who wanted chic clothes she could throw on and live in, there seemed to be nothing at all and yet again Stella mourned the passing of Milly Munro, who had understood that women's bodies weren't clothes hangers and that their lives were complicated so their outfits should be simple.

If Stella were a designer she would make up samples and get ordinary people to wear them. Only when she was sure they could last without creasing ruinously, bagging at the knees, puckering at the seams, pilling or pulling threads, would she go into production. And she would ask her testers lots of questions: how did you feel in it, did you get compliments or admiring glances, did it make you more confident, sexier or happier?

Of course, she wasn't a designer. Working with Milly Munro, the more she learnt the more certain she became that she didn't have what it took: the talent, the drive or the willingness to take risks. While Milly was lovely there was an inner toughness there that Stella suspected she herself lacked.

For a while, when the fertility treatments were dragging them down, Ray tried to convince her to go back to college and retrain in fashion design – he even offered to support her financially. But Stella was so set on a baby she hadn't wanted to admit she might need a plan B. Later, after she and Ray had split, he'd mentioned it again but by then she felt so discouraged by life, so lacking in light and enthusiasm, sticking with what she knew had seemed best.

If there had been a baby almost everything would be different, Stella was certain. She and Ray would still be together, and she would have given up her job, or at least cut down to part-time. There might have been a second child – a boy and a girl had always been the dream – and she would have been busy with nap times, story times and play dates; Stella felt cheated of all that.

She sat on the edge of the fountain beside the town hall, listening to the water playing over it, smelling the sweet scent of fresh bread coming from the bakery, watching two old priests meandering slowly across the piazza, deep in conversation. Stella wouldn't be here if life had turned out that way. She would never have written to Leo and swapped her home for Villa Rosa, or met Raffaella and Tosca. All the hormone injections, blood tests and scans, in the end everything in life had turned on those failed fertility treatments, and this was where she had ended up; how random was that?

Stella might have sat there for ages, remembering and wondering, but in her bag she had the shopping list Francesca had written out and it was time to make a start on gathering what was needed.

Walking back towards the market stalls, she paused to exchange a smile with the butcher leaning in his shop doorway and a tentative *buongiorno* with a woman she often saw drinking her morning coffee in the same bar. At the stalls, she didn't haggle the way she had seen Raffaella do, but she got the sense they weren't charging her the tourist prices any more.

Still, she was startled by how much it cost and had to make a couple of trips back to the car to carry everything. Francesca must have over-stretched herself with a menu that was far too complicated and Stella could imagine the frazzle of an afternoon that lay ahead as she tried to put it all together. Help was needed and it was Raffaella who sprang to mind. Not only was she a cook, Stella had noticed how Francesca seemed slightly cowed by her.

Instead of driving straight back to Villa Rosa she took the road down to the harbour. She found Raffaella crouched down in her courtyard, repotting herbs, her fingers steeped in soil and her body clad in black again.

'*Buongiorno*,' Stella called. 'I have news.'

Raffaella raised her head. 'You've spoken to Tosca?' she asked hopefully.

'I haven't, sorry. Have you not heard from her either?'

'No, I've tried calling and knocked on her door a couple of times but there's no answer. I suppose she might have gone away but it seems unlikely.'

'Roberto Russo is missing too,' Stella told her. 'You don't think they've gone off together?'

'Who knows with Tosca?' Raffaella seemed worried. 'The other night when that story came tumbling out I thought she was reaching some sort of crisis point, that she was starting not to believe the lies she's been telling herself.'

'What lies?'

'About what she really wants: a man to love her, a quiet life, security; how can you dream so big for so long then suddenly start thinking small? She has always been ambitious. That is Tosca. She hasn't changed as much as she likes to think.'

Seeing how anxious she seemed, Stella tried to reassure her. 'She's been very flirtatious with Roberto, you know. He was texting her the other day. It's possible they're holed up together in a hotel somewhere.'

'Maybe.' Raffaella sounded doubtful. 'My concern is that she's shut herself away and is unable to face any of us. I thought I was helping when I pushed her to talk the other night, but what if I've made things worse? Remember how withdrawn she was afterwards? She hardly said another word.'

'I could knock on her door if you like,' Stella offered. 'Although if she won't open up for you then she's unlikely to want to speak to me.'

'It's worth trying. Her place is two doors along, the one with the green shutters.' Raffaella put down the pot of rosemary she was holding, stood up and stretched. 'But you said you had news. What is it?'

'Nothing important, only that I have neighbours; a man and his son have rented the place next door to Villa Rosa. They seem nice actually and Francesca is very excited. She's invited them to dinner tonight and is planning on doing all the cooking herself.'

'Oh yes.' Raffaella sounded uninterested.

'Here's what she had me buy.' Stella pulled out the long shopping list.

Raffaella glanced at it. 'What is she going to make?'

'Some long, complicated menu that's bound to go badly. I was hoping you might come and sort her out – and stay for dinner too obviously.'

Raffaella held up her soil-covered hands. 'Today I'm gardening, not cooking.'

'Please come,' Stella begged.

'I'm still feeling blue. I'm not in the right mood at all.'

'But food makes everything better, doesn't it? You told me that.'

Raffaella managed a dry laugh. 'I'm sure I didn't use those exact words.'

'It was something like it. Please, please, please.'

'*Va bene*, Stella, *va bene*. I will go and scrub my hands.'

'Thank you.' Stella smiled. 'You've saved me.'

'I'll bring some of Antonio's vinegars with me, and one or two other things. I won't be long. Try to stop Francesca doing anything disastrous in the meantime.'

'OK ... and I'll knock on Tosca's door on my way back to the car.'

'Yes, please do.' Raffaella sounded grim again.

Aside from the colour of the shutters, Tosca's house was the twin of Raffaella's; she even had a few pots of herbs outside the door. Stella knocked, then waited a while and knocked again. No one came. She tried sending a quick text: *I'm outside. Are you home?* But there was no reply and, giving up, she made her way to the car.

Driving back to Villa Rosa, she managed to convince herself that Tosca was with Roberto. With both of them disappearing at the same time, it was the obvious conclusion. Hopefully they were together now enjoying some romance and passion, and there was no need to worry.

Francesca for one wasn't buying into the idea. She gave an emphatic shake of the head when Stella shared her news.

'No, no, Roberto won't be with Tosca, he'll be in Bali surfing, I'm certain of it. That's where he was the last time, some small place the family can't get to him. He's not interested in the linen business, doesn't want the responsibility, but Angelica can't accept that. Tell me, how did the old woman seem to you when you saw her in the shop?'

'Not happy.'

Francesca smiled. 'Good.'

'Doesn't this make things worse for you, though? If Roberto has really gone then Gennaro will have to stay living with his mother indefinitely.'

'That's what she will want. But why should she always have things her way?' Francesca was wearing a witchy expression. 'Maybe she's about to find out she can't control all of us.'

The news her mother-in-law was working behind the counter of the linen shop instead of her put Francesca in such a good mood she didn't even show signs of minding when she heard Raffaella was to share her kitchen and help prepare the dinner party. As she unpacked the shopping, she started to run through the dishes she was planning to make.

Stella headed her off. 'Let's have some coffee and wait for Raffaella. She's looking forward to an afternoon cooking with you. She said not to get going without her.'

As soon as she walked through the door Raffaella took control, as Stella had known she would. She checked the contents of the bags and jars cluttering every surface and listened to Francesca then remade her menu, cutting the more complicated dishes and adding a few of her own. Francesca tried to argue but was silenced by a glare.

'First we need to have a quick lunch,' Raffaella declared. 'Stella, put some of the cheese and the prosciutto out on the table; Francesca, make a salad. And there is bread? Yes, good. We will eat then we will cook.'

The afternoon was a productive one. Flanked by two busy cooks Stella made herself useful, washing dishes, stirring a sauce, pulling out platters and serving bowls as they were needed. Raffaella and Francesca did the tasting, discussing whether a dish needed more seasoning or perhaps the acid of a little vinegar to liven the palate, both absorbed in what they were creating.

'You know, Francesca, you're not so bad at this.' Raffaella sounded surprised. 'Have you ever considered training as a chef?'

She frowned. 'Not really. I imagine it would be very hard work?'

'And long hours,' Raffaella agreed. 'You have to love it.'

'This is what I love,' Francesca said. 'Cooking for friends, entertaining. You would think the Russo family would throw a lot of dinners but they never do. Angelica has no real friends and Gennaro is always too busy. It's boring. When that big house is mine I will fill it with people and parties.'

'When it's yours?' Stella asked quizzically.

'Sooner or later it will be. I just have to get rid of Angelica. Now she's working in the linen shop it would make sense for her to live in the little apartment above it. More convenient, don't you think?'

'My old place, it would be perfect for one,' agreed Raffaella. 'And actually Angelica lived there for a while years ago so it would be like going home.'

'Exactly.' Francesca grinned happily. 'Then Gennaro and I will have the house and we can start a family like he wants and begin living our own lives. It all makes sense; he just doesn't see it yet.'

'Francesca, you are such a schemer.' Stella couldn't help smiling. 'Do you really think you can pull it off?'

'Why not? So far things are working out the way I want them to, aren't they?'

'But you said you wanted to go to Rome, have a career, see the world?' pointed out Stella. 'What happened to all of that?'

Francesca shrugged. 'Did I?'

'Yes, you did. I distinctly remember.'

Raffaella seemed amused. 'What people say they want and what they really want are often two different things, Stella. Have you not noticed that yet?'

'I want what I've always wanted, right from the beginning when I married Gennaro,' said Francesca defensively.

'Let me guess,' said Raffaella. 'You want to be *Signora* Russo, to have the house, the status, the wealth, most of all to be rid of your mother-in-law. That's what all this is about, not travel and freedom. Am I right?'

Francesca tilted her chin. 'We can still travel, Gennaro and I. We can do all sorts of things once we're in charge of our own lives. I'm only trying to make that happen a little sooner. I can't wait around for it any longer.'

It was early evening when Neil and Otis came over to join them. The setting sun was throwing a golden light across the terrace and they sat outside with glasses of icy limoncello, letting the last rays of the sun warm their skin.

Stella had changed into a different, slinkier dress. Neil was wearing jeans, a crease carefully ironed into them, and a shirt with a retro pattern that she rather liked. He was questioning Raffaella about the area, where they should go now they had a car, what they should see, and Francesca kept jumping in to contradict the advice she gave. 'No, that's not the best beach. There is another one further south that is sandier and prettier. Neil and Otis would prefer it, I'm sure.'

The dinner was a long one. They lingered over every course: pillows of pasta filled with ricotta and a walnut pesto, a chicken dish flavoured with rosemary from the garden, artichokes steamed and served in deep bowls with their juices, scallops lazing in their shells amid a light lemony sauce, parcels of savoy cabbage leaves stuffed with spiced meat and pine nuts, and then berries soaked in fig vinegar and a creamy tiramisu. They ate until the moon was overhead and the table lit by candles, and even Otis couldn't manage another mouthful.

Neil opened another bottle of wine. 'That was one of the best meals I've eaten and I've been to a lot of good restaurants in my time,' he declared.

'I didn't have very much to do with it,' Stella was quick to admit. 'It would have been salad and an omelette if I'd been in charge.'

'I'm not much of a cook either, otherwise I'd invite you back to our place. Perhaps we could take you out in Triento one night instead.' Neil turned to Francesca. 'Is there a restaurant you'd recommend?'

'No need to go all the way to Triento; there is a pizza place a little way up the road,' she told him.

'After all this amazing food we'll have to do a bit better than pizza.'

'No, no,' she assured him, 'it's very good. Better to avoid Triento for now. At night that road is a nightmare, so many accidents, so you should wait until you're more used to it.'

Scraping back her chair, Raffaella got to her feet. 'Francesca is right about the road. I'm tired and shouldn't wait any longer to drive it. Sorry, Stella, I'm leaving you with dirty dishes.'

'Don't worry, there'll be plenty of time to wash up in the morning.'

Francesca sprang from her chair. 'Otis and I will do it. You stay here, Stella, have another glass of wine – you don't have to drive anywhere after all.'

Stella lit the fire and sat with Neil in the circle of its

warmth, glasses topped up. As they talked they kept finding things in common: books they liked, places they loved; things they found funny or infuriating. They were so deep in conversation neither of them noticed Francesca and Otis had finished cleaning the kitchen and both had slipped away to their beds.

'The stars are amazing.' Neil tilted back his head. 'I suppose there are no city lights to ruin them, just a few houses and that statue illuminated on the hill, and everything else is blackness with pinpricks dotted across it.'

'Dramatic, isn't it? I love sitting out here at night.'

'We should go down to the beach, look at the sky from there,' he suggested. 'It's not far to walk, is it?'

'Not really, I guess the quickest way would be down through the garden and over the rocks. There's a pathway but I don't fancy it in the dark. By road it will take a little longer.'

'Let's do it. We need a walk after all that eating; it'll help the digestion.' Neil patted his flat stomach. 'There must be a torch, surely. I'll go back to my place and have a look if you like.'

'Leo's got one. It's in the storeroom; I'll grab it.'

By torchlight they walked the silent lanes, giggling like kids on an adventure, past houses with their shutters closed and their rows of vines and vegetables all in darkness, through a tunnel beneath the railway line and past the empty car park until they reached the steps that led down to the beach.

'Careful now. Here, you take the torch,' said Neil.

The beach was all theirs; footsteps crunching over the pebbles, waves crashing on the shore, but still they spoke in whispers as though concerned about disturbing someone.

'How cold is the water?' asked Neil.

'Pretty chilly – at least it was the other day.'

He kicked off his sandals. 'I'm going in for a paddle to see.'

Stella watched as he walked into waves tipped by moon-light and heard him gasp as the chill hit him. 'It's lovely,' he called back to her. 'Come in.'

'You're lying.'

He laughed. 'No, I'm not. I'm going in deeper. I might even have a swim. Come in.'

'I don't have a towel with me or a swimsuit,' she pointed out.

'It's dark and there's no one here to see. Come on, Stella, let's do it. I dare you. Don't be wussy.'

'But I am a wuss.'

He laughed again. 'I don't believe that for a second.'

Self-consciously, Stella slipped behind a wall of rock and stripped off to her underwear, thankful it was sensible, plain cotton, but still feeling ridiculously daring. As quickly as possible she ran across the sand and into water so icy it took her breath away.

'You crazy woman,' called Neil, heading back to the shore to throw off his own clothes and join her.

They paddled out beyond the gently breaking waves until the water felt like silk against their skin. Floating on her back, face to the sky, Stella said, 'Look at the stars now.'

Neil sighed. 'A couple of days ago I was in a panic trying to finish up work, pack bags, find the passports, and get to the plane on time. Now I'm here swimming under the stars. Life's not all bad, is it?'

'I've never been swimming in the sea after dark before,' Stella confessed.

'Me neither. It's what holidays are for, though, isn't it? Moments like this. Escaping your everyday self.'

Stella tried to recall her everyday self. She seemed almost a stranger, that woman with a life as neat and restrained as the clothes hanging in her wardrobe. Was this new bold-ness only a holiday feeling? Once the sand had been shaken from the bottom of her suitcase and the photographs shown around would she put away this other version of herself? As the waves washed her gently back in towards the shore, Stella realised that she hoped not.

Dear Stella, how are things going? I heard from my friend Rosie today and she says she saw you in the village. Apparently your houseguest is sticking around. I hope Francesca isn't being a nuisance. I know how she can be pushy but this is your time at Villa Rosa, so if you don't want her there you must tell her so. Use me as a reason if you need to, say I'm very fussy about the house or something (actually that's probably true!). I expect she'll be offended but that can't be helped. And really it is a bit too much expecting someone she hardly knows to give her houseroom indefinitely.

Rosie tells me you seem happy and very relaxed. She says she invited you to Sunday lunch. So you are getting to know my friends and I am getting to know yours. It adds an interesting new twist to this house swap, doesn't it? I am finding it endlessly interesting actually! Leo.

Stella, sorry if this text wakes you but I've seen a light on in Tosca's place. She's there! Come over first thing in the morning – we need to make a plan. Raffaella.

The art of hoping

Stella planned to outfox Francesca with another early wake-up but found her already in the kitchen waiting, moka pot full of coffee, and primed with questions.

'How was it last night after I left?'

'Fine.' Stella opened the fridge to see what leftovers she could pick at for breakfast.

'Did you and Neil go somewhere together? I saw torch-light and heard voices.'

'We walked to the beach.' Stella dug a spoon into the tiramisu and took a taste. 'Mm, even better now than it was yesterday.'

'What time did you get back?'

'Not sure, but I'd say it was fairly late.'

'And?'

'And nothing; I went to my bed and he went to his, if that's what you're asking.'

'That seems a wasted opportunity.'

'Francesca, I've only just met him.'

'He likes you; I can tell. And he's attractive, so what's stopping you? You must have at least kissed?'

'No!'

'Really?' Francesca sounded disappointed. 'He won't be around for long, you know. You shouldn't waste too much time, not if you like him.'

'I'll just rush over now and seduce him then, shall I?'

'I'm serious, Stella; if you want something then you have to make it happen. You can't wait around, hoping.'

'What I want is another coffee and some more of this tira-misu for breakfast and then I need to pay a visit to Raffaella. That's as far as my plans go for now.'

'You're forgetting that we're all going out for pizza.' Francesca smiled. 'So you will have another chance.'

When Stella had read Leo's email very late the night before she had been feeling warm towards Francesca and hadn't thought an excuse to get rid of her was needed. Now she was reconsidering. Clumsy attempts at matchmaking had never been her favourite thing but this time she was finding it especially discomforting.

For there had been a moment, right at the end of the evening, when they were saying goodbye at the gates of Villa Rosa, she had thought Neil was going to kiss her. Not even a moment, more a heartbeat or two, then he stepped back and gave her a lopsided smile that might have meant anything.

Stella had whispered goodnight and slipped away quickly. Damp-haired still from her swim, skin taut and salty, she had felt relieved, and leaning back against the locked door of Villa Rosa, tried to work out why. Oddly enough, Leo seemed to be the reason. She was free to kiss whoever she wanted but not right there, not just outside the gates of his house; it would have felt wrong somehow, disloyal. How could she explain that to Francesca, who saw life in such stark black and white because she had never had a reason not to.

Driving the coast road, the blue expanse of sea at her shoulder, Stella remembered how once she had hoped life would make more sense as she got older; instead it only seemed more complicated. A kiss was always more than just a kiss at her age; it brought expectations and hopes with it. A kiss changed the game.

Taking the road down to the harbour, she sighed, half-wishing Neil had never appeared and everything had stayed simple. Now he was going to be there, in her mind and on her doorstep, for two whole weeks. Stella hoped whatever happened, they would both handle it graciously.

The harbour was busy by the time she arrived and Stella had to park on the hillside and walk the rest of the way. Today the place looked perfect, sun shining, sleek yachts bobbing on a sheen of still water, trawlers moored against the sea wall, a pale gold crescent of sand with children playing, their parents drinking coffee at the tables of the café just above. But somewhere, in one of those houses facing out on it all, a woman was feeling so low she wouldn't answer her door or take a phone call. What were they going to do about Tosca? Make a plan, Raffaella had said, but Stella couldn't imagine what it might be.

The door to Raffaella's house had been left ajar for her, but still she knocked and called out a greeting before walking in.

'Hello, it's me.'

'Yes, yes, come in. You're late. I expected you earlier.'

'We didn't arrange a time,' pointed out Stella, and then she realised Raffaella was wearing the red dress again, orange scarf arranged expertly round her neck. 'Oh, look at you.'

'Today needs some colour,' she said.

Stella was glad to see her like this. Perhaps those bright clothes really might help make a difference. 'Have you thought of what we should do about Tosca?'

'I spent half the night lying awake and came up with all sorts of wild plans until at last I realised we should behave the way she would in our position: demand a response and refuse to go away until we get it. She will be in a rage when she does answer the door but we'll deal with that when it happens. OK?'

Stella didn't have a better idea. 'Fine, if you think that's the way, let's do it.'

'One more thing.' Raffaella rummaged in the drawer of a

wooden dresser, and in producing a shiny red bangle, slipped it on her arm. 'There, I think that completes the look, don't you?'

'Perfect.' Stella was pleased.

Standing on Tosca's doorstep, Raffaella outlined the finer details of the plan. 'I'll knock and ring the bell repeatedly. You call her. I have the number of the house phone here for you, too. Just keep dialling and letting it ring. We are going to drive her crazy.'

'You're right, she'll be furious.'

'Yes, she will; but that's better than unhappy, isn't it?'

'I guess so.' Stella wasn't confident of success. 'I suppose we can only give it a go. We have to do something.'

Tosca held out for longer than Stella had imagined she might. They rang and knocked for almost an hour, Raffaella refusing to give up, until at last the door opened a crack and a torrent of angry Italian poured through.

Raffaella put her shoulder to the door, pushing. So much smaller and lighter, Tosca didn't have the strength to resist for long. Even Stella recognised the Italian words she was shouting as curses.

She looked tired. Her skin was waxy and she seemed to have dropped weight, her cheekbones standing out from her face in stark relief, her eyes glinting with anger and smaller without the make-up she usually layered on them. Now she was shouting in English.

'Leave me in peace. Can't the two of you take a hint? I don't want to see you; I don't want to see anyone; I want … I want …' She stopped, stared at Raffaella as if noticing her for the first time. 'What are you wearing?'

'My new outfit. Do you like it?'

Tosca's expression was distrustful.

'I'm out of mourning now,' Raffaella told her.

'Yesterday I saw you from my bedroom window and you were wearing black,' Tosca pointed out.

'Yes, I was. But I don't have to be the same person today that I was yesterday,' said Raffaella. 'I can change if I choose to.'

'Good for you, but that doesn't give you an excuse for this crazy behaviour. Who do you think you are, hammering on my door for half the morning?' Tosca was haughty.

'I'm your friend; I'm all the family you've got left. Are you going to let me in or do we have to stand on the doorstep yelling at each other like a couple of common fishermen's daughters?'

'Isn't that what we are?' Tosca stepped aside but not quite far enough for them to pass.

'We are that and we are so much more. Let us in, Tosca. Just let us in.'

Where Raffaella's home was filled with layers of people's lives, this one was so plain it might have been a holiday rental. The furniture looked cheap and the walls were bare aside from a couple of framed photographs and a small nook with a dusty statue of Our Lady. Stella was surprised. She had expected Tosca's private space to look as stylish as she did but it seemed she hadn't bothered to make any effort at all.

'I suppose you want coffee?' Tosca sounded resigned.

Raffaella nodded. 'Do you have any food? No, of course not. Stella, please will you go back to my house. There are some biscotti in the cupboard; bring them and whatever else you feel like.'

Stella did as she was told. Suspecting the pair needed a few moments alone, she didn't rush, checking the fridge and cupboards and putting bread and cheese into a basket along with the biscotti Raffaella had requested.

By the time she got back the atmosphere had changed. Both women were sitting at the kitchen table and to Stella it looked as if Tosca may have been crying.

'Now eat,' Raffaella said, unpacking the basket.

'Eat, eat, that's all I hear from you. It's not the solution to everything, you know,' Tosca responded.

'You are half-starved; it's not attractive.'

'Who cares?'

'You will when we're speed-dating and you look a hundred years old.'

'There will be no speed-dating,' Tosca huffed. 'No one is interested.'

'Actually lots of people are interested. While you've been shut away here I've been getting organised. The date is set, I've made a flyer, put the word out.' Raffaella said it so airily even Stella was convinced she might be telling the truth.

'Really?' Tosca sounded more dubious.

'Obviously there is still a lot to do. The internet.' Raffaella waved a hand dismissively. 'That's your department. I can't do this all alone, you know.'

'And you think this is going to cheer me up?'

'No.' Raffaella gestured towards her own dress. 'I'm out of mourning and I'm the one who needs cheering up. A good friend would help me.'

Tosca shook her head. 'You're an incorrigible old woman.'

Raffaella pressed her lips together but failed to stop a smile. 'I hope so.'

It turned out that Raffaella had been lying, or exaggerating a little, as she preferred to call it. There was no flyer and no interest in their speed-dating evening, she admitted as soon as they left Tosca's place, having extracted a promise that she would join them later for pizza.

'I'm sure you can make a flyer, can't you?' she said to Stella briskly. 'You have a computer.'

'No printer, though.'

'The post office in Triento will print things. You can distribute the flyer around the bars and shops while you're there and then tomorrow drive around taking them further afield.'

'Exactly what will I say on these flyers?'

'Speed-dating on Saturday evening at six thirty p.m. The venue is my *trattoria*. Drinks and nibbles provided, all welcome. I'll write the words out for you in Italian. You'll only need to copy them.'

If Stella organised something she liked to do it properly. 'Saturday is little more than a week away,' she pointed out. 'It seems too soon. People will have to RSVP after all.'

'We can't wait any longer. This is about getting Tosca excited about life again, giving her a reason to leave the house and rejoin the world. It's a one-off event so it doesn't matter if it's a little chaotic; actually it will be more fun.'

'We will need someone to adjudicate.' Stella was focused on the practicalities.

'Francesca is the one for that obviously; doesn't she love bossing people around?' said Raffaella.

'Yes, but she may still be in hiding in Villa Rosa ... although I do hope not,' Stella admitted.

'I'm sure everything will be sorted out for her by then, one way or another.'

'Really?'

Raffaella nodded. 'I will be very impressed if she gets the better of Angelica Russo, and I'm beginning to think she has a chance. She knows exactly what she wants and that's half the battle.'

Dear Leo, speed-dating is back on! Long story but now it's Raffaella in charge of things so it's sure to happen – that woman is a doer. The big night is just over a week away and we're in a frenzy trying to work up as much interest as we can. We're holding it at Raffaella's trattoria. Shame you're not here – you could come and boost the numbers!

Thanks for your suggestion re using you as an excuse to get rid of Francesca. I did consider it (she was being especially trying) but there's a part of me that wants to see how her scheming turns out. She thinks she's going to get exactly what she wants but may well be underestimating her mother-in-law.

And yes, on Sunday I'm going to have lunch at your friend Rosie's place. Francesca is invited too but seems terrified to leave Villa Rosa in case someone spots her and tells her husband. So I'm taking my new neighbours instead. Oh, that's right, I forgot to say that an English man and his son have rented the place next door. They're great company and Neil – that's the man – is keen to see the olive estate.

I ought to go. I'm supposed to be designing and distributing a flyer for the speed-dating evening and I'm procrastinating.

Are you sure you don't want to come? You could fly over for the weekend! Stella.

It was nice having a project. Stella was rather proud of her design for the flyer and it caused some excitement when she had copies printed off at the post office. Both the staff and customers were intrigued; and one young woman chased her down the street to ask if there was an age limit.

'No, everybody is welcome, like the flyer says. It's just a fun evening, a chance to get together and maybe meet new people,' said Stella.

'No one has ever done anything like this round here before. Was it your idea?'

'Francesca Russo from the linen shop is running things,' replied Stella, although she hadn't asked her yet. 'She'll be an excellent adjudicator, I think.'

'Oh yes, I know Francesca – this is a great plan.' The woman laughed. 'I'm definitely coming and I may bring my aunt.'

There were reactions to make Stella smile everywhere she went. The butcher lamented that he was married and his wife surely wouldn't let him attend. The woman in the pharmacy asked for extra flyers for her friends, the stallholders in the market called friendly insults to one another.

'Speed-dating, Carlo, you should do it. If a woman doesn't have time to get to know you properly you may have a chance with her.'

'Speed-dating? You've never done anything at speed in your life, Matteo.'

From one end of Triento to the other, Stella's flyers provoked so much interest she began to worry so many people would turn up that the *trattoria* might prove too small to hold them all. It also seemed that far more women than men were going to come and she wasn't sure how they would manage that.

'Stop worrying,' Raffaella said, when she phoned her in a minor panic. 'If you start telling the men we have too many women then I'm quite sure it will work out. When you've finished in the village bring some flyers down here and I'll help you take them round.'

'It all seems so disorganised,' Stella said anxiously.

'When Ciro and I opened the doors of the *trattoria* each day we never knew how many customers would appear – none at all or double the number we could comfortably handle. Somehow we always managed with whatever the moment threw at us. This will be the same.'

'OK.' Stella tried to feel reassured. 'I'll come down to you now. Just wait till you see people's faces when they read the flyer.'

'Don't forget to put one through Tosca's door,' Raffaella reminded her. 'She's the reason we're doing this, after all.'

After so much rushing about, it was a relief to get back to Villa Rosa and sit out in the shade on the terrace with a cup of tea and her laptop to check for emails. Her mood lifted when she saw that there was one from Leo.

Dear Stella, I wish I could see the people of Triento speed-dating one another. I'm smiling just thinking about it. If only I could join in, but the weekends are busy as that's when most of the volunteers come to help and I need to be here co-ordinating. We've finished preparing the ground now and we're starting to plant. It's important not to leave that too late in case (by some remote chance) the summer is a dry one. And I'm enjoying it now. All the dull paperwork and the meetings are finished with. Getting in there, dirtying my hands, seeing things go into the ground and the area start to green is my favourite part of the process – well, that and the cold beer at the end of the day.

So sadly speed-dating will have to happen without me. I look forward to hearing about it, though. I wonder if there will be any unexpected romances? Just think, people may fall in love thanks to you and eventually babies may be born. Who knows what ripples will spread from this one thing you do. You may help change the landscape of Triento for ever. Leo.

Oh no, Leo, don't make me feel any more responsible. Raffaella keeps telling me to calm down, that Italians expect a healthy level of chaos but I'm really not the person to leave these kinds of things to chance.

I'll be very surprised if any romances spring from the evening. Even Tosca seems to be having second thoughts. When I dropped off a flyer to her place earlier she rolled her eyes and when I reminded her the whole thing was her idea she said, 'That doesn't necessarily mean it is a good one.' How ironic would it be if she didn't turn up?

It's probably for the best that you're not tempted to abandon your garden and come. I'm concerned the whole thing is going to be a fiasco. Argh! Stella.

Hi Stella – I have to admit I thought it was a mad idea myself. Surely you could meet every single person in Triento if you stood in the main piazza for long enough. If I were you I would be delivering flyers further afield – but I expect you've thought of that. And if it's any comfort sometimes the ideas I've thought good are the ones that have turned into a fiasco and things that seemed to have no chance of working have surprised me.

Also I'm sure your friend Raffaella will provide excellent drinks and nibbles! Leo.

The pizza place Francesca had been so determined they should go to was tucked into the hillside, a low-slung building with an outdoor dining area and a view towards the sunset. Claiming the best table, they sat down, Francesca not especially subtle about making sure Neil was positioned right beside Stella.

Wine was ordered and bottles of sparkling water delivered to the table. By the time Tosca arrived they were eating fried croquettes of potato with stringy melted cheese at their centre. She had managed to restore her appearance since they had left her that morning. Now her hair fell in soft waves, the paleness of her skin was hidden beneath make-up and a dress in oyster shaded silk brought some shape to her too-slim figure. Still, to Stella's eyes she looked delicate, and not especially happy to be there.

'Raffaella tells me this is the place where they put fries on the pizza,' she said disparagingly, once she'd introduced herself to Neil and Otis.

'They only do that for the tourists and children,' Francesca hurried to explain. 'Just smell the pizza cooking now, the mozzarella bubbling and the prosciutto roasting and the fragrance of fresh basil. Delicious, yes?'

'Hmm.' Sounding unconvinced Tosca picked up a menu. 'There are better places to eat but I'm sure you've got your reasons for choosing this one.'

'I like it here,' Francesca insisted.

'Of course you do,' Tosca said. 'Oh and I hear a rumour that your brother-in-law Roberto left rather suddenly? Is that true?'

'He's run away again. It's what he does whenever there is too much pressure from Angelica. He takes his surfboard and finds a place to escape to.'

'Who can blame him?' Tosca didn't seem especially troubled. 'Not me, certainly.'

'I thought you two were getting on rather well.'

'He is fun,' Tosca said coolly. 'Good company.'

'I'm sure he'll be back when he runs out of money. And he'll expect to fit in again like he was never away; that's what always happens. But it may take a while so I wouldn't wait around.'

'You are always full of such excellent advice, Francesca, thank you.'

Francesca gave her a wary look. 'I just meant—'

'Yes, yes, I know what you meant. There's no need to spell it out any further.' Tosca sounded amused. 'Try to be a little more subtle, *cara*. You'll find people appreciate it.'

Stella hoped she was as indifferent as she seemed about Roberto's disappearance. It was so very hard to tell with Tosca. She liked to be in charge of the way people felt about her, Stella knew that. And tonight, with her beauty so fragile, she could see how just easy it would be to hurt her.

The waiter brought out a carafe of white wine along with dishes of glossy-coated green olives, crunchy savoury biscuits and salty nuts for them to snack on. He filled their glasses and they clinked them with whomever they could reach down the length of the table.

As they grazed on the food Stella noticed how transfixed Neil seemed by Tosca. In turn Stella watched him, wondering what was going through his mind. Of course, he must find her attractive, with her glossy lips and kohl-lined eyes, her cheekbones slanting and her extra slenderness.

Finally Neil cleared his throat and asked, 'Tosca, I was just wondering, have you ever done any modelling?'

She eyed him over her menu. 'Not really. I did something like it for a while, years back, but not proper modelling.'

'Your face, your bone structure, you'd be perfect,' Neil told her.

Tosca laughed dismissively. 'Really? I'm a little old, don't you think? Modelling is only for the younger girls.'

'That's changing.'

'I'm sure it isn't, not really. Maybe there are one or two designers who use an older woman as a novelty but that doesn't make for a career.'

'Actually you're wrong,' said Neil bluntly.

Tosca seemed taken aback. 'I am?'

'Companies like mine, we're aiming our eyewear at mature people and we're always looking for the right faces to help sell our products – beautiful, aspirational, yes, but not young. My marketing manager complains constantly how difficult it is to cast the right people.'

'You should send Tosca's photograph to her,' put in Francesca.

'I was kind of working up to asking if I might,' Neil admitted.

'Thanks, but I'm not interested.' Tosca dismissed him.

'Really, that's a shame. Worth a try though, and I should give you my card in case you ever change your mind—'

Francesca interrupted. 'He only wants to send a picture,

Tosca. It's not like you're signing a contract. You should let him. I could take one now with my phone.'

'Francesca, no …' Stella tried to caution her but she wasn't interested in listening.

'What's the point in being so glamorous if you're not going to use it to your advantage?' she said. 'You could make money from this, good money, and who knows where it might lead? I don't understand why you won't even think about it. If I looked like you do then I'd jump at the chance to be a model.'

'I expect you would.' Tosca turned to Raffaella. 'Surely you have an opinion to share?'

She shook her head. 'Not me.'

'That doesn't seem very likely.'

'I'm a changed woman, as I told you earlier.'

'Your clothes have changed but that's all.'

'My clothes are only the beginning. Tomorrow morning Benedetto and Maria are coming to see me. I'm going to offer them the lease on the *trattoria* like you suggested. It's time for a new stage of my life, a real change. I'm ready for it.'

Tosca stared at her, eyes narrowing. 'And you think I should be ready for change too? Is that it?'

'No, that's not it at all; quite the opposite.'

The two women glared at each other across the table and switched to talking in Italian, Francesca looking from one to the other as they volleyed words back and forth.

Neil seemed uncomfortable. 'Did I cause this?' he asked Stella in a low voice.

'It's been brewing for a while.'

'They sound angry. What are they saying, do you think?'

'I don't speak Italian but as I understand it both have strong opinions on how the other should live her life. It may not sound like it but actually they're the best of friends.'

The two women had raised their voices and were talking

over each other. 'You're right, it doesn't sound like it at all,' said Neil.

'You know, I think you're right – I can imagine how Tosca would get lots of work as a model,' Stella told him. 'She's not tall enough for the catwalk but I bet she photographs like a dream.'

'Yes, it's a shame. I have a new range I'd love to shoot on her – reading glasses, very cool ones in retro styles. But if she's not interested—'

Raffaella stopped shouting and said to Neil in English, 'She is interested.'

Tosca hissed at her. Throwing down her menu, she reached for her bag, got to her feet and swept out of the pizzeria without a backward glance.

'Oh dear,' said Neil.

'She is bored,' Raffaella told him. 'She wasn't born for a peaceful life. She likes glamour and excitement, wearing beautiful clothes and going to stylish places. She flourishes in big cities with crowds of people, noise and drama. She will be interested in your proposition; it's just a matter of timing. Give me your card and I'll make sure she gets it when she's in a more receptive mood.'

'Sure.' Neil passed it over. 'I can't imagine that she'll change her mind though. She seemed pretty definite to me.'

Raffaella shrugged. 'We'll see.'

A waiter had been circling the table and now saw his chance, darting in to take their orders, scribbling them quickly onto his notepad, as though in a rush to get away before another scrap started.

Darkness fell and they sat in a pool of warm yellow light, teasing a conversation along, pleased when the pizza finally arrived and talk could be replaced by eating.

Francesca hadn't lied about how good it was; thin crusts were perfectly charred at the edges, toppings molten on the tongue, a generous slick of oily tomato puddled with buffalo mozzarella and littered with prosciutto and basil. Even Raffaella nodded her approval. 'Almost as good as my husband Ciro's pizza used to be, but not quite.'

As soon as their plates were clean, Francesca started yawning theatrically and complaining of exhaustion. She couldn't have been more obvious.

'Would you mind dropping me back at Villa Rosa?' she asked Raffaella. 'Maybe Otis is tired and would like to come too? Then Stella and Neil can stay on and have a last drink. There's no need for them to rush.'

'Of course, if that's what you want. I'm tired too and tomorrow will be a busy day. I have my meeting about the *trattoria* first thing and then Stella and I have a lot of work to do delivering more flyers for our speed-dating event. Ah yes, I need to talk to you about that, Francesca. Let's discuss it in the car.'

'Speed-dating event?' asked Neil.

'*Si, si.*' Raffaella rummaged in her handbag. 'I have some of the leaflets here. I was going to leave a few with the waiter. Stella will tell you about it. You should join us, *signore*. Everybody is welcome.'

'Please come,' Stella begged him. 'It's happening next Saturday night and I don't think we're going to have any men, just loads of women.'

Otis had been very quiet all evening, playing with his phone, seemingly not listening to the conversation; now he spoke up. 'Dad's not into stuff like that.'

'It's just for fun, really,' Stella reassured him, 'a bit of a laugh. He'd be into that, wouldn't he?'

Otis set his face into a frown and didn't bother to answer.

Neil glanced at him anxiously. 'We'll see,' he said. 'In the meantime I'm keen on that last drink. Something sweet to finish off with, do you think?'

For Stella the evening ended just as the one before, with her and Neil outside the gates of Villa Rosa, saying goodnight.

This time she was aware that his son might be watching from the window of the neighbouring house, that anxious frown on his face again. Perhaps Neil was thinking the same.

'I guess I won't see you tomorrow if you're busy helping your friend,' he said.

'What are your plans?'

'If it's hot we'll hang out by the pool, otherwise I'll see what Otis wants to do.'

'Have fun together, either way.'

'Stella, I ...' He paused and she waited for him to finish. 'Perhaps you could swing by for a drink tomorrow evening once you've handed out all your flyers. I'm sure we'll be here.'

'A drink sounds good.' She pushed open the gate. 'Goodbye for now, then.'

He stood and watched her go. 'Yeah, goodbye,' she heard him say softly as she crossed the terrace.

Dear Leo, I'd been planning to swim every day and get fit but instead all I seem to be doing is eating and drinking. Tonight we had pizza in that place up the hill. Francesca swore it would be delicious and it truly was. I polished off the whole thing and now I can hardly move.

Oh well, I expect there will be plenty of opportunities to get fit when I'm back in London. Any idea when that might be? I know we said we'd leave things reasonably open-ended but I'll need time to get to grips with the idea of leaving Villa Rosa. I'm very at home here; I'm starting to feel as though I belong. Hopefully someday there will be a chance to come back. Life is unpredictable, though, isn't it? You can't bank on anything – watching my boss die so quickly taught me that. I'm quite sure Milly still had places she wanted to see and things she planned to do but she ran out of time. So I'm just happy to be here right now, having this adventure, getting to know a small part of a different country ... being surprised by it and myself.

I'm full of wine and pizza and I'm getting very sleepy so I'm going to put my laptop down and turn out the light. Thanks for listening, Leo. It's good to have you to confide in. I really hope you're well and not missing home too much – Stella.

Dear Stella, don't worry. I won't rush you away from Villa Rosa. Even when I finish there will be work for me to do in Napoli. It seems such a shame for you to miss being beside the sea at the height of the summer. Had you thought of staying on, renting a place perhaps, maybe even the one next door? That way we'd meet. I'd like that. It would be good to have the chance to get to know you properly; to swim in the sea together and sit on the beach. I have a feeling we'd get on well.

Of course, who knows what's going to happen at your speed-dating event? Perhaps you'll be married to the butcher and living in Triento by the time I get back there! Leo.

Hi Leo, the butcher is already married – he told me so himself. That's not a bad idea about the house next door, though. I've seen inside and it's nowhere near as nice as Villa Rosa but it has a pool and a bit of a garden so I'm sure I could stand it. It would be great to meet you at last – and we'd be neighbours! I suppose that would mean we'd stop sending emails? I look forward to finding them in my inbox. I'd miss them. Stella.

The road to love

Francesca actually sulked when she realised Stella had spent the night at Villa Rosa alone. She turned her back and refused to speak as she made morning coffee and remained aloof as they sat outside to drink it.

'Honestly, what's wrong with you?' asked Stella, losing patience.

'Women like you and Tosca, that's what's wrong.' Francesca made a face as if she had tasted something bitter. 'All these opportunities present themselves and you refuse to take them. I'm not interested, you say. I don't understand it.'

'Perhaps we need to make sure they are the right opportunities,' suggested Stella.

'And what if you wait so long they disappear?'

Stella looked at Francesca. She was edging near to attractive with her long dark hair, almond eyes and olive skin but there was a definite sharpness to her features that gave her a sly look and her mouth twisted a little when she smiled. She was smart though and almost certainly ambitious. What had her life been like growing up in a small, tucked-away place like Triento?

'I'm guessing you didn't have so many opportunities yourself,' said Stella.

'Only one and that was Gennaro. Other girls were interested in him but I made him like me best. I made him adore me.'

'Did you adore him?'

'Yes, of course.' Francesca was indignant. 'I wouldn't

have married him otherwise and certainly I wouldn't have stayed for all these years listening to him promise that soon we'd have a place of our own but never having it happen. I've been forced to make my own opportunities. They don't come along for me the way they do for you and Tosca.'

Stella stared out at the view. Each morning it seemed subtly different. Today the blue of the sea was choppy with white caps, and clouds were hanging low in the sky, soft light filtering through. She could smell woodsmoke from some smallholder's fire and hear the hooting horns of impatient drivers roaring along on the road above them.

'Your poor husband, not knowing that you're here; he must be so worried,' she said.

'He knows I can look after myself wherever I am.'

'Haven't you made him wait long enough?'

'Maybe,' Francesca admitted. 'Raffaella tells me I have a deadline. She wants me to preside over the speed-dating and says I must speak to Gennaro by then and sort things out one way or another.'

'What if he refuses to go along with your demands?'

'Then I will leave him,' Francesca said flatly. 'I don't want to but I will.'

Sidestepping the suggestion of another Italian lesson, Stella set off for a walk around the coast, this time heading south and finding the path steeper and crumbling in places. She hadn't got far when it seemed too perilous to carry on so, choosing a smooth rock, she sat down and, closing her eyes, basked in the sunshine.

Stella thought about Raffaella, who would be preparing for her meeting by now and ready to sign over the *trattoria* to a struggling couple from Naples, at least for the summer. She thought of Tosca, so quick to reject the idea she could be a model, afraid of failing again, of not meeting her own high standards. And she thought of Francesca, who needed to be convinced to get in the car and drive up to her husband in Triento, preferably today. Here on the rocks was a good place for thinking, peaceful and still, with a sailboat on the horizon the only sign of the world continuing on around her.

It wasn't until she climbed the steps back up to Villa Rosa that Stella noticed the gardening crew had been again and left without her seeing them. The lawn was mowed with edges neatened and all the dropped pomegranate flowers raked away; the tomato plants in the vegetable bed had been attached to stakes and between the rows neatly weeded. If she rented the house next door she might still be here when those tomatoes ripened and were picked, still here to taste their sweetness. But the place was likely to be pricey in the height of the season and with no paid work on the horizon Stella had to take care not to be extravagant. It wouldn't be the same anyway, that stark, impersonal house, not after Villa Rosa.

There was no sign of Francesca in the kitchen. Stella went round the house and walked back through the garden, calling her name, but she had made herself scarce. Possibly she was hiding out at Neil's place, waiting until Stella had driven away and there was no chance of her being coerced into Triento to face her husband. While it seemed as good a time as any to resolve things, clearly Francesca had other ideas.

Stella drove to the village alone, stopping in at her favourite bar for another coffee and walking past the linen shop to glance in on Angelica, already at her station, her face locked into its usual unfriendly grimace. At the post office she paid for more flyers to be printed off, provoking another ripple of interest when she told the woman behind the counter that she was going to distribute them in some of the surrounding villages.

'Don't bother with San Nicola. The men there are brutes, every one of them,' the woman advised her.

'Right, OK,' said Stella, still amazed at how engaged people seemed to be with the idea of speed-dating.

'Are you hoping to find an Italian romance for yourself?' the woman asked.

Stella took the stack of leaflets from the counter. 'Not really, I'm doing this for a friend.'

'Oh, a friend.' She gave a knowing smile. 'Yes, of course.'

Raffaella had written out a list of places they should visit and marked on a map the ones allocated to Stella. She seemed businesslike and brisk today, making no mention of her morning's meeting, with no time for niceties at all, it seemed.

'We have a lot of ground to cover so let's get on with it,' she said.

'Wouldn't it be more fun if we did this together?' suggested Stella.

'It will be faster if we split up, more efficient.'

'OK then.' Stella was disappointed.

'If you need company why not knock on Tosca's door? I don't see why we should be the ones running round while she sits at home and makes no effort.'

Stella didn't hold out much hope of Tosca even opening the door, never mind being keen to spend a day handing out leaflets. Nevertheless she tried.

'Tosca, hello,' she called, hammering out a rhythm with the brass doorknocker. 'Open up, please. I need a favour.'

'Again?' The door swung open and Tosca peered around it. She was wearing a white towelling bathrobe, her hair caught up in a messy topknot. 'Are you never to give me a peaceful morning? What favour?'

Stella waved the map at her. 'I have all these places to deliver flyers to and don't want to get lost driving to them.'

'Where is *she*?'

'You mean Raffaella? She's taken off by herself and is in

239

a bit of an odd state, actually. She had that meeting with Benedetto and Maria this morning; maybe it didn't go so well.'

'Hardly surprising ... she can be so unreasonable and stubborn. I hope she hasn't ruined her chances with them.'

'I didn't dare ask her,' Stella admitted. 'She didn't seem in the mood for questions.'

'Such a diva,' Tosca murmured. 'Oh well, it seems I will have to help you then. Come in for a moment while I get ready.'

It took considerably longer than a moment. Stella occupied herself examining the few personal items on display. In the kitchen three framed photographs hung on the wall. One was a large black-and-white portrait of a couple standing ramrod straight and staring gravely at the camera. She assumed these were Tosca's parents. The others were formal shots of small babies in christening gowns. In the living room there was another picture she presumed was of the same children but older now, a little girl holding her sister on her knee, both of them smiling.

Tosca found her staring at it. 'That is Annunziata. She died not long after the photograph was taken; a high fever, complications, it was very sudden and it broke my parents' hearts. I have only a hazy memory of her. To me, growing up, it always seemed like Raffaella was my big sister.'

'Did she look after you?' asked Stella.

'Oh yes, and she told me what to do all the time, just as she does today. I didn't mind it so much then. Now it drives me insane.'

'I never had sisters or brothers,' Stella said. 'My mother had several miscarriages so sadly it was just me. I do have a friend who is a bit like Raffaella though, one that likes to boss me round – Birdie, she's called. Usually it turns out that she's right.'

'Raffaella isn't right nearly as often as she likes to think.'

'Maybe she is this time though,' Stella said hesitantly, 'about the modelling I mean.'

'Oh no ... I'm not going to drive round in a car with you for half the day while you nag me,' Tosca warned her.

'I think you should consider it, that's all,' Stella dared suggest. 'Opportunities don't come along all that often, as someone pointed out to me very recently. But I'm not going to nag you, I promise.'

'Good. Let's go then and get this done.'

Tosca seemed to blossom with attention, whether it came from men or other women. She was a born performer, realised Stella as she trailed in her wake through the bars and shops of nearby villages. Everywhere she made an entrance, drawing people in and charming them, becoming more energised even as Stella was flagging.

The full force of Tosca's charisma was saved for men, especially those who were well dressed and without a wedding band on their fingers. Stella couldn't understand what she said to them but it was clear they were flattered, and most nodded and smiled as they folded flyers and slipped them into jacket pockets.

'Enough, we need a break,' said Stella. 'I'm starving and it's way past lunchtime.'

'Let's go to one more place.'

'Are we likely to find food there?'

Next on the list was a mountain town, perched high and almost deserted. There was only one small *trattoria* and the patron, a brusque older man, looked at his watch and shook his head when they asked to see a menu.

Tosca wasn't prepared to take no for an answer. She leaned her elbows on the counter and stretching forward, flashed a smile and said something in Italian to make him laugh. She gestured at Stella and pulled a rueful expression; she kept talking and he kept laughing.

'*Va bene, va bene.*' He poured a couple of glasses of wine, pushed them towards Tosca, and nodded at a table. 'No menu,' he said to Stella in English, waggling a finger in her face. '*Lagane e ceci*, two plates, *e basta.*'

'What is *lagane e ceci*?' she asked Tosca, as they sat down at the table.

'It's what he's making for his own lunch, a peasant dish of pasta and chickpeas; a little heavy for me but it seems we have left it too late for any other choices.'

'Nice of him to cook extra for us.'

She smiled. 'I'm not sure that nice has anything to do with it.'

The dish was a humble one, thick ribbons of pasta, softened tomato, nuggets of chickpeas and a mild burn of chilli, all slick with olive oil and served in a ceramic bowl chipped at its edges.

The patron pulled up a chair and ate with them, dabbing the oil from his lips with his apron. He wasn't an especially attractive man but Tosca held his gaze as she talked to him and let him feel that he might be.

He refused to take any cash for the food, accepting only one of the flyers, reading it, eyebrows raised.

'That one will come, just you see,' Tosca said, as they left.

'He's crazy about you and he's going to be disappointed.'

'Maybe he'll find someone else he likes; that's the point of speed-dating. Perhaps we'll create all sorts of matches, change people's lives.'

'That's what Leo says. The thought makes me feel slightly nervous ... the whole thing does, to be honest.'

'It's going to happen so no point worrying.' Tosca sounded upbeat. 'So where next is on the list? We still have some flyers left, don't we?'

Driving back through the gates of Villa Rosa, the last flyer finally given away and Tosca dropped back home, Stella felt exhausted. It had been a long day with a lot of time spent on the road, her at the wheel for far longer than she was used to. Without much enthusiasm, she recalled Neil's invitation for an evening drink. Really she ought to go – it might seem impolite if she didn't.

However, when Stella wandered over she noticed Neil's rental car wasn't there. The front door was locked, and although she knocked on it just in case, there was no sign of anyone around. Villa Rosa too was all closed up and in darkness. Stella made her own drink, with the last of Leo's gin and some rather flat tonic, and sat outside alone with it.

She was considering what there might be to cook for dinner when she heard the sound of an engine then car doors slamming. Wherever Neil had been, he was back it seemed. Francesca's voice called out goodnight and a few moments later she appeared through the gates, toting a beach bag, a smile on her face.

'*Ciao*, Stella,' she called.

'Hi, where have you been? I thought you weren't supposed to be leaving the house.'

'We went to the beach, Neil, Otis and me. But not the local one, a lovely sandy beach I know of further south. We had a beautiful day together. Neil wanted to ask you along but we couldn't find you. Sorry … I hope you don't feel left out.'

'No of course not, I was busy anyway so I couldn't have come.'

'Is that gin you're drinking?'

'There's none left.' Stella knew she was sounding tetchy. 'Actually Neil had invited me over to his place for drinks but he must have forgotten.'

'He thought we'd be back earlier, I expect. My fault for insisting on going so far. But you could go over now. I'm sure he'll be pleased to see you.'

'No, it's late and I'm tired. That's OK, there'll be another time. And there's wine in the fridge,' said Stella, trying to sound warmer. 'I'll get you a glass.'

'I'll fetch it. Do you want one too? You've nearly finished that. And I stopped off to buy fish on the way back so we have plenty for dinner. You will miss me when I've gone, you know.' Her tone was teasing. 'I am the perfect houseguest.'

Stella smiled. 'I don't know about perfect but the fish was a good idea. I'll find Leo's torch and go and pick something from the garden to go with it.'

Dear Leo, I had a candlelit dinner with Francesca this evening, outside, just the two of us, very romantic! She says I'll miss her when she's gone but still isn't giving any clue when that might be. She did do a good job with the fish – it was all crispy and lemony on the outside, and succulent through the middle. That fish was so amazingly fresh; she bought it from the boats. And the salad I put together came straight from your garden with a lemon from the tree squeezed over it and a heavy drizzle of that olive oil your friend Rosie gave me. It was the perfect meal, really, and Francesca managed not to torment me with any of her ridiculous ideas while we were eating it.

It's funny how other people see you, isn't it? I think Francesca imagines I've had it easy, that I don't appreciate all the advantages I've got, that I'm spoilt, even. But then life to her is straightforward; she knows what she wants and is completely focused on it. I can remember being like that once not so long ago. Too many things didn't go my way and I changed.

I have to say it is exasperating having her act superior; like she has it all worked out and I don't have a clue. There is this tiny, mean part of me that would quite like to see life come up and slap her on the face a couple of times. I don't feel like that deep down of course. I hope her husband allows himself to be manipulated into doing what she wants and they have babies and are happy. Of course, that's what I hope although I suspect she'll be unbearably pleased with herself if it happens.

How are things with you? Is work still going well? Do you think you'll manage to catch up with Birdie again before she goes on holiday? Stella.

Dear Stella, I had a drink with Birdie this evening, and her new girlfriend Emma joined us. I'm told that you'll be furious that I've met her before you. Birdie says to calm down and promises to send you photographs of them both from Scotland. They are talking about buying matching kilts; I think they're joking but at times I misread the English sense of humour so I can't promise you won't be seeing a lot of tartan. Anyway they seem very happy in that way some couples are when they first fall in love and everything seems rosier. Have you ever felt like that?

Of course I had to observe them very closely as I knew you would want details. Emma is striking, tall and very attractive, obviously intelligent. She does something in IT that she refused to explain because she said I wouldn't understand it. I wasn't at all offended as I'm certain she's right.

They touch a lot, they make eye contact; to me they seemed like people who are very sure about themselves and each other. But then I was looking at them from the outside and, as you say, things can appear very different viewed from that perspective. From the inside life always seems more humbling, doesn't it?

Gardening is humbling. You put a seedling into rich, well-prepared soil and it rewards you by wilting, looking sad and sickly for a few days. Usually it will rally, but not always. Sometimes for no obvious reason they wither and die. Or later on they catch diseases, are eaten by insects, get blown over in a high wind. The world is a dangerous and uncertain place, even if you're a plant. Someone like Francesca, who has had such a small life that everything in it seems straightforward, who may go to her grave feeling that way – I'm not sure if I envy her or feel sorry for all she's missing out on …

Right, I have finished my beer. It was never my drink of choice in Italy but here in London I have embraced it. And surely it doesn't count as drinking alone when I'm chatting to you on email as I sip it. That's what I'm telling myself anyway!

You are going to Rosie's for Sunday lunch tomorrow, yes? It is always an occasion. Have fun!

Oh and I am so envious of that fresh fish and the salad from my garden. It feels like everything I eat here comes out of plastic. Leo.

A long Italian lunch

Francesca couldn't make up her mind. One moment she was joining them for lunch at the olive estate, the next she wasn't so sure. Stella presumed she couldn't bear the idea of missing out.

'I've told Rosie that you're coming. Do you want me to text her again to let her know you've changed your mind?'

'Yes, no ... oh just give me a minute.' She was exasperating.

'Francesca, it's a simple invitation for lunch.'

'OK, but do you promise we'll go directly there? No stopping in Triento on the way?'

'There's no need for us to do that. I've got some wine here we can take.'

'Then I'll come ... definitely ... I think so.'

'You know there will be other people going besides us?' Stella felt she had to remind her.

'Yes but there's no chance of Gennaro being there. He will be eating at home with his mother; with me gone she will be doing all the cooking.' A satisfied smile spread over Francesca's face. 'Can you imagine how bad the food is?'

Stella could imagine it. Thinking of Gennaro, sitting in that sterile dining room, picking over some unappetising meal, most probably in silence, made her feel even more sorry for him.

'I hope he misses me more with every mouthful he takes,' Francesca said cheerfully.

Neil had offered to do the driving so they all piled into his car, Stella in the back seat next to Otis, Francesca wearing her disguise of hat and sunglasses, sitting low in the passenger seat, overly dramatic, as if she were playing a role in some spy movie.

Stella couldn't help finding it amusing. But perhaps Francesca's husband really was still combing the streets looking for her and worried sick that something bad had happened. The casual way she was prepared to hurt him was hardly funny.

'The Santi family are famously good cooks,' she was telling Neil now. 'I can't wait to see their place. We've never been invited there because my mother-in-law doesn't like them.'

'Does she like anyone?' Stella wondered.

'A few – the priests, the mayor, some of the boutique hoteliers who always buy our linens, the owners of the better restaurants. She gets along with the people she thinks matter.'

Neil laughed. 'She sounds awful.'

'Oh yes,' agreed Francesca. 'Actually I'm not sure what she has against the Santi family. It will be some offence taken years ago and never forgotten. They are successful people. Their olive oil is the very highest quality and is sold around the world. Perhaps she's jealous.'

They saw the trees before they reached the gates of the estate. There were so many of them, marching up the hills in neat lines, thousands of trees with silver-green leaves stretching away in every direction.

'Wow, that is some olive grove,' said Neil.

Pulling through the gates, Neil parked beneath a stand of well-spaced young trees, where other people had left their cars. They found everyone gathered in a courtyard that lay between a three-storey house and a smaller, older building with lemon trees espaliered over its trellis.

Rosie wasn't difficult to spot, fair-haired among so many dark heads. She looked coolly English in a floral print tea dress but greeted them like an Italian with warm kisses on both cheeks.

'I'm not going to introduce you to everyone because you'll never remember any of the names,' she said. 'But these are my husband Enzo's relatives, some of them at least. He has five sisters and they all have lots of children. Plus there are some cousins here, his parents of course, a few good friends.'

'How do you manage to cook for so many?' asked Stella.

'His sisters have helped me today. And actually before I married I used to be a food stylist, so it's sort of my thing. Come and meet Enzo and I'll pour you an *aperitivo*.'

Enzo had a sleek, wealthy look to him, with short greying hair and caramel skin, although his eyes and his brow were deeply furrowed.

'Ah, you are Leo's friend,' he said when he was introduced to Stella. 'It's a shame he's not here. I'd like him to see how his garden is doing.'

'Show it to Stella and she'll let him know,' Rosie suggested. 'I'm sure she and her friends would like a tour. Lunch is under control. The *antipasti* will be out by the time you get back.'

Enzo led them to the garden he seemed so proud of. It rose up a gentle slope behind a barn and was backed by a grove of old olive trees, their trunks twisted and split, their branches unpruned. Stella recognised it as a more undisciplined version of the garden at Villa Rosa with rows of straggling artichoke plants, sunflowers shooting up between them, beans racing over bamboo frames, rosemary taking over in the herb beds, marigolds opening their golden heads at the edges.

'My father takes care of all of this,' explained Enzo. 'He is supposed to be retired but he can't stop working. At least now he has the garden and he leaves the trees to me; I have that to thank Leo for. Papa used to pace up and down the groves, keeping an eye on everything; now this is his job and he lets me do mine.'

'An operation like this must take a lot to run,' said Stella. 'Has the estate been in your family for long?'

'My great-grandfather established it and I'll pass it on to my son.' Enzo smiled. 'Someday I'll step aside and be the one who tends this garden.'

He seemed so certain of the route he was meant to follow, very like Francesca in a way. Stella was finding herself beginning to envy people who believed life could be arranged so neatly.

'What if your son doesn't want to be an olive farmer?' she asked.

Enzo frowned. 'The groves are in his blood. Already he knows how to prune and helps at the harvest. Perhaps there will be a time when he looks for more excitement but I'm sure he'll come back and settle down eventually. Tradition is still very strong in this part of Italy. And family is the most important thing for many of us.'

He might have sounded smug had he not been so solemn. And when he had them pile into an old Land Rover so he could show them the full reach of the groves, Stella got more idea of how hard he must have to work to maintain his legacy.

By the time they got back from driving across the Santi acreage, trestle tables had been set beneath the gnarled old trees and covered in jugs of wine, baskets of bread and platters groaning with garlicky olives, roughly hewn salami and shards of grainy yellow cheese.

'We are very rustic,' Rosie told them. 'Sit wherever you want and help yourself.'

Stella was about to follow the others and take a place at the table when Enzo stopped her.

'*Signora*, a moment if you don't mind,' he said, his voice low.

She glanced back at him in surprise. 'Yes?'

'Francesca Russo, she is a friend of yours?'

Stella nodded.

'In the village people are saying she has run away from her husband and disappeared. But my wife tells me she is staying with you at Villa Rosa?'

'That's right, she is.' Stella saw the disapproval on his face. 'Just for a short time while she sorts herself out.'

'Her husband doesn't know this?'

'Not yet,' Stella admitted.

He stared at her for a moment. 'I see.'

Stella felt ashamed; perhaps he meant her to. 'I'm sure she's planning to talk to him soon.'

'I hope so.' His tone remained stern but he managed the trace of a smile and motioning towards the table with a hand, he added, 'There is nothing to be done right now. Please take a seat, *signora*, and enjoy your lunch.'

The noise level was intense. Everybody seemed to be shouting and no one doing any listening. This was how Stella had imagined a real Italian lunch would be, lively and chaotic. She smiled over at Neil, who was sitting beside Francesca on the other side of the table.

'Crazy,' she mouthed.

He nodded and smiled back, raising his glass to her.

Enzo's sisters ferried trays of baked pasta over to the table. More courses followed: red peppers blistered over the wood-fired barbecue, plates of tiny fishes fried in the lightest of batters, hunks of roasted lamb in an oily sauce of anchovies, parsley and garlic.

Someone brought their car closer and parked it with the doors wide open, blasting out Italian pop music from its stereo. An older couple got up and started dancing, the teenagers rolling their eyes at them, too cool to join in even if they were tempted to. At the far end of the table an argument briefly raged before ending in laughter. Otis was hanging out with a gang of other boys and seemed to be making himself understood with the help of sign language and a smartphone; Neil was smoking a cigar; Francesca got up to dance; Enzo's sister Concetta waved a tea towel aloft in time to the music.

'Do you do this every week?' Stella asked Rosie.

'Not usually with so many people but yes, Sundays are about family. This is when Enzo is happiest, with everyone he loves together at his table. It has become much more important to him as he's got older.'

'I can understand that,' said Stella. 'I don't really have any family left now.'

'No, me neither. I'm lucky to be part of all this. In London I still have a few good friends but that's all.'

'So you never miss it – your life there, your career?'

'Now and then, but I think I would miss Italy more. I belong here now. It took me a while to get used to the idea and to some people I'll always be an outsider, but not to the ones that count. Why do you ask? Have you been missing home while you've been here?'

'No, I'm totally in love with Italy; in fact I've been thinking about extending my stay. But even if I do, I'm only postponing the inevitable. I'll have to go back eventually.'

'Why do you have to?' asked Rosie. 'Couldn't you make a life here if you wanted?'

'I don't speak Italian.'

She shrugged. 'So learn it.'

'Francesca has been trying to teach me but I'm not a very good student. I suppose if I set my mind to it I'd get better.'

'Is that the only barrier, the language? There are no people you have to return to? No job.'

'Only my apartment, but I could rent that out.'

'So you are free. What have you got to lose?'

'Nothing at all,' Stella admitted.

The music was turned up even louder and, with conversation impossible, Rosie poured them both more wine then pulled her up to dance in the tree-dappled sunshine. Stella couldn't remember the last time she had moved her limbs to music. For a bit she jiggled about self-consciously and then a Michael Jackson track came on, one she had danced to in clubs when she was younger, and she let loose, arms in the air, hips swinging, letting the beat take her with it.

Afterwards, dropping back down on a chair, pink-cheeked and breathless, Stella watched as the others danced on. Rosie was up with Neil now, managing a reasonable jive to a song that belonged to a generation even older than theirs.

To Stella it seemed as if Rosie was good at living. It might very easily grind you down, a place like this: all the hard work and the weight of tradition, the forests of olive trees almost touching the horizon, lovely but monotonous. Somehow she must have found a way to make the best of things with her serious-faced husband and her son whose life was all planned for him.

If Stella did stay in Triento she wasn't sure she would ever feel a part of it like Rosie did. She was older for a start so there wouldn't be a family to anchor her, or a place with a pull as strong as this estate must have.

How long would it take to learn Italian well enough to get a job in a bar or even a souvenir shop for a bit of extra cash? Could she find another house swap to keep the bills down in the meantime? If she lost the holiday feeling and made Italy her home would she continue to love it so much? The questions danced through Stella's mind as she listened to the music and watched Neil with Rosie, jiving.

When the track finished they parted and Neil held out his hand to Stella. 'Come on then, have a dance with me.'

She stood up and stepped towards him as the next track began. It was out of pace with the others, a slower number, much too moody to jive to.

His arms went round her shoulders and hers round his waist. He was so much taller than her but it felt reassuring rather than awkward. Stella moved with him, not speaking. Over his shoulder she could see other couples dancing: Francesca awkwardly with one of the teenagers, Rosie with Enzo, his sisters with their husbands. In the trees coloured lights were glowing and the day's light was fading. Coffee had been brewed and set on the table, dishes of sweet treats distributed. There, holding a plate and eating from it steadily, was Otis. He was watching them, realised Stella, his expression blank and unreadable. It was so uncomfortable she felt her skin prickle. When the track finished she was almost relieved to hand Neil over to one of Enzo's sisters, a round-bodied woman in a smock-like dress. Otis dropped his gaze and started fiddling with his phone again, although Stella noticed every now and then he darted a look as if checking up on them.

Lunch became dinner, the leftover pasta was brought out again, a fresh salad made by one of the sisters, more bread was sliced, more cheeses appeared. Families began to drift away after they had eaten for the second time. Car horns sounded their goodbyes as they drove out through the gates.

'Thank you,' Stella told Rosie.

'For lunch? Any time.'

'Thank you for what you said. You're right that there isn't much to lose. All the risk lies in doing nothing.'

Dear Leo, I can't sleep. Your friend Rosie put an idea in my head this afternoon and it's buzzing round in there still. She pointed out that there's no real reason for me to come back to England; that I could stay in Italy if I wanted to, live here permanently even. The thought had never occurred to me. I've lived in London all my life, different parts of it but always the same city. It's my home and I've loved it but I think the only reason I haven't moved on is a lack of imagination. It never seemed possible; and suddenly it does. Friends are the only real reason to go back and I have some here now – Raffaella, Tosca, even Francesca (although she horrifies me at times!) and you too I guess, despite us never having met.

It's very late and perhaps in the morning I'll think differently, but right now I feel curious about living a life here, at least for a while, and seeing what comes of it. The idea is exciting.

I suspect I'm never going to get to sleep ... Stella.

More drama than necessary

Dear Stella, I hope you managed to close your eyes last night. I wonder how you're feeling about it all this morning. Have you changed your mind or is your head back to buzzing again? I know what I would do in your place but I'm not going to say because this is something you must decide for yourself. Actually I hope you've already decided. Leo.

There must have been a moment when she had put her laptop aside and turned off the light but Stella had no memory of doing either of those things. She recalled looking at rental properties and language courses, then reading the blogs of other English people who had settled in Italy and felt the need to share their highs and lows, but she couldn't remember closing her eyes or what she had dreamed of.

Leo's reply to her email perplexed her. Why was he being so cryptic? It wasn't like him and she found it frustrating as his opinion seemed worth having.

Raffaella was the one other person it might be useful to talk to. Stella sent her a text suggesting they meet for breakfast in Triento. A few minutes later she had a reply.

Yes, good idea. See you in the café in the piazza in about an hour. R.

Showering and dressing as quickly as she could in white shorts and a loose linen shirt the colour of watermelon, Stella left Villa Rosa without seeing Francesca. There were a few things she wanted to say to her but they would have to wait.

It was a sunny morning with the village busier than usual and Stella was lucky to find an empty table at the café. Raffaella arrived ten minutes later, resplendent in colour once again, this time a bright turquoise dress Stella hadn't seen before.

'You look great,' she said. 'That shade suits you.'

'Ciro used to tell me that too. He liked it when I wore this. But today I'm making the effort just for you, Stella.'

'Well I appreciate it.'

They ordered coffee and Stella picked out her favourite pastry, although she was aware of the waistband of her shorts feeling tighter and thought if she were to live here for any length of time she might have to cut out the regular treats.

Raffaella seemed not to have any appetite. She had chosen a plain *cornetto* and tore off the end, kneading it between her fingers, fidgeting rather than eating.

'I have a dilemma,' she said.

'Yes, me too actually,' Stella told her. 'But you go first.'

'*Va bene.* The other morning I had that meeting to talk about leasing out my *trattoria* for the summer. Benedetto and Maria are very keen. They wanted to give notice on their place beside the statue straight away because really it's a disaster and they are losing money. But I told them no, they should wait while I talk to my lawyer. I ought to do that today but I'm not sure if I'm ready.'

'What's stopping you?'

'I keep thinking if they have my *trattoria*, then what do I have? What is my purpose?'

'You could retire,' suggested Stella. 'Spend more time in London with your grandchildren, take life easy over summer instead of working so hard.'

'I'll be nobody.'

'You'll be you still. The *trattoria* isn't your whole identity.'

'It's what has brought me respect and what I've taken

pride in for all these years.' Raffaella sighed. 'What should I do, lease it to them or run it myself for another summer?'

Listening to her, Stella understood why Leo had been careful not to share his opinion. 'No one else can make this decision for you,' she said, echoing his advice.

'I know that and yet still I can't seem to do it,' Raffaella said. 'I've never thought of myself as a person who lacked courage but right now it's failing me. And those people, I've raised their hopes and I need to let them know one way or the other.'

Stella was still considering how best to reply when the commotion began. First the sound of a siren and then an ambulance, screaming into the piazza and stopping outside the linen shop, the paramedics racing inside, the sound of a woman's voice raised in hysteria.

Raffaella looked at her. 'Is that Angelica in there screaming?'

'I think it might be.'

'How odd. Let's go and see what's going on.'

The scene that met their eyes was a disturbing one. Angelica was lying on the ground in front of the counter, thrashing around, screaming at the paramedics.

Backed up against the shelves of linen, white-faced and wide-eyed, was a middle-aged woman. 'Oh my God, is she all right?' she was saying in English.

Stella turned to her. 'What's happening?'

The woman seemed relieved to hear another English voice. 'I think she's having a heart attack. I was in here having a look around when suddenly she started gasping then made this awful noise and fell to the ground unconscious. I managed to put her in the recovery position and call an ambulance ... and then she started yelling when she came round. What is she saying? Do you understand?'

'No, but my friend might.' Stella looked at Raffaella for an answer. 'Can you make it out?'

'She is refusing to go to the hospital. She says she is dying and they must bring her son to her straight away because she doesn't have long.'

'Oh no.' Stella lowered her voice. 'I'd better call Francesca.'

'I wouldn't,' said Raffaella quietly. 'Not unless it's to tell her that she's being outmanoeuvred.'

'Seriously?' Stella thought the old woman seemed genuinely distressed and in pain. 'Are you sure?'

'Quite sure; she is good, though, I will give her that.'

Angelica must have caught sight of them standing there because she called out Raffaella's name and then her yelling became a low but still dramatic moaning. The paramedics had brought in a stretcher and were trying to strap her into it but she pushed them away with surprising strength.

Raffaella moved closer, saying something in a sharp voice that was enough to still Angelica for the few moments the paramedics needed. Following them out to the ambulance, she continued talking to her, in lower and more calming tones.

From the doorway, Stella saw the stretcher being loaded and watched the ambulance set off, Angelica inside it, with another noisy whine of its siren. Beside her the English woman was still quivering.

'I think she's going to be OK,' Stella comforted her. 'My friend doesn't think it's her heart, possibly just a panic attack.'

'It was very dramatic; I thought she was a goner.' The woman breathed out heavily. 'I feel quite unsteady myself now.'

'Why don't you go over to the bar and see if they'll make you a cup of tea,' suggested Stella.

She seemed reluctant to leave the shop, reliving exactly what had happened, what she had said and done, and repeating it several times, before allowing herself to be steered out towards the café, amid Stella's admonishments to take it easy because she'd had a shock.

Raffaella was standing behind the counter by the time she got back, looking about her with a strange expression on her face. 'All these years since I worked here, it hasn't really changed much. I think even some of the designs are still the same as back then.'

'What was it you told Angelica to make her calm down?' Stella asked.

'That she'd end up in the psychiatric ward if she wasn't careful ... and then I said we'd call Gennaro and look after the shop until someone came.'

'Poor Gennaro,' said Stella, not for the first time. 'You think she did this to get his attention?'

'Of course, and it will work. They will do all the tests and find nothing is wrong, still it will be enough to scare him.'

'I suppose now Francesca doesn't have a chance of getting her mother-in-law out of her house?'

'Not unless she is much cleverer than she seems. The other son Roberto, maybe this will bring him home. And then Angelica will have everything the way she wants.'

'Francesca claims she'll leave Gennaro if he won't put her first.'

'Poor man, what a wife and mother to have to choose between.' Raffaella sighed and pulled her phone from her bag. 'I suppose I'd better see if I can find his number and let him know.'

Dear Leo, I've left Raffaella working in the linen shop. Long story but the short version is that Angelica Russo had some sort of turn and was carted off to hospital so Raffaella stepped in to look after things. She seemed almost pleased about it. She worked there years ago apparently and I guess it must bring back memories. Anyway, I had been planning to ask for her advice – you know, about whether I should stay or go – but things took their dramatic turn before I was able to. And now

I've realised no one else can make this choice for me (which is basically what you said!).

So I'm back at Villa Rosa, weighing up the pros and cons again. I know what I want but the idea is daunting. Not so much all the things I'd have to do – learn Italian properly, find a place to live, rent out my apartment, etc. – but making a leap in a direction I never expected to take.

Thankfully I have the place to myself right now. Francesca has disappeared somewhere; she may have gone on another outing with the people from next door as their car is missing too. In a minute I'm going to sweep up the dropped bougainvillea petals from the terrace, then potter in the garden and pick some salad for my lunch. Perhaps later I'll go for a swim. Hopefully by the end of the day I'll have made some bigger, more important plans. Stella.

Even the beach was busier today; small groups had put down towels on its pebbly surface or brought their own sun loungers, children were splashing in the shallows, a boy was fishing from the rocks, a girl parading the tideline in the tiniest of bikinis.

Stella had brought a book but didn't have the concentration required to read it. She sat leaning back against an expanse of rock warmed by the sun, stretching out her legs and letting the waves cool her toes. If she stayed in Triento she could come to the beach every day over summer. It was a lovely idea but not enough to swing a decision.

Later, swimming out into the bay, Stella thought of herself as two people. One was right here, her body striking through seawater and her head full of new ideas, the other was where she had always been, at her desk at Milly Munro's, answering emails, keeping the place running smoothly. Stella saw herself hunched over a keyboard, saw the little vase of fabric flowers she kept on her desk and the sketches of the next collection up on the wall, imagined Milly calling some request, the scattered chat of her colleagues. It had been such a wrench to lose it all but she wasn't the same Stella any more; her life had shifted and she had discovered new parts of herself; she could never be as content with that old routine. Hadn't she wanted a more interesting life? Wasn't that what she was longing for? This was her chance.

Towelling herself dry on the shore, she felt refreshed. On the walk back to Villa Rosa her decision firmed and by the time she strolled through the gates it seemed there was only one thing to do.

She saw that Francesca was back. Neil must have helped her pull out the table-tennis set and now she and Otis were playing a frantic ping-pong match out on the terrace. With her cheeks so flushed and her ponytail flying, she looked much younger. Otis seemed to be beating her and there were shrieks of protest and appeals to Neil to adjudicate.

He smiled when he saw Stella. 'Where did you disappear to? I was going to suggest we all headed to the beach together but there was no sign of you this morning when I called by.'

'I went by myself.' Stella brushed her fingers through her wet hair. 'It was good to get some exercise.'

'Do you fancy a walk now, or have you done enough?' He glanced over at the ping-pong in progress. 'I'm trying to avoid getting involved in this.'

'Sure, I'll come for a walk. Just let me change out of my wet swimming costume.'

They took the narrow path that snaked down to the coast and over the rocks, Stella walking behind Neil with a view of his neat fair head and square shoulders. For a while he strode ahead and then he paused beneath the shade of a pine tree and waited for her to catch up.

'Otis is having a good time,' he said. 'Coming away together is working out the way I hoped.'

'That's great,' said Stella.

'This holiday is all about him, doing the things he likes and spending time together. In a couple of years he won't be interested in hanging out with his dad. That's what everyone keeps telling me anyway.'

'My friends say the same,' she agreed, wondering where this was leading.

'I was thinking when we get home, and back to normal, perhaps we might see a bit of each other, you and I? Otis spends four nights a week with his mum, you see.'

It had been so long since anyone had asked Stella out, since she had even met a man who might. She looked at Neil, seemingly so perfect for her right down to the crease in his trousers, and said, 'That would be lovely, but the thing is I'm not going back to normal.'

'Sorry?' He sounded confused.

'I'm planning to stay in Triento. I've lost myself here just like you said I might.'

'Are you serious?'

She nodded happily. 'I made the decision this afternoon.'

'Me and my terrible timing,' Neil said ruefully. Then he stepped closer, setting a hand on her shoulder. 'I really like you. I was hoping to get a chance to see how things might work out between us.'

'I like you too.' With him so near, she had to tilt her chin upwards to see his face properly.

It was an easy move for Neil to drop his head and touch his lips to hers. His mouth brushed lightly, then with more firmness, and there was a short and shivery flare of pleasure down Stella's spine before he pulled away and his grey-green eyes stared at her seriously. 'Is your mind completely made up?'

She took a breath. 'I'll be back in London from time to time but yes, it is.'

His hand dropped from her shoulder. 'I'm envious of

you really. If I didn't have Otis and my business I might do something similar. I've reached that point where I keep wondering, is this it? But life is too complicated. I'm not in a position to put myself first right now.'

'That is exactly what I'm doing,' Stella realised, surprised. 'I hadn't thought of it like that. I'm putting myself first. There's no reason why I shouldn't.'

They walked back together more slowly; and at Villa Rosa, while Neil challenged his son to a game of ping-pong then proceeded to let him win, Stella sat with Francesca, allowing herself a small moment of regret. Neil was a nice guy. She could imagine him perfectly suiting her old life, getting on with her friends, making plans for things they'd both enjoy, being the sort of man Birdie would describe as her type. But Stella's old life didn't fit her so well any more. Perhaps even her type was beginning to change.

As she half-watched the ping-pong game progressing, Stella tried to find a way to tell Francesca about her mother-in-law's sudden illness. She expected anger or frustration as a reaction, but while she was describing the scene at the linen shop – the terrible screaming and the ambulance arriving – Francesca's expression stayed stony and for a long while she was silent.

'What will you do now?' Stella asked.

Francesca gave a quick shake of her head. 'I'm thinking,' was all she said. And then she stood up and, taking her drink with her, headed alone down the steps towards the rocky cliffs. It was a good place to think, remembered Stella, who hoped she might find some answers there.

Dear Leo, it's the end of the day now and I managed to make that decision. I'm staying; it's definite! I've only told one other person besides you so please don't mention it to Birdie if you happen to be in touch as I'd like to tell her myself. She'll be the one I'll miss most, especially not being able to catch up for lunch at a moment's notice, but then things are changing for her too, so perhaps I was going to have to get used to that anyhow.

I'm excited as much as afraid by what the future holds. Remember how once I described my life as a clean slate? It feels as if I've made the tiniest scribble and now there's the potential to fill it in with lots of colour and interest.

First there are practicalities of course, most importantly finding somewhere to live once you return to Villa Rosa. I'll be sad to pack up and leave this house but hopefully you'll invite me back and we can sit on the terrace together and have drinks and watch the sun setting. Imagine that! Stella.

Dear Stella, I am cheering. How do you write that? Whooh? To me this seems the right thing to do. You can keep your apartment and London will be here if things don't work out, but I hope that they will. And yes, you are invited to come to Villa Rosa for drinks on the terrace and long lunches. And in the summer when the sea is calmer I'll attach the iron ladder to the rocks and we will swim together from there into the deeper water. I'm looking forward to all of that but most of all to meeting you at long last after all these emails that we've sent. Well done, my friend. I'm pleased for you. Leo.

The many benefits of interfering

Stella kept on waiting for Francesca to say something. For two days now she had been unusually taciturn. On the first they had driven for miles to a sandy beach and yesterday they had gone together on an outing chosen from Leo's scrapbook, a walk beneath the trees in a national park an hour's drive away, inland through the mountains. She hadn't been much of a companion either time.

'I'm still thinking,' Francesca replied every time she tried to engage her in any sort of conversation about her future.

Even when Stella broke her own news, there was only a flicker of interest.

'You should rent somewhere with two bedrooms in case I have to move in with you,' she said flatly.

Now she was in the garden, hoeing between the rows of tomato plants, having never taken the slightest interest in the grounds of Villa Rosa before. Stella wondered if she could tempt her out for lunch. There were plans to meet Tosca and Raffaella and eat at some place by the harbour but that was too near Triento, she supposed, with a chance of Francesca running into someone who would tell her husband they had spotted her.

Feeling only mildly guilty for leaving her alone, because she needed a break from all that brooding silence, Stella dressed in her blue Milly Munro dress. She was starting to get tired of the clothes she had brought to Italy with her. A new skirt or top would give her a lift but she hadn't seen anything in Triento she would consider spending money on.

Stella had a rule that she only bought things she loved. There were no rejects in her closets, no barely worn impulse buys or things that didn't suit her. Milly had taught her how to curate a wardrobe, had been almost motherly as she had explained the value of pieces that worked together, the rudiments of creating your own style from clothes other people had designed. So while Stella had the urge to treat herself, perhaps to a new frock to wear for the speed-dating evening, she wasn't going to invest unless the perfect item presented itself. She thought again of Rosie's outfits and how she had meant to ask where she shopped for them. On her trips back to London, she suspected, or in Rome or Naples maybe. Possibly there was a fabulous store nearby that she had failed to come across, but Stella doubted it.

The blue shift dress was fine for now. Stella checked with Francesca one last time to be absolutely sure she didn't want to come along, then reversed the car out of the gates, and with a poop on the horn and a wave to Neil who was sunning himself on the balcony next door, she set off up the hill.

It hadn't been too awkward between her and Neil since their kiss on the cliff-top. They had been careful not to mention it again and had carried on much as before. Most likely Francesca would be irate to know of the missed opportunity but Stella had let go of any regrets easily enough. One kiss wasn't enough to send her home, not now she had made up her mind it was time for change; not now she was finally feeling excited about the future.

She found Raffaella ready and waiting at her place, wearing the orange scarf again but this time teamed with a green dress covered in tiny pale blue polka dots.

'Does this work?' she asked, tugging at the scarf to cover a patch of bare skin at the neckline.

'Yes, although it would look good without that scarf.'

'The neckline is too low. All my old clothes feel wrong for me now,' Raffaella complained. 'Too young somehow, although it's only been three years since I last wore them. I suppose I've got so used to being covered up in black.'

'I could take you shopping again,' Stella offered, pleased to have the chance to do something for her. 'It would be fun. And after all we need new outfits with our big night coming up.'

'Ah yes, the speed-dating. A woman in Triento stopped me yesterday to ask if it was going to be a regular event.'

'What did you tell her?'

Raffaella laughed. 'I said to ask Francesca Russo and that the whole thing was her idea.'

Stella assumed they would meet Tosca at whatever restaurant they were going to but for some reason Raffaella was determined to have her come to the house first, so all of them could walk there together.

'She'll be late, so I'll make coffee for us to have while we wait.'

Sitting at the kitchen table, Stella watched as she ground the beans and filled the moka pot. 'Did you make a decision yet about the *trattoria*?' she asked.

'Yes, but that has to wait for Tosca too. You will see why soon ... well, I hope so.'

It was half an hour before she appeared, Raffaella refusing to be drawn into answering any of Stella's questions. At last there was Tosca on the doorstep, glamorous in gold-rimmed sunglasses and a short dress that showed off lots of smooth skin toasted by the sun to a light caramel.

'Where are we going exactly?' she asked. 'Not very far if we're walking, I hope, because I'll never make it in these heels.'

'What are shoes for if not for walking in?' sniffed Raffaella. 'Why put on a pair that prevent it?'

'Because I like to wear heels and I don't particularly like walking,' Tosca replied.

'And what if you needed to run for some reason?'

'Run?' Tosca laughed. 'Then undoubtedly the situation would be so dire it wouldn't matter what I was wearing. Stop pestering and tell me where I'm having lunch.'

'At the only place down here in the harbour that serves really good food.'

'Your *trattoria*?' Stella guessed.

'Not quite,' Raffaella told her. 'But come and I'll show you.'

They walked towards the far end of the point. Stella noticed someone had set out lots of chairs and tables shaded by sun umbrellas right outside Raffaella's *trattoria*. The specials board was propped up against the wall and covered in writing; a few of the tables were occupied but not too many.

'So we are going to your place then,' said Stella.

Raffaella paused to take in the scene then gave a tiny nod as if she found it satisfactory. 'Yes, but it's not mine any more, not really.'

Benedetto came out to welcome them, his smile wide and his greeting effusive. There was some discussion about which was the best table and only when that was decided and they were comfortably seated, and three glasses of chilled rose wine had been poured, did Raffaella explain.

'Tosca and I made a pact,' she told Stella. 'My side of it was that I would stop postponing the inevitable. The tourists are arriving now. If they are to do enough business over summer to make it through winter then Maria and Benedetto can't afford to waste more time.'

'So you've leased it to them already?' Stella was amazed at how fast she had worked.

'Not exactly. Tosca's proposal was that I should let them have it for a very small fee while they're still paying rent on that other place. And once they are clear of it we will begin our formal agreement. They opened yesterday with a limited menu. It went quietly but well enough for them to be encouraged. Apparently I have to stay out of things, try not to interfere. That's right, isn't it, Tosca?'

Tosca sipped her wine and nodded. 'You will be tempted; you won't be able to resist.'

Stella turned to her. 'So what was your side of the pact?' she asked, although she had a suspicion what the answer would be.

'Apparently I am going to become a model.' Tosca looked down at her wine glass, twirling its stem between her fingers. 'I'll try anyway because that's the deal I've made with Raffaella. Yesterday I emailed some photos of myself to your friend Neil and his company is interested in me going to London for a casting. They've also suggested an agent I should speak to, one that specialises in older models, so there may be other work ... or there may not.'

'I think there will be,' Stella told her. 'You've got such a great look. And maybe you could do some acting, too.'

'One step at a time,' Tosca said quietly. 'This might not work after all. But I'm going to give it a try and my friend Raffaella tells me that's the important thing.'

'At least I won't have to put up with you complaining all the time about how bored you are. Surely it's impossible to be bored in London,' said Raffaella. 'And there'll be no need to resort to flirting with unsuitable boys either.'

'Unsuitable boys? I don't know what you're talking about,' Tosca said lightly. 'I hope you're not going to get even crazier now you've given up this place. It's a risk, you know.'

Benedetto brought out the first dishes: sweet razor clams drizzled in orange vinegar, a salad of fennel and citrus, a platter of langoustines with a lime-spiked salsa.

They talked about how Raffaella might occupy herself now she knew for sure she wasn't spending her entire summer in a kitchen. 'I'm not a person to sit around doing nothing,' she maintained.

'Write a cookbook then,' suggested Stella.

Raffaella dismissed the idea. 'There are enough of those in the world. It doesn't need another from me.'

'Come to London,' Tosca suggested.

'For a visit maybe,' she agreed, 'but only for a short while. This is where I want to be.'

'Yes, me too,' said Stella. 'This is exactly where I want to be.' And then she told them of her decision to stay on in Triento.

Tosca seemed surprised, Raffaella not so much. 'What was it that made up your mind?' she asked.

'I realised I wanted my future to be different from my past,' Stella told her. 'I'm still not sure what I'll do here. I'm thinking I might open up a little shop, just a small one selling clothes that will appeal to the tourists as well as some of the more stylish local women. It's only a dream at the moment and I need to learn some Italian before I do anything else. But, Raffaella, if it happens, maybe you could help me?'

'I don't know anything about fashion,' she pointed out.

'No, but you've worked in a shop and you understand Triento.'

'She will take over,' Tosca warned.

Raffaella rolled her eyes at her. 'As Stella says, it's no more than a dream right now. How would I take over?'

'You'll find a way.' Tosca laughed. 'You always do.'

'Actually I'm going to help Antonio plan a restaurant for the vinegar estate. It's not the start of a romance so don't give me such a look, Tosca. I can never replace Ciro and I don't want to try. Better to make a new life, I think, than have a pale copy of the old one. But Antonio and I are friends. I will enjoy helping him. And after that, Stella, perhaps I may be able to help you. In the meantime I have a very good suggestion.'

'Of course you do,' said Tosca. 'Please tell me it isn't another pact. One of them is enough for now.'

'Not a pact; an idea – if Stella is living here and you are going to be in London why don't you stay in each other's houses? It will save you money, yes? And with Stella as my neighbour I might not miss you constantly annoying me quite so much, *cara*.'

Stella was keen on the idea. 'If the timing was right that would be ideal. I'm all for another house swap.'

Leaning back in her chair, Raffaella raised her glass. 'Here's to me interfering.'

Stella's phone rang as she was walking back to the car. It was a local number she didn't recognise and she answered to hear Rosie's voice, a thread of worry running through it.

'Have I caught you at a bad time? Can you talk?'

'Yes, sure,' said Stella, opening the car door to let some of the heat out before she climbed in.

'It's about Enzo. You know how family is so important to him? Well, he also has a tendency to get involved with other people's families if he thinks there is something wrong and he can help.'

'He interferes,' prompted Stella.

'Exactly. I asked him not to but he rang Gennaro Russo and told him he would find his wife at Villa Rosa. He felt it was his duty to do so. I'm sorry.'

'No need to apologise.' Stella sat in the driver's seat and swung her legs inside. 'I've been feeling bad about Gennaro. It's actually a relief that he knows where she is now.'

'I hope things work out.'

'Me too. Thanks for letting me know.'

Stella drove back to Villa Rosa with some trepidation as she was certain Gennaro wouldn't have wasted much time. Would he be angry with Francesca? Was he the violent type, given to shouting and smashing things? He hadn't seemed that way to her but then she had met him only once so couldn't be sure.

There was no one to be seen when she arrived. The table-tennis set had been abandoned on the terrace; there was an empty coffee cup on the table and beside it an ashtray with the stubs of a couple of cigarettes. Did Gennaro smoke? She couldn't recall.

Stella checked the kitchen and the gardens but all was quiet there too. Heading into the main house she found them both in the living room, side by side on the sofa, silent and tear-stained, not touching, not really moving at all.

'Oh,' she said, taking a step back. 'Sorry to interrupt you.'

Gennaro stared at her, a steady and unreadable gaze. '*Signora*,' he said.

'I'll go upstairs and get out of your way.'

'*Grazie, signora*,' he replied.

It was half an hour before she heard the front door slamming shut. By then Stella had rearranged the clothes in her wardrobe and refolded the contents of her drawers, all the time wondering what was being said downstairs. After that there was no noise at all. She waited five minutes and couldn't stand it any longer.

'Well?' she said, finding Francesca sitting alone in the dimly lit room, staring out through the half-shuttered window.

'He won't say how he found me.' Francesca didn't look at her. 'He was here for an hour before you arrived, talking and talking.'

'Was he furious with you?'

'No, only sad and that was worse.' Her voice broke and she put her hands over her face for a moment. 'He wants me to go home and promises that once he's sure his mother's health is OK we'll move out. He says I don't have to work in the shop if I don't want to; I can do whatever I choose. He thinks Roberto might come back and take on more responsibility and then we'll have a holiday together. I've heard all those things before but I've never seen him like he was this afternoon.'

Her voice wobbled again and she turned her face away. Stella stood in the doorway, feeling desperately sorry for her.

'He cried,' Francesca said. 'He's been so worried; he thought he might never see me again; he was scared what might have happened. It's what I wanted but ... now I've seen him and I know ... I'm so sorry ...'

She was sobbing properly now, fat tears running down her cheeks, her shoulders shaking. Sitting down beside her, Stella said helplessly, 'Oh, sweetheart.'

'Now it will be worse because Angelica won't let me forget what I've done. She'll make me pay when Gennaro isn't looking.'

'You're going to go back home then? You've decided?'

Francesca let out a shaky breath. 'He's coming to get me in half an hour. He said he'd give me time to talk to you and pack my stuff. He says we love each other and we can make it work ... but I don't know.'

'You don't know if you love each other?'

'No, of course we do ... we always have. But when I go back nothing will have changed and I'll still be unhappy.'

'What if I came and helped you in the linen shop part-time?' Stella asked. 'I wouldn't ask for payment, I'd be doing it for the experience. And when things are quiet you could teach me Italian. It would be a huge help, actually.'

'Really?' Francesca sounded unsure.

'Yes, it would be fun, I think. And you know how much I love that shop.'

'What about Angelica?'

'Well,' said Stella thoughtfully. 'With her health in doubt I wonder if she should really be on her own in that big house all day? If I were Gennaro I would hire someone, perhaps a housekeeper or paid companion, to keep an eye on her and make sure the place is running smoothly, to clean and cook, that sort of thing – and then, of course, you won't have to.'

The corners of Francesca's mouth lifted; it wasn't a smile

exactly but she seemed faintly cheered. 'That's clever,' she said.

Stella put an arm round her and gave her shoulders a quick squeeze. 'Shall we go and pack your suitcase then?'

Francesca leaned in and hugged her back. 'Thank you. I'm glad you're staying in Triento. I think I'm going to need a friend like you.'

Dear Leo, I have the house to myself at last. Gennaro came and took Francesca home late this afternoon and there was an emotional scene with lots of crying and hugging. He even thanked me for looking after her, which made me feel so guilty because if she hadn't been able to stay at Villa Rosa, I'm sure things would have been resolved much sooner. There was a small glimpse of the old Francesca just before she left. She whispered to me that she's had an idea; I hate to think what it might be.

Anyway, now I'm enjoying a moment of respite. I'm at the kitchen table with a glass of limoncello and in a minute I'm going to have some cheese, bread and salad for supper. Then I'll sit outside beneath the pergola and watch the sky turn pink and the sun sink into the sea, and now I know I'm not leaving Triento any time soon the beauty of the end of another day won't feel so bittersweet.

It's nearly time for our speed-dating event, so expect to hear all the details in my next email. Stand by! Love Stella.

Hi Birdie. Still no picture of you and Emma, despite your promises. I imagine that's because you're having a fabulous time in Scotland and haven't given me a thought? No, I don't want you to feel guilty, just like you don't have to feel bad about not getting out here to visit me. As it turns out you still have plenty of time. I'm staying. Indefinitely. Long story, but if you and Emma need another holiday this summer then I'll be making sure I have a spare room so you know where to come.

I can't lie; I'm daunted at the prospect of making such a big change, but I had to do it sooner or later, didn't I? There was no point carrying on the same way for ever.

Hey, Birdie, I hope you're both happy up there in your matching kilts. I miss you. I love you. Stella.

Ending with a beginning

The first thought that came into Stella's head that morning was that she should feign an illness, a stomach bug or migraine, anything to get out of the evening ahead. She really didn't feel like going speed-dating; and Tosca, the person they were doing it for, had lost interest completely, forgetting she was supposed to be lonely and looking for love, talking only of London and model agents and who she needed to email right away. Her ambition had returned with a vengeance, it seemed.

Stella had suggested cancelling the event but Raffaella remained adamant. Too many people were promising to turn up, and besides, this would be the perfect opportunity for Benedetto and Maria to get the word out that they had taken over the *trattoria*. They were planning a selection of delicious nibbles. They were very excited. It was far too late for a change of mind.

Her only hope of avoiding it was to come up with an excuse, one good enough to convince everyone that she couldn't possibly be there. A sudden stomach bug seemed her best option, some sort of horribly infectious thing she didn't want to pass on to people.

Stella spent the morning on the beach. The lido had opened, meaning it was officially summertime, and she celebrated by hiring a sun lounger and lying on it in a semi-dazed state. This was her final week of laziness. From Monday she would be helping out in the linen shop, mostly on folding duty at first, according to Francesca.

Stretching her arms above her head, Stella considered going for a swim but really couldn't be bothered. Much nicer to lie here, body slick with sun cream, skin warm and sandy, watching beach life go on around her. There was a couple playing racquet games, an old man with a stomach like a camel's hump quietly snoring on his lounger, babies of course and toddlers playing in the sand. Stella could only watch them for a little while before she had to look away, back to the racquet game.

Pangs of hunger drove her from the comfort of the sun lounger. She bought a slice of oily pizza and a cold beer from the bar on the cliff and sat at a wobbly table beneath the trees while she finished them. Noticing the tips of her shoulders had begun to turn pink, she decided she'd had enough sun for the day and, knotting a towel round her neck like a shawl, she started on the walk back to Villa Rosa.

Perhaps she might email Leo this afternoon. He would be busy working with no time to get back to her but she liked the feeling of anticipation, knowing a reply was coming eventually.

As she walked a stretch of promenade with a crumbling stone balustrade and a view back towards the blue of the bay, Stella wondered how it might be when she and Leo finally met. Hopefully not too awkward after all the contact they'd had, but it was impossible to be sure.

What would Leo think of her? Was he going to like her? Might they become close? Or would they catch up for one drink and not bother to see each other again? Stella supposed it would be a while before she found out as even when Leo had finished in London he had his business in Naples to attend to.

Back at the house she had a quick shower then braced herself to phone Raffaella.

'I'm not feeling great,' Stella lied. 'I think I may be coming down with something.'

'Nonsense,' Raffaella dismissed her.

'Really, I'm feeling queasy,' Stella insisted.

'Yes, yes, aren't we all? Get down here as soon as you can. We need help setting the place up. Francesca's got some sort of plan. She's closed the linen shop early and is down here issuing commands.'

'But I ...' Stella paused. 'What kind of plan?'

'I haven't got time to go into it now. You'll have to come and find out,' Raffaella said, before hanging up.

Stella smiled to herself. She should have known better than to think she could deceive her friend. It looked like she was going speed-dating whether she wanted to or not. Although she hadn't bought anything new in the end, there was this one dress she hadn't worn yet, not a restrained Milly Munro but a cheap silk in bright colours that Birdie had brought back from a trip to India. Stella never felt entirely like herself when she was wearing it but this evening that might be a good thing.

She threw it on and left the house, her hair still beachy and her face mostly free of make-up. The air-conditioning in Leo's car had gone on the fritz so she opened the windows and let the warm wind blast her. Turning up the stereo, she chair-danced to terrible Italian pop songs all the way to the harbour. If she had to spend an evening speed-dating then she may as well enjoy it.

Francesca had a clipboard. She was jabbing her finger at it and calling out instructions. The tables and chairs had to be arranged a certain way inside and out, with numbers placed on each of them. She would sit on a raised plinth that Benedetto was trying to put together from old packing cases.

'I've printed off forms and got plenty of pens,' she told Stella. 'When people arrive they'll register – the women with me, the men with Raffaella – and then we'll make up name badges to give them.'

'I thought Raffaella was taking part?' Stella protested.

'I need her so she can't,' said Francesca. 'I may need you later, too. But right now you can go and help Maria polish up the glasses.'

'Where's Tosca?'

Francesca glanced up from her clipboard. 'Tosca? We won't see her for a while surely. She'll be wanting to make an entrance.'

Relieved that there was a possibility she wouldn't have to speed-date anyone, Stella went to find Maria. She didn't seem to need much help but Stella picked up a clean cloth anyway and stood beside her wiping dust from champagne flutes and wine glasses. When they had finished Maria took her into the kitchen to taste some of the food she had prepared. Crostini topped with a cream of fava beans and flakes of smoked tuna, *pizzette* spread with a smoky *bagna càuda*, bite-sized meatballs with a crunch of pine nuts and a hit of chilli.

'This *trattoria* is going to be good to us, I think,' said Maria.

'Better than the place by the statue?'

'Oh yes, already we are doing so much more business and if we get busier I will have to get my cousin from Napoli to come and help me in the kitchen.'

'Leo will be pleased.'

'Leo has helped change our lives, Raffaella too.' Maria arranged more crostini on a platter. 'Many of the customers who have come in so far have been old regulars and disappointed not to see her. They've talked about eating here when her husband was alive and most describe the food as simple but perfect. I have a lot to live up to.'

'I'm sure you'll manage it. Soon people will be flocking back for your cooking and we'll be fighting for a table.'

'For good friends we will always make space, you can be sure of it,' promised Maria.

*

By 6 p.m. it felt like a party, so many people crowding together, helping themselves to glasses of Prosecco from the tray that Stella had been told to carry round.

'People get one free drink and then they must pay,' Francesca instructed, but Stella had already lost track of who'd had what.

'We should have restricted the numbers,' she said, slightly panicked. 'Or set age limits. This is out of control.'

'It's fine,' Francesca told her. 'Everyone is welcome to mix and mingle. In a moment we'll start taking registrations for the speed-dating and those we can't fit in can come back next time.'

'Next time?' Stella said weakly. Then her eyes settled on a curious sight – a woman who looked very like Angelica, dressed in a ruffled blouse and a skirt that almost touched the floor, was talking to Antonio from the vinegar estate, dimpling and laughing at something he was saying.

'Francesca, is that your mother-in-law?'

'It is.' She sounded pleased with herself. 'I made Gennaro ask her to come along and keep an eye on me. While she's spying she may meet someone, you never know – if not tonight, then next time. That's my best idea. I think it's my only hope of getting rid of her.'

'She looks happy ... as if she's genuinely having fun.' Stella was amazed.

Francesca glanced over quickly. 'Ah yes, the rule about the Prosecco doesn't apply to her. Keep filling her glass.'

Queues formed, chaotic ones that snaked between the tables. People kept breaking out to greet a friend then trying to force their way back in. Stella saw faces she recognised: the man from the café in the mountain town who had cooked pasta for their lunch, one of the waitresses from the bar in Triento, men and women she had given flyers to. She helped Francesca by writing out their name badges and showing them to tables.

Barely half of those who had come along were seated, the ones that couldn't be fitted in forming a noisy circle round them to watch the proceedings, an air of excitement among them all. Francesca stood and rang a hand bell to get their attention.

'Speed-daters please listen carefully,' she called in Italian. 'You will each get five minutes to talk and then I will ring this bell and the men will move to the next table. You must make a note of anyone you want to see again. At the end of the night give your form to me and I will see where there are matches. By this time next week I will let you all know how many you have and after that it's up to you to get in touch. Is that clear? Any questions?'

A chorus of voices called back, telling her to get on with things. Francesca grinned, and holding the bell above her head, rang it loudly for the speed-dating to begin.

No one noticed Tosca make her entrance. She was late, dressed all in white and picking her way over the cobbles carefully in her heels. 'Did I start all this?' she said when she saw Stella. 'It's completely insane.'

'You may have started it but you can't take part. We're over-subscribed.'

Tosca surveyed the scene. 'So many people looking for love.'

'It's a disaster actually. We've got older women dating younger men; hopefully they don't mind.'

'What exactly is wrong with older women dating younger men?' Tosca took the last glass of Prosecco from the tray and gave Stella a defiant look. 'I'm going to see if Neil is here. He said he might come along.'

Stella went inside, where the noise was even more deafening, and had Benedetto pour her a drink. She offered to help out some more but he told her to enjoy herself. Taking her glass, she went back to join the circle of onlookers. Francesca had rung her bell by then and at each table new couples were starting afresh. The body language was interesting. One woman had her arms crossed over her chest defensively while the man she was dating slumped in his chair, legs apart. There was a couple that clearly knew one another and were laughing to find themselves in such a situation; a pair of youngsters shyly gazing out from beneath their fringes; and beyond them Antonio paired with a woman much too frail-looking for him but still leaning forward on his elbows listening intently to what she was saying.

Stella's eyes met those of a man standing opposite. He must have been watching her, as carefully as she had been all the others. Holding her gaze, he gave her a hesitant smile.

There was something familiar about him, she realised. She knew his face, but from where? It took a few moments before she worked it out because his grey hair was much shorter than it had been in the only two photographs she had seen of him and his skin was not as tanned.

'Leo?' she called, disbelieving. 'Is that you?'

He couldn't hear her over the racket. Smiling again, he held his hands in the air, and shrugged. They were broad hands, hands that were used to hard physical work – Stella could tell that even in the dusky light.

He gestured away from the throng and tilted his head. She nodded in reply. Pushing her way through, stepping on toes and squeezing past hot bodies breathing Prosecco fumes, she panicked that she might not be able to find him. But he was there, a little beyond the edge of the crowd, waiting.

'Leo?' Stella asked again.

'I came all the way from London to this speed-dating event and, can you believe it, I couldn't get in.' His voice was soft and low, his words shaped by an accent that was stronger than she had expected.

'Leo,' she said. 'It's actually you.'

'Yes, it is actually me.' He was smiling. 'I thought I would surprise you.'

'It worked. I don't know if I could be more surprised than I am right now.'

'Do you need to stay or can we get away from all this?'

'Let's get away; it's madness; I've had enough.'

Together they walked back along the point and sat down on the stone steps leading down to the small stretch of beach, side by side, a hand's breadth between them, looking back towards the party at the *trattoria*.

'I thought you were too busy to come,' said Stella.

'Truthfully I am but I decided I couldn't miss an event as unique as Triento speed-dating.'

'Perhaps not so unique – Francesca is already talking about holding another one.'

He laughed. 'So I didn't need to book that last-minute flight and rush over, is that what you're telling me?'

It was the weirdest feeling, thought Stella, this sense of familiarity with a stranger. She had shared things with Leo in her emails that she would hesitate to say aloud to many of her friends and now here he was, and she hardly knew him at all.

'How long are you here for?' she asked.

'Only for a couple of days. I'm staying with Rosie and Enzo. You're invited to lunch tomorrow, by the way. I hope you'll come.'

There was a moment of silence, not uncomfortable but reflective. Then Leo's voice filled it. 'You know, you're not quite how I expected you to be.'

She was startled. 'Really, in what way?'

'I thought you'd be more intimidating since you worked in fashion and seem to have such definite tastes and style, but instead you look like you belong here.'

'I'm beginning to feel as if I do.'

When she turned her head she could see his profile. He

had a strong face: a broad forehead, a straight nose and square jawline. There was a faintly musky scent to him, a pleasant one without the chemical sting of cologne, and he was wearing dark jeans and a loose linen shirt.

'You're not exactly how I imagined either,' said Stella. 'In my head I always pictured you in gardening clothes, dirty workpants, muddy boots and a hat.'

He laughed. 'I look like that much of the time, and I'm probably happiest that way, but I can smarten myself up. I don't always have a spade in my hand.'

'Leo?'

'Hmm?'

'This is a bit freaky, isn't it? Being sort of friends but also strangers at the same time.'

'I'm not sure I like it,' he agreed. 'I think we should try to get the being strangers part over with as quickly as we can.'

'OK but how?'

'What about if we try this?' He touched her cheek and as her face turned towards his, he leaned in and kissed her, very softly and not for long. 'How is that? Any better?'

Stella took a shaky breath. She couldn't quite believe this was happening. 'Not really ... perhaps if we tried again,' she half-whispered.

This time his arms wrapped around her, and his kiss was long and deep, until she stopped noticing the noise booming from the *trattoria*, and the moment became only about his lips on hers and his hand running down her spine and the solidity of the muscles in his back as her fingertips pressed into them.

Gasping a little as they parted, Stella laughed. 'Yes, it's definitely making a difference now.'

She pushed her face into his shoulder and smelt the natural muskiness of his skin again. He ran his fingers through the salty tangle of her hair.

'A little more then?' he asked and she nodded.

They kissed, then they talked, then they kissed again. Down beside the beach, sheltered in semi-darkness, they heard the sound of the party fading, people calling their goodnights in loud, Prosecco-laced voices. The lights went out as bars and cafés closed until there was only silvery moonlight to see each other by.

Stella heard Raffaella calling her name. 'Is that you down there on the beach? Oh yes, I see. Vinegar dinner at my place next week – Antonio is coming, Tosca too. See you then.'

'My friends,' Stella told Leo. 'If you were here for longer, you could meet them.'

'Next time then; soon, I hope.'

Somewhere there was music playing – an old Neapolitan love song Stella recognised from the record Leo had given her. She leaned against him, closed her eyes and listened.

'This song seems so sad,' she murmured. 'It sounds as if it's about loss. Is it?'

Leo paused and listened to the words. 'Things end,' he said, 'other things begin, you never know where life will lead and that's how it is.'

And then he smoothed his hands over the slippery silk of her dress and kissed her once more.

Dear Stella, I didn't want to leave you tonight. It was tempting to stay on that beach beside you until morning. And now I'm sitting up in bed in Rosie's guest room writing to you instead of sleeping, even though I know that before too long you will be coming here for lunch and we'll have some more time together.

We are still strangers, of course. And yet I have a feeling about you. I had it every time I read one of your emails and when I saw you standing in that crowd in your colourful dress, and when we spoke, and when we kissed, that feeling only got stronger. I think we won't be strangers for long.

You told me your life is a clean slate. If that's still the case then I hope there is a space somewhere for you to write my name on it. Leo.

Dear Reader,

I hope my books go into the world and do some good; that this one has taken you away from your everyday life and directly to the warmth, scenes, scents and flavours of southern Italy.

Actually, I know this book has already done a little bit of good, thanks to a man called Martin Smith who bid to have a character in it named after his sister-in-law, Nicky Bird, to raise funds for the charity Look Good, Feel Better. Obviously the real Nicky Bird bears no resemblance to the character of Birdie – except that I'm told she's a great friend, so they have that in common.

Thanks are due as always to the teams at Orion, Hachette NZ and Hachette Australia and to my agent Caroline Sheldon. Also grateful thanks to Clara and Antonio DeSio whose house has appeared in several of my novels in the guise of Villa Rosa, to Jo McCarroll for sending me on assignment for *NZ Gardener* magazine and helping to inspire Leo's passion for growing things, and to Pamela Stirling of the *Listener* for being such a supportive editor over the period I've been writing this novel.

And finally, thanks to my lovely husband, Carne Bidwill, for providing IT support and the best ever margaritas.

ALSO BY NICKY PELLEGRINO

*Two feuding families, two love stories
and a lot of delicious Italian food . . .*

Although settled in London, the Martinellis are a typical Italian family: fighting, eating and loving in equal measure. Now Pieta's sister is getting married and she will make the wedding gown. But she is distracted by a series of mysteries. Why is her father feuding with another Italian family? Why is her mother so troubled? And could the man she's always secretly cared for really be getting married to someone else?

As the wedding draws nearer, Pieta uncovers the secrets that have made her family what it is – and may stand between her and happiness . . .

'*The Italian Wedding*, a feast of food and love, a terrific read.'
Beattiesbookblog

'If your soul needs some nourishing, *The
Italian Wedding* is a great pick.'
MiNDFOOD Magazine

'Nicky Pellegrino has crafted a feast not
just for the mind but the mouth.'
boomerangbooks.com

'The elements of drama, history, romance and passion are layered, flavoured, tasted and left to simmer, not unlike the Italian recipes which are scattered throughout the book . . . I absolutely loved it!'
Stephanie Zajkowski, tvnz.co.nz

Luca Amore runs a cooking school in the Sicilian mountain town of Favio. He's taught many people how to cook the dishes passed down to him by generations of Amore women. As he readies himself for yet another course he expects it to be much like all the others. He will cook, he will take his clients to visit vineyards and olive groves, they will eat together, become friends, and then, after a fortnight, they will pack up and head home to whatever corner of the globe they came from.

But there is a surprise in store for Luca.

This time there are four women booked in to The Food of Love Cookery School. Each one is at a turning point in her life. Each one is looking for something more than new cooking skills from her time in Sicily. Luca doesn't realise it yet but this group of women is going to change his life. And for Moll, Tricia, Valerie and Poppy, after this journey, nothing will ever be the same.

'Nicky Pellegrino not only knows her Sicilian recipes and cooking traditions, she also keeps an immaculate beat throughout her tale.'
Sainsbury's Magazine

Two women, one house – one at the beginning of her life, one nearing
the end. Alice is in London, working in the kitchen of a top restaurant
and determined to live life fast and to the full. Babetta is living in a
lonely house in southern Italy and trying to hang on to the quiet life
she has made for herself.

When the two women meet one summer life changes for both of
them. This is a novel about what we run from, and the places that make
us stop and consider. Drenched in sunshine, it's about friendship and
growing up, food and love.

'A slice of pure sunshine'
Good Housekeeping

**'An amazing book . . . it's a wonderful and enchanting
read . . . one of those books you want to read and
reread. It's endearing, entertaining and inspiring.'**
Novelicious.com

**'The author delivers not only on every sensory front – combining
her love and knowledge of food with her passion for the Italian
coast – but also with her energetic writing, layering every
character with shades of darkness and believable charisma.'**
The Australian Women's Weekly

Can a city
hold the key
to happiness?

One Summer in Venice

Nicky Pellegrino

*In the maze of Venice's canals, one woman sets
herself a goal to find the ten things that could be
the key to her happiness*

'This isn't a mid-life crisis OK? For a start I'm not old enough yet to have
one of those. I'm calling it a happiness project. I've stolen an entire summer from my life and by the time it's over I plan to leave this place with
a list in my hand. The ten things that make me happy, that's all I want
to know.'

Addolorata Martinelli knows she should be happy. She has everything
she thought she wanted – her own business, a husband, a child. So why
does she feel as if something is missing? Then when her restaurant, Little
Italy, is slated by a reviewer, she realises that she's lost the one thing she
thought she could always count on – her love of food.

So Addolorata heads to Venice for a summer alone, aiming to find the
ten things that make her happy. Once she's found them, she'll construct
a new life around her ten things, but will they include her life in London?

'Genuine heart and true observation.'
Elizabeth Buchan